IVORY'S FIGHT (SPECIAL FORCES: OPERATION ALPHA)

PREY SECURITY: ARTEMIS TEAM
BOOK ONE

JANE BLYTHE

Dear Readers,

Welcome to the Special Forces: Operation Alpha Fan-Fiction world!

If you are new to this amazing world, in a nutshell the author wrote a story using one or more of my characters in it. Sometimes that character has a major role in the story, and other times they are only mentioned briefly. This is perfectly legal and allowable because they are going through Aces Press to publish the story.

This book is entirely the work of the author who wrote it. While I might have assisted with brainstorming and other ideas about which of my characters to use, I didn't have any part in the process or writing or editing the story.

I'm proud and excited that so many authors loved my characters enough that they wanted to write them into their own story. Thank you for supporting them, and me!

READ ON!
Xoxo
Susan Stoker

I'd like to thank everyone who played a part in bringing this story to life. Particularly my mom who is always there to share her thoughts and opinions with me. The wonderful Amy Queau of Q Designs who made the stunning cover. And my lovely editor Lisa Edwards for all her encouragement and for all the hard work she puts into polishing my work.

CHAPTER ONE

December 24th
  7:19 P.M.

WHAT A GREAT WAY TO spend Christmas Eve.

Insert a heavy dose of sarcasm right here.

Ivory Smith did her best to ignore the metal cuffs circling her wrists. The man who'd put them on her had made sure they were tight, and she could already feel blood smearing her skin from where the rusty metal was cutting in.

Not that anybody here cared that she was bleeding.

Here she was nothing but a piece of meat. One to be sold to the highest bidder. She had no rights and no control over what happened to her.

The future was always uncertain.

One second in time could change everything.

That was what had happened to her.

Now she was here, chained to a brick wall which was cold and rough against her bare skin, her arms secured above her head. They'd long since gone numb, and she was stretched until her five-foot-one frame was pulled tight. Her muscles had well passed the stage of cramping, the best she could do to relieve the strain was to balance on her tiptoes every now and then to try to relax out her legs.

It wasn't the awkward and painful position that had her stomach swirling and her pulse racing, it was what was coming next.

Shoved into the back of a van, a bag had been thrown over her head before something was slammed into the side of her temple, knocking her unconscious. Young woman, walking alone at night, kidnapped, she knew what was going on. These men weren't your average kidnappers, they were human traffickers.

When she'd woken up, she'd been thrown over a giant of a man's shoulder and carried from the van into an old-looking house. The man had brought her into this room which seemed to be some sort of showroom. She had been placed on a small stadium, about two feet off the flagstone floor, then chained to the wall.

Ivory knew why she was on show.

A buyer, or multiple buyers, would soon be arriving to browse the wares.

She was the wares.

Well, not just her, there was another woman who appeared to be about her age, early twenties, and then there were six young girls, no older than nine or ten, also naked and chained to the wall.

Anger burned so brightly inside her she almost believed it was possible to spontaneously burst into flames. How could someone do something so sick as to buy and sell little girls?

Was there anything more evil?

The children had been crying earlier, but the eight of them had been in this room for what had to be close to two hours, and the girls had eventually grown quiet after crying themselves out. The youngest of the girls, who couldn't be more than six was directly across the room from Ivory. Despite being the youngest, she was also the quietest, she hadn't wept like the older girls, she'd just stood there, watching the men who manhandled her and the others with a regal sort of anger.

Had the child been hurt before?

Did she know what was going to happen to her?

Had she already accepted her fate?

Ivory's heart wept for the small girl. So young, so tiny, so innocent, no child should ever be treated like this.

Voices signaled that people were approaching, and just like that, the panic in the room—that had been simmering away at a low boil—was suddenly turned up high. Terrified eyes darted toward the large double doors at one end of the room. It was a sunroom of sorts, with brick walls on three sides and the fourth made of glass as was the ceiling. Today was cold, rain pummeling through the gray afternoon, but on a bright summer's day it would be stiflingly hot in here. Not that anyone would care the girls were suffering.

One of the children whimpered and another started crying. Ivory would have risked their abductor's wrath by offering some sort of consolation, but the men had put ball gags on her and the other adult. The drool that wet her skin was more annoying than anything else, and certainly much better than what was to come.

The doors into the house remained closed, but the double doors leading out to the beautiful gardens were opened and three men stepped inside. One carried a large umbrella, which he held over the other two. He was dressed all in black and had a large gun holstered at his hip, clearly the muscle. One of the other men was dressed in a crisp navy-blue suit, his thick, dark hair slicked back, glasses perched on the end of his nose.

But it was the third man who immediately dominated the space.

Dressed in black jeans slung low on his hips, a white shirt, and a black leather jacket, he wore sunglasses despite the dreary day, and his black hair was gelled, so it stood on end about two inches up. He carried himself with an air of confidence, almost arrogance, and just from the way he held himself she knew he was a dangerous man.

They always were.

Mean too.

And with more money than any person could ever hope to use in one lifetime.

"As you can see, we have a small offering today, but I'm sure something to cater to your needs," the man in the blue suit spoke in a cultured voice. Another man who had more money than morals. Suit man had been here when she arrived. He'd given her a thorough perusal, poking and prodding at her as though she were a product he needed to inspect to be able to figure out its price. Ivory had endured the inspection with a stoicism born of the life she'd led, but that didn't mean she didn't harbor fantasies about ripping the man's filthy fingers right from his hand. Fingers that had touched her most intimate parts without a single care over what he was going to do to her.

"If there's nothing here that meets with your approval you can either wait until we have another offer, or you can put in a custom order. It does cost quite a bit more because of the extra effort in procuring what you would like, but it does mean you can have a girl who meets every one of your criteria," suit man continued. A slick salesman only he wasn't selling cars he was selling women.

Sexy man—had she really just thought of the sick, twisted monster as *sexy*?—okay, hot man merely nodded, and then began to roam the room. He bypassed the children, which was at least some small saving grace, and went to the other woman first, standing before her and examining her with a complete lack of emotion.

Anger buffeted at her, and she had to fight not to struggle pointlessly against the chains. It wouldn't do any good—certainly wasn't going to change anything—but it would make her feel so much better to kick out at him even if she was punished for it. If hot man thought he was going to buy himself some submissive, terrified, broken woman in her then he was going to be in for the shock of his life.

Moving on he came to stand in front of her. Removing his shades, he gave her an appraising onceover, taking in her pale skin, slim physique, and pale blonde hair. She noted that his gaze paused on the few white lines marring her otherwise perfect complexion, old scars from another man who thought women were possessions not people.

"I'll take her," he announced, sliding his shades back on.

Just like that.

Sold.

"Of course, good choice, she is a beauty, and there's a fire about her that says she'll be very enjoyable to break," suit man said with a smile she wanted to smack off his face. "Once you've paid, we can prepare her if you wish to receive her a certain way. We have a full wardrobe, and hair and makeup facilities."

Instead of answering, hot man pulled a cell phone from his back pocket, tapped away at it for a moment, and then slid it back into his pocket. "Money is transferred, and I'd prefer to take her as she is, I have a Christmas engagement tonight I can't miss, and I'd like to be on my way as soon as possible."

Suit man pulled out a tablet and obviously brought up his banking app because he nodded approvingly when he must have seen the pending transfer. Pulling out a key, he stepped up onto her podium and unlocked the cuffs at her wrists.

Painful pins and needles stabbed at her as soon as her arms dropped to hang listlessly at her sides, and she couldn't take a swing at either suit man or hot man even if she allowed herself to.

Which she wouldn't because she couldn't risk it.

Hot man wrapped a hand around her wrist, showing no concern for the pain in her arms as blood flow returned, and yanked her off the podium, making her stumble, her cramped muscles not ready to support her yet.

Not that he cared.

He pulled her along with him toward the door that led to the house, and she had no choice but to follow along as the pet she now was.

Just as he was leading her through the door, the garden doors opened, and a man stepped through.

Ivory gasped.

No.

It couldn't be.

Yet it was.

The little girls were her mission, the reason she was here. The reason she'd deliberately placed herself in an area of Mexico known to be riddled with human traffickers. One, in particular, she believed might be in possession of the kidnapped children. It was why she'd allowed herself to be abducted even though she could have taken down the kidnappers without breaking a sweat. And why she hadn't fought back when she was poked, prodded, and chained up.

But the man who had just entered the room was one she thought she would never lay eyes on again. One who had bought her and several other young girls two decades ago.

One that elite Prey Security operative Ivory Smith wouldn't allow to walk free this time.

* * *

DECEMBER 24TH
8:02 P.M.

ALL ROMAN WANTED to do was get out of this house.

Keeping his grip on the young woman he'd just bought, he moved with long steps through the winding corridors of the house. With her much shorter legs, the girl struggled to keep up, but his skin felt too tight like if he didn't get out of here now then he was going to lose it.

That was the last thing he could do.

Never before had he done something like this, and it hadn't gone like he'd thought it would. He hadn't expected there to be children involved.

Damn. The youngest couldn't have been more than five or six.

Just a baby.

While it had been his choice to come here, he hadn't expected the one-two punch of the small children and then the gorgeous woman eyeing him with a mixture of venom and fury that had his blood threatening to rush south and embarrass him.

How could he respond to her like that?

She was naked, chained to the wall, and had been abducted with the purpose of being sold. Being attracted to

7

her was completely unprofessional, and Special Agent Roman Morales of the US Drug Enforcement Administration felt it down to his bones.

Cold.

Emotionless.

Robot.

Ruthless.

Uncaring.

Just a few of the adjectives his colleagues had thrown at him. Well, most of it had been said behind his back, but he knew how everybody saw him, he just had no inclination to go about changing their opinions.

Mostly because they weren't wrong.

He absolutely was all of those things, and it was one of the reasons he had joined the DEA after leaving Delta Force. He'd intended to be a lifer in the military but after his sister's murder things had changed.

Now here he was, fighting a completely different kind of war.

One that he'd thought he was cut out for given the fact he was cold and emotionless like a ruthless and uncaring robot. Turns out maybe he was wrong. Maybe he couldn't go through with this.

There had to be something wrong with him if he could feel attracted to a woman who had been abducted and brutalized. He knew what these kinds of men were like, just because he couldn't see any fresh cuts or bruises didn't mean they hadn't hurt her.

And those scars ...

That had been what had cut through his hard shell. Roman had known he needed to get out of here now before he did something that would blow this mission to hell before it even got started. If he wanted to catch a notorious drug trafficker—and he did because the man was also responsible for Roman's sister's murder—then he needed to keep his head on his shoulders.

Why was that suddenly so hard?

As he dragged her out the front door, the woman tried to pull out of his grip, only she wasn't pulling in the direction of the thick rainforest that surrounded the house, instead, she was pulling at him as though she wanted to get back inside. The poor thing was probably so traumatized that she didn't know which way was up. She was probably also terrified about what he was going to do to her when he got her away from here. Perhaps there was a sort of security in staying at the house, at least she knew what to expect there.

Even though he wanted to tell her who he was and that she was perfectly safe with him, he couldn't break the charade until they were far away from here. Inside, he'd come perilously close to decking Richard Bouquet, head of the El Compradores. They were a relatively new trafficking ring that had risen in the wake of El Entregar's destruction at the hands of the renowned Prey Security who had managed to disassemble the largest trafficking ring in the world. It was only the fact that this mission was personal to him—if he failed a drug lord didn't just remain free, but the man who killed his sister went unpunished—that had him refraining from beating the man to a bloody pulp.

He had to hold it together.

There wasn't any choice.

Which was why instead of stopping to remove the ball gag the woman was wearing and tend to the bleeding wounds on her wrists, to reassure her that she didn't have to be afraid anymore, he merely snatched her up, slung her unceremoniously over his shoulder, and carried her to his rental.

With no choice but to treat her as he would if he had really come here to purchase himself a sex slave, he opened the trunk and dumped her inside it. Fire shot at him from the blue eyes of the woman, and he consoled himself with the thought that she was strong, she would get through this ordeal, he had to believe that. Had to believe that he hadn't further traumatized her with this charade.

Pulling out a plastic zip tie, he yanked her arms behind her back and secured them, guilty about having to put the unyielding plastic flush against her raw wounds. Next, he secured her ankles, and from the mumbling through the gag she was aiming his way he was pretty sure she was telling him exactly what she thought of him.

Needing to get away from her, he slammed the trunk closed and slid into the driver's seat. Music blasted into the car as soon as he turned the engine on, and he took a moment to lean his head back against the headrest and rake his fingers through his rain-soaked hair.

Why was he all of a sudden struggling with this mission?

He'd wanted it, argued his case to get it when his boss thought it was too much given his personal connection to the man he was hunting. It wasn't like he hadn't known that human traffickers dealt in children as well as adults. He'd known that, studied Richard Bouquet in great detail, and was well aware of the fact that the man had been known to sell children as young as twelve months old to sick perverts. The man would acquire anything that his customers required, from infants to the elderly and anything in between. Any nationality, any physical traits, you could even request a particular hobby or occupation. Whatever you wanted El Compradores would find for you. At a price of course.

Knowing he better get out of here before he stormed back in there and strangled the man with his bare hands, Roman started driving. The house he'd rented for his stay in Colombia was about ten miles from Richard's estate. He'd wanted to be close by so if there was any chance he could have partaken in the raid to bring the man down then he could do so. It had taken months to build this alias, months of networking and building underworld connections to get an invite to use Richard's services, and while he couldn't do anything to ruin his cover if there was a way to be involved— however small—in the coming raid to take down El Compradores he wanted in.

The pounding of the rain on the car's roof went some way to soothing his strung-out nerves, and the music blocked out any screams the woman might be making. He didn't want to feel her pain and terror, he had learned to shut himself down to other's pain a long time ago, and he didn't want some trafficking victim changing that.

All he had to do was get her to his house, tell her who he was, then call in his boss and hand the woman over to the embassy to get her safely back to her home. Then they would bring in another DEA agent to play his slave when he moved on to the next stage of his plan.

By the time he pulled into the driveway he had a blinding headache, which had at least helped his emotions to stabilize again, so it was an even trade. Once the car was in the garage and the door was down—he didn't want the woman trying to run before he could explain—he got out of the car and popped the trunk.

As predicted, the little spitfire was shooting daggers at him as he gathered her into his arms, and he was pretty sure that if he didn't explain fast, she would indeed take any opportunity to run.

Juggling her in his arms he unlocked the interior door that led from the garage to the house and carried her inside, through a large laundry room, and into the lounge room where he set her on the couch. Roman quickly shed his jacket so he could remove his shirt and wrap it around the woman's small frame.

Surprise flickered in her eyes at the gesture, and she didn't fight him when he cut the zip ties at her ankles, and then the ones binding her wrists.

"You don't need to be afraid, I won't hurt you," he explained as he unbuckled the ball gag. Roman was no expert in dealing with victims, they never usually connected with him as though they could sense somehow he had absolutely nothing in the way of comfort or reassurance to offer them, but today there was nobody else here to do it.

Still, he knew what she needed to meet her physical needs, a fire in the fireplace, something to wear besides his shirt, food and water, painkillers, and treatment for her wounds. Those were all things he could provide.

"I'm a DEA agent," he told her as he stood, but at the exact second he took his eyes off her, the woman sprung from the couch with a speed he hadn't anticipated. With strength he never could have guessed she possessed, she swept his legs out from under him, knocked him down, and twisted his arm behind his back, using pressure points and physics to render him all but helpless. Him, a six-foot-two, two hundred and ten pound, trained Delta Force operative had just been taken down by a tiny little thing who was barely five foot tall and couldn't weigh in at triple digits.

"Wait," she said, her voice raspy no doubt from a dry throat thanks to the ball gag and her treatment by El Compradores. "What did you just say?"

"I'm a DEA agent," Roman repeated as he wondered who in the hell this woman was. One thing was for sure, she was no helpless trafficking victim.

CHAPTER TWO

December 24th
    8:30 P.M.

"You're a what?" Ivory asked, sure she must have somehow misheard even though he'd said the same thing twice now.

He'd said he was DEA. The only question was whether or not she believed him.

"I'm working an undercover op. My name is Roman Morales. My badge is hidden in a secret compartment in the third kitchen drawer beneath a bunch of utensils."

Was he telling the truth?

To find out she'd have to release the hold she had on him and she wasn't sure she was ready to do that just yet. When he'd brought her here, he had given her his shirt, and he'd tried to reassure her right before she'd jumped him. Even though she had his arm twisted and was using pressure points to keep him under control, he still had a foot and a hundred pounds on her. If he really wanted to, he could take her out.

Beneath her, she could feel his corded muscles tense with restraint. He didn't want to hurt her so he was allowing her the illusion of being in control. She'd bet anything this man had served in the military before joining the DEA. This wasn't her first rodeo, she'd done this before, taken down a man who thought he'd bought her with nothing but her hands. Wasn't like she could have a weapon on her when she allowed herself to be kidnapped. Roman was the only man who she had ever believed could crush her if he so chose.

Slowly, she released her hold on him, ending the charade. If he really was DEA then they were on the same team. As she took a step back, suddenly far too aware of the fact that she was naked except for his shirt around her shoulders, Roman moved equally as slowly. Keeping his hands held out, palms up, showing her he was no threat to her, he walked backward into the kitchen.

A small smile quirked up one side of her mouth. Even though they both knew he would win if the two of them went hand to hand, the fact he didn't want to turn his back on her at least said he viewed her as a threat. It was the very fact that most people didn't see her as one that allowed her to go undercover and do what she did, but she liked that Roman acknowledged that she was in fact quite capable of eliminating threats.

"Here, see?" Roman tossed her a badge, which she caught easily and confirmed that he was in fact Roman Morales a DEA Special Agent.

Relieved to know he was actually one of the good guys, Ivory nodded, then set the badge on the coffee table and sunk down onto the couch, suddenly exhausted. Her muscles were achy from too long being chained to the wall in Richard Bouquet's house, then in the trunk of the car. She also had a headache, her wrists were caked in dried blood, she was thirsty, and she was still in shock over the man she'd seen as Roman was taking her away.

All in all, she was ready for her team to arrive so she could tell them what she knew. Then she wanted to take a long hot bath and take a nice long nap so she was well rested to go after the monster of her nightmares.

"Can I take a look at your wounds?" Roman asked, approaching cautiously and she laughed, causing him to eye her like he wasn't completely sure she wasn't going to knock him down again just for fun.

"If you have a first aid kit, I can do it myself. And maybe some clothes too? And water? Oh, and something to eat if you have anything, fruit maybe?"

He frowned like he didn't know what to make of her but nodded and left her in the living room while he disappeared, presumably to get her something to wear. While she waited, Ivory slipped her arms into the shirt and buttoned it up. It had a warm, woodsy smell to it, strong, powerful, kind of like Roman himself and she didn't even attempt to analyze why she got a soft feeling in her belly by wearing it.

"Sweatpants, sweatshirt, socks, and, uh, underwear," Roman announced as he came back into the room, carrying the clothing over to the couch, but carefully not getting too close. Seemed while she trusted him, he still didn't quite trust her, although he hadn't asked her who she was yet.

"Thanks," she said as she took the clothes and started putting them on.

"They're probably a little too big, I wasn't sure what size the woman I would be buying would be and you're a tiny little thing."

"Took you down," she reminded him with a grin, and he frowned at her again.

"You going to tell me who you are now?" he asked when she sat down to pull on the socks.

"Ivory Smith. I'm part of Prey Security's Artemis Team. I'm positive you're familiar with Prey." Even if he hadn't been in the military Prey regularly worked alongside various alphabet agencies including the DEA. Prey was one of the best security companies in the world, a billion-dollar business that did everything from private security to the wealthy to black ops missions for the government. Artemis Team was a team of four women based out of the West Coast offices, run by a team of former SEALs under the authority of Eagle Oswald, CEO and founder of Prey. The company was run by Eagle and his five siblings and had branched out from the original Alpha team to include Bravo, Charlie, and Delta teams, then the West Coast teams, Artemis and Athena teams around four years ago. Now they were adding search and rescue, serial killer hunters, and a K9 unit.

"You work for Prey?" Roman seemed surprised by that and she fought back a surge of irritation.

"Because I'm a woman I can't work for Prey? Don't let Raven, Sparrow, Dove, Olivia, Hope, and Maddy hear you say that." Raven, Sparrow, and Dove were Eagle's three younger sisters, and Olivia was his wife. Hope was married to Falcon Oswald, and Maddy had married Hawk just after Thanksgiving.

"I wasn't implying a woman can't work at Prey," he said as he went into the kitchen and retrieved a bottle of water and an apple, both of which he brought to her. "I just wasn't sure Artemis and Athena teams actually existed. You guys are like legends in the spec ops world. No one knows your identities."

"Can't do what we do if our faces are plastered all over the place," she said as she took the bottle, cracked the lid, then took a long drink. "This is not how I thought today was going to play out."

"What was your mission?"

She wasn't going to tell him about the man, that was personal to her and her sisters, so she said, "The girls. We got word that a shipment of little girls had been taken from the US to Colombia and Prey was hired to find them."

"So, you got yourself abducted on purpose hoping to get taken to the same place?"

"Yep. I have a couple of trackers implanted. Once my team knew where I was, they could go in and get them. A dozen girls were in that shipment though and only six at Richard Bouquet's place, which means we have another six girls to find."

"How did you know it would work?"

"I didn't."

"That's crazy."

Ivory shrugged. "No crazier than what you did. I knew my team would track me, come for me. It's not the first time I've done it."

"Crazy," he muttered again, this time under his breath, and she couldn't really argue. It was a little crazy, but it was all she and her sisters knew to do with their lives. "How about I take a look at your wrists, looks like there's some rust in the wounds and we don't want them getting infected."

It was on the tip of her tongue to tell him that she could quite easily clean and bandage the wounds herself, but for some reason, she kind of liked the idea of his large hands touching her, so instead she nodded.

Neither of them spoke as he took a seat beside her on the couch and opened the first aid kit. His touch was gentle as he cleaned out the wounds on her wrists, then applied antibiotic cream before bandaging them.

When he turned his attention to the lump on her head, Ivory got a fluttery feeling in her stomach.

She'd never had a man touch her this way, so gently and softly.

Gentle and soft weren't words she'd immediately think of when she looked at Roman, but despite his size and the hardness in his nearly black eyes, he was being so careful with her.

"Did they do this to you when they kidnapped you?" he asked as his long fingers probed the lump.

"Yes," she replied, the word coming out a little breathily.

"You lose consciousness?"

"Yes."

"Dizziness, nausea?"

"I'm okay." No point in telling him both had been present when she'd woken up at Richard's house, everything had worked out in the end.

"How many fingers am I holding up?"

She smiled at his fussing. "Three."

"Blurred vision? Double vision?"

"I'm fine," she assured him. If he was this freaked by the idea of her having one head injury, she'd hate for him to find out about more serious injuries she'd sustained on missions, or the causes of the scars he'd been looking at back at Richard's house.

"Fine," he echoed. Only this time his eyes met hers and she felt this invisible thread pulling her toward him.

Her gaze dropped to his lips.

She wanted to know what they felt like pressed against her own.

Would he taste as strong alpha male as his scent?

His head dipped and she leaned in, almost mesmerized by the sudden desire swirling through her body.

"I hope we're not interrupting."

* * *

DECEMBER 24ᵀᴴ
8:44 P.M.

THE SOUND of the voice had Roman springing away from Ivory.

Had he really been about to kiss her?

What had he been thinking?

He had little time for women and no desire for any romantic entanglements. The last thing he needed was to risk getting a woman pregnant and passing on his defective genes.

"Since I know you're capable of taking down a threat, I take it you know them," he said, allowing his voice to go hard as he started repacking the first aid kit, ignoring the three women who had entered the house.

If Ivory was the least bit embarrassed about their near kiss, she didn't show it, just stood and hurried over to the newcomers, throwing her arms around a woman with mahogany hair. Next, she hugged the brunette, then finally a woman with black hair and green eyes which were currently narrowed on him like he carried the plague.

"He's not in cuffs," the green-eyed woman stated as though that wasn't abundantly obvious.

"He's DEA," Ivory explained. "Roman Morales, he's undercover."

Although two of the women relaxed, their hands moving away from their weapons, the one with green eyes continued to stare at him skeptically. Instead of responding, she pulled out a cell phone and tapped away at it. "I'll have Raven or Olivia confirm his identity."

Ivory rolled her eyes. "I checked his badge."

"Yeah, because that can't be faked," green eyes muttered, causing Ivory to roll her eyes again.

"Sorry about Pearl, she doesn't trust anyone and she can be a bit of a killjoy," Ivory explained as she walked back to the couch, picked up the apple he'd given her, and took a big bite. "Mmm, delicious," she said as her tongue darted out to catch a drop of apple juice from her bottom lip, and he had to quickly look away before he did something to embarrass himself. Like getting a hard-on.

Ridiculous.

He was acting like an idiot.

Which annoyed him more than anything else. So Ivory was sexy, gorgeous, had the ability to take him down—which wasn't something a lot of men could do let alone a tiny woman—and didn't seem hardened by her job.

"I'm Opal," the woman with the mahogany hair said, "and that's Lacey," she pointed at the brunette. "Ivory, are you hurt?" Opal crossed the room and fussed around Ivory who smiled indulgently at her.

Lacey gave him a sexy smirk and a lazy once over and although the woman was stunning, she didn't do anything for him. Pearl was still glaring at him, and he knew they wouldn't share much with him until she got confirmation he was who he said he was.

A minute later, Pearl announced to the room, "He checks out. Raven called one of our DEA contacts and they vouched for him."

"I didn't doubt him, Pearl," Ivory said, finishing off her apple, resting back against the fluffy couch cushions, and tucking her feet up beneath her. She looked exhausted, no wonder after what she'd just put herself through, and he felt the unusual urge to make sure she took care of herself and got the rest she needed.

To fight off the unwanted concerns about a stranger, he stood and headed into the kitchen. It was late, but he hadn't eaten dinner yet, he'd been too anxious to make sure everything went down the way it was supposed to. He knew Ivory wouldn't have been given anything at El Compradores and he doubted her team had eaten either.

Cooking was what he did to relax. As a kid, they'd been lucky to have ramen noodles and boxed mac and cheese for dinner. When he'd gone out on his own for the first time, he'd been determined to learn to cook real food. In the military, and even sometimes now at the DEA, he had to eat MREs and other packaged food but when he could he preferred homemade meals made from scratch.

As he started rifling through the cupboard to find enough food to cook for five, he watched as the other women hovered around Ivory talking in hushed whispers and wondered what was going on. It wasn't really any of his business. As far as his mission was concerned, he could go right back to what he'd planned. Purchasing a woman had been all for show, he'd always intended to set her free as soon as they got back here. He just needed to make sure the man he was hunting was aware of his purchase, and that when he turned up to try to make contact with him, he came with a woman in tow. That woman would be a trained agent not the woman he bought, but his target wouldn't know that.

Still, he was mildly interested in what Ivory and her team were whispering about. She'd told him she was sent in to try to get a lead on the missing girls, but there had been a man entering the room just as he was leaving with her, and she'd become agitated upon seeing him.

Once he had lightly battered fish frying and fresh vegetables steaming, he wandered over to the couch. Immediately the women stopped talking.

"This doesn't concern you," Pearl snapped, and he could see that even knowing he was actually one of the good guys she still wasn't prepared to trust him.

"Pearl," Ivory rebuked. "Sorry about her, she doesn't play well with others. We should tell him."

"DEA won't have information Prey doesn't," Lacey said.

"Still, I have an idea and I'll need him for it, so I vote that we tell him, but if you all don't want to then we won't," Ivory said, but she didn't sound happy about it. It was clear the four women were close, and that they were reluctant to let outsiders in.

He should respect their wishes, head back to the kitchen and leave them to it, but he found instead that he perched on the edge of the coffee table and looked expectantly from one woman to the other until his gaze landed on Ivory.

"Fine, tell him," Pearl said with a dramatic sigh.

Ivory huffed a chuckle. "Ease up on him, he didn't hurt me, he was quite the gentleman all things considered."

"Fine," Pearl said again, but this time her voice lost its hard edge. "Thank you for taking care of her."

"I can take care of myself," Ivory muttered, and he didn't doubt that was completely true. With a last glance at her team, when they nodded, she faced him, all traces of humor gone, and he found himself wanting to bring it back. "We were all abducted when we were very young, under five. We were all sold to the same man."

"The man you saw today," he said.

"Yes. We don't know his real name, we were made to call him Master. He kept us locked away on a remote property surrounded by an electrified fence. We lived there until we were teenagers, he trained us to become killers. His own personal army," Ivory explained.

Cold chills immediately prickled his skin.

Roman thought his own upbringing had been messed up, but Ivory and her team took the cake.

"Are you sure it was him you saw today?" he asked.

Ivory's blue eyes met his directly. "Positive. We were rescued by Prey, Eagle helped us, took care of us, and because we were so well trained, he asked us if we would like to work for him. Of course, we said yes. A chance to take out men like the one who bought us, no way we could turn that down."

"We looked for him," Lacey added.

"But so far even with all of Prey's resources we haven't had any luck," Opal said.

"Until today." A fierceness in Ivory's eyes told him he wasn't going to like whatever she had to say next.

This woman seemed to manage to bring out a protective streak he hadn't even realized he had. Joining the military had been about getting out of the hell he'd lived in as a kid. He could never afford college so enlisting seemed like the best path for him to take. A path that would keep him on the straight and narrow. Once there, his natural competitiveness had led him to try to make it to the elite Delta Force. Of course he'd liked fighting for his country, ridding the world of trash, but it wasn't why he'd joined.

But Ivory lit a protectiveness inside him, and he was positive whatever she had planned none of them, including him, were going to like.

"So, let's hear it," he said.

"Hear what?" Ivory asked, all big blue eyes and innocent smile, twirling a lock of hair around her finger like she wasn't some highly trained undercover operative.

"Whatever plan you have cooked up in that pretty head of yours." The words were out before he could stop them, and he hardened his gaze so the women thought he was mocking her rather than being deadly serious.

Ivory merely grinned like she could see inside his head and knew he was attracted to her. "We can't let him go, we might not get another chance at him. You have to take me back."

CHAPTER THREE

December 25th
12:23 A.M.

"HOW MUCH LONGER ARE YOU going to be sulking?" Ivory asked Roman. She had to fight back a grin. He was pretty adorable with the pouting routine and giving her the silent treatment was kind of cute too. Annoying definitely, but also kind of sweet considering the reason he didn't want to go through with her plan was because he was worried about her getting hurt.

While she was no masochist, she was also no stranger to pain. It was sometimes something you had to endure to get the payoff you wanted, and there was no better payoff than getting the man who had kidnapped her and her sisters and done unspeakable things to them.

None.

If to achieve that goal she had to take a beating or whatever other punishment Richard Bouquet would hand out, then that was what she would do.

"I'm not sulking." Roman tossed a glare her way.

This time she couldn't hold back a laugh. "If you say so."

"Your sisters didn't like your idea either," he reminded her as though she'd forgotten the argument they'd had over the delicious dinner he'd cooked for them.

"They'll get over it, and they'll agree to it, you're going to be the only holdout." It was true. Her sisters wouldn't like the idea of her deliberately putting herself in a dangerous situation—again—but they were also logical like her, and logic dictated that this was the best way to get what they all wanted.

There was no way her sisters would pass up this opportunity.

"I could call my boss, have you arrested and taken back Stateside," he threatened, only they both knew it was an empty threat.

"What exactly would you charge me with? I don't have any drugs in my system, and you found me at the house of a human trafficker, naked and chained to the wall." There was no way to miss the flare of heat in his eyes at the word naked, and she was pleased to know she wasn't the only one feeling this crazy chemistry between them.

Tearing his gaze away from her, he studied the fire crackling in the fireplace. Her team had left. While getting a lead on the Master was something none of them could overlook it also didn't change the primary mission objective.

They had to find the girls, but they also wanted to find the buyers. Finding a buyer meant rescuing any other slaves they may have, and sometimes even recovering bodies of former slaves, which meant being able to give closure to their families.

Closure was so important, Ivory knew that from experience.

She'd been less than two years old when the Master had kidnapped her. She'd had no memories of her parents or her life before and hadn't known if anyone was missing her or trying to find her. After they were eventually rescued by Prey, Raven Oswald had looked into each of their backgrounds and Ivory had learned that her parents had been murdered in a home invasion, but that her mom had hidden her and saved her life. With no family to take her in, she had been placed in foster care, and been kidnapped while in the system. Of course, her disappearance had been investigated but with no family to fight for her, her case had eventually slipped through the cracks.

Knowing she'd had parents who had loved her, who might very well have sacrificed their own lives for her had helped a lot. Someone had wanted her, she'd been important to someone, and belonged somewhere.

Of course there was her team—sisters as they thought of one another—and she loved them so much, loved everyone at Prey who had done so much for her and made her part of their extended family. She and her team had promised it would always be just the four of them, that nobody would ever come between them and break them up.

Ivory cast a glance at the strong man staring into the flames.

Some nights she got lonely, climbing into her empty bed, and she wondered what it would be like to have a man in her life. It would have to be a man who saw and respected her strength and independence, who could cope with her job and with the issues she had because of her childhood. A man who could see past all of that to get to the real Ivory, the one only a few caught a glimpse of.

"There has to be another way," Roman said, breaking her train of thought.

"If you have another plan, I'm open to hearing it." Her team had brought her clothes so she was more comfortable now in her own sweats, and she'd taken a shower and had a full belly. All she really needed was sleep, but she was way too wired for that.

Roman turned to face her, his expression dark as he examined her from the other end of the sofa. He'd been careful to place the distance between them after her team left and she had to wonder if he was as baffled by his attraction to her as she was by hers to him.

"No, I don't have another plan," he growled. Clearly, that frustrated him.

Alpha men, what could you do with them? They carried the weight of the world on their shoulders and thought they were responsible for taking care of everyone.

Only she wasn't a normal woman.

No way she could have been given the way she'd been raised.

If there was one thing Ivory Smith knew how to do, it was take care of herself.

Reaching over, she rested a hand on his forearm. Corded muscles rippled beneath her touch and although he tensed, he didn't pull away as she expected him to. "Roman, I know you don't like it, but we told you what that man did to us." Well, the basics, she wasn't sure he could handle knowing the details of just how bad it had been. "You can't ask me to let him get away."

"Why are you the one taking all the risks while your sisters sit safe and sound in the van?"

"This is what I'm good at. They've all done it too, but I'm the one who seems to get kidnapped more when I play bait. Pearl is too angry, Lacey is too flirty and self-confident, and Opal had a panic attack when she tried it, we almost lost her."

Before Ivory could get lost in the memory, she shook herself and gave Roman what she thought was a confident smile. "I look sweet and innocent. I'm never seen as a threat, it just makes sense that I'm the one who usually does this. And it's not like the others aren't in danger too. After I get the man restrained, they come in which usually includes shooting their way through the man's guards. Then we go back and shut the seller down if we can."

Dark eyes studied her, deep orbs of inky blackness that seemed full of emotion he fought ruthlessly to control. "You don't have panic attacks letting those men do what they do to you?"

"No."

"You're not angry about everything you've been through? About the sick world we live in?"

"Oh, I'm angry, I'm just better at controlling it than Pearl."

"You're not confident in your body?"

A pleasant flush warmed her. "I'm plenty confident in my body."

"You don't flirt?" A husky quality to his voice had her skin tingling and her nipples pebbling.

How long had it been since she'd been with a man?

Much too long.

She liked sex for the most part, although it had taken her a while to get to that point. More often than not, they were working one mission or another. Most involved human trafficking although not all of them, but all of them involved a tremendous amount of time and planning. When she wasn't working, she'd had the odd boyfriend, but usually, they seemed like work, like she had to pretend to be someone she wasn't, and so things eventually fizzled out. Ivory was content to enjoy her Prey family and live vicariously through Lacey's always entertaining tales of her love life.

"I've been known to flirt," she murmured, looking down to realize her hand was still on his arm.

What would he do if she kissed him?

She wanted to, had barely been able to think of anything else since she learned he was DEA and not some sick pervert who bought trafficked women.

He was a dangerous man, she could tell that just by looking at him, but at his heart he had to be a good man to do what he did.

"You know," she said as she leaned forward, "it's after midnight, that means it's Christmas Day. Merry Christmas, Roman." Ivory touched her lips to his in a soft, sweet kiss, and tried not to let the warmth inside her grow into a fiery inferno she'd have no chance of putting out. One thing was clear, Roman had I don't do relationships all but tattooed on his forehead, and she didn't want to wind up hurt and nursing a broken heart.

* * *

DECEMBER 25TH
1:08 A.M.

"I DON'T LIKE THIS."

Ivory rolled her eyes at him. Again. "I know. You've told me. Several times. No not several times, I think the definition of several is more than two but not a lot. You've definitely told me you don't like this plan a *lot* of times. A whole lot of times."

"You talk too much," he muttered under his breath, making her laugh.

"Maybe *you* don't talk enough," she countered, and Roman found himself fighting a smile.

How was this woman so positive all the time given what he knew about her past?

Surely, she should be a little more affected by everything she'd been through. How could she be abducted, trained from toddlerhood to become a killer, willingly allowing herself to be taken by human traffickers and be not only so completely normal but so happy?

He'd love to know her secret.

Because he was bitter and cold thanks to his own sordid life story.

"Your team knows you're going back in?" he asked as they stared each other down from either side of the couch. Well, he was the one staring, she was watching him with something akin to curiosity, like she was trying to figure him out, get a read on him. Good luck with that. Nobody got inside his head.

"You know they do. I wouldn't operate without them just like you wouldn't operate without yours. I assume you called your boss already and told them you found me there. I hope you also asked them to hold off on whatever raid they have planned until we see if the man who kidnapped me and my sisters is still there. If he's not, and we raid the house too early, we might lose this lead."

"I told my boss," he acknowledged. While he hadn't been forthcoming about his case, Ivory hadn't asked many questions. He didn't want to lie to her, but he also didn't want to confess that this case was as personal to him as finding this man was to her.

"And?" she prompted.

"And he agreed to hold off on the raid until tomorrow."

Ivory let out a long breath. "Thank you." There was pure

gratitude in her eyes, and it made him uncomfortable. Why did the woman have to be so open? Couldn't she keep this a simple business transaction between them?

Although, that implied he would go along with her crazy plan.

Who was he kidding?

Of course he was going to go along with it.

Because she'd asked him to.

"You know if I take you back, pretend that you weren't worth what I paid, there's a chance he might kill you," Roman said. The idea of Ivory no longer existing left him feeling almost ... bereft. Which was as crazy as it was ridiculous.

"He won't," Ivory said with a confidence he wished he felt.

"You can't know that."

"Course I can. How is he going to make any money off me if he kills me?" Her blue eyes dared him to counter that argument, but for some reason, all he could do was stare at her lips.

She'd kissed him earlier.

He hadn't stopped her.

Worse, he'd liked it.

"I'll give you a choice."

"Yeah?" Somehow he tore his gaze from her lips and focused them on her eyes instead.

"You can take me back to Richard's and demand a refund so I can get a second chance at finding the man who stole me, or you and I can spend Christmas Day upstairs in your bed making love while we wait for your team to arrive tomorrow."

"We're not having sex," he blurted out, even though every drop of blood in his body dropped south of the border.

"I don't know if I should be offended or amused by that declaration," Ivory said. Instead of looking the least bit offended, she laughed like his discomfort was amusing to her. Like she knew without a shadow of a doubt how badly he wanted to bury himself inside her and lose control, just for a few minutes.

Doing his best not to let her know how tempted he was to follow up on option B, he kept his voice hard when he spoke. "If they don't kill you then they'll hurt you. Badly." While he hadn't had a lot to do with human traffickers—he worked with the DEA where obviously they were more focused on drugs—it didn't mean he wasn't aware of how these men worked. They believed he had been truly there to purchase a woman. If he returned said woman claiming she didn't meet his standards, then Ivory would be the one to pay the price. Chances were, she was right when she said they wouldn't kill her, but they could make her wish they had.

"Roman." Her tone softened, became gentle like a soft caress against his soul, and she moved closer again, placing her hand on his knee. It was small and warm, but it packed a powerful punch just lying there. This was a woman who held the power to turn his entire carefully constructed world upside down. "I only need a short time there, long enough to see if I can get any intel from him. He's probably long gone, but I might be able to get something, I can't pass up this opportunity, you get that right? Because I might never get another chance. I'm not asking you to give up your mission. All I'm asking is that you do this for me and then I'll leave and you can get back to what you came to Colombia for."

There was a part of him, some deep primitive part that appeared to be unaffected by his bad childhood and poor genes, that wanted to beg her to stay.

But it was a part of himself best ignored.

"You can always offer to buy me back at a discount," she suggested. "That way you give me enough time to see if I can find anything out, but you don't have to deal with the guilt of what happens to me after you leave me there."

Guilt.

If he left her behind and she was badly injured or even killed before his team moved in tomorrow morning, he would blame himself.

"Please."

It was the whispered plea that did it. The desperation behind that one word. How could he not offer her a chance to gather intel on the man who had hurt her so badly when he was here to do the same thing?

It wasn't as though guilt wasn't already a part of his life.

If he hadn't been so pig-headed, so utterly arrogant and confident, then his sister would likely still be alive.

"Fine," he snapped.

Relief washed over her, and she placed her hands on his shoulders and touched a kiss to his cheek. "Thank you."

As she pulled back their eyes met and immediately the air around them changed. Becoming supercharged with the sexual tension that seemed to ripple between them whenever they were close.

Why hadn't he picked the other woman?

Something had drawn him to Ivory even before he knew anything about her. Buying one of the children wouldn't have worked with his plan, no way one of his colleagues could pretend to be a child, but he hadn't so much as stepped in the door when he knew it was the woman with the long white locks that he needed.

Needed.

Was it possible to need a woman?

He'd made it through thirty-two years without one. There hadn't even been a time when he remembered needing his mother. He and his sister spent so much time in and out of the foster system, even when they were placed back with their biological parents, he never relied on them. Roman made his own meals, got himself to and from school, made sure his homework was done, and signed his own permission slips so he could go on field trips and play sports as he got older.

He had worked hard to get to where he was, and he'd done it all on his own.

So why did this woman make him want more?

Why did she make him feel like everything he had achieved wasn't enough?

Although his body practically begged him to take what Ivory was offering, seek comfort in her sweet kisses, he ruthlessly shoved those thoughts away and stood. "All right," he said on a sigh. "Let's get this over with."

The sooner he got this woman her answers and sent her out of his life the happier he would be.

Or maybe it felt more like the safer he would be.

One tiny woman wasn't going to mess up the life he'd created or have him longing for something that could never be. The sooner he sent Ivory Smith on her way the sooner he could get back to his op.

That had to be his focus.

Justice for his sister.

Lusting after Ivory had no part in a mission of revenge.

CHAPTER FOUR

December 25th
2:26 A.M.

PREDICTABLY, Roman had come up with at least a dozen concerns and arguments after agreeing to her plan.

Ivory thought it was kind of sweet the way he worried. To look at him you wouldn't think he was a worrier. Roman was so big and had the whole tough guy routine down to an exact science. She would have laughed about it, but she was currently trussed up in the trunk of Roman's car, right where she'd been when he'd taken her from here.

Then she'd thought he was a sick monster she was about to have detained, now she couldn't deny she was a little nervous about what was to come. It certainly wasn't like she was going to enjoy this, it was just that she had objectively weighed the pros and cons and decided that allowing herself to be beaten—or whatever else Richard Bouquet decided to have done to her—was worth a chance at finding a lead on the Master.

There was a chance there was no lead there to find, but it was a chance she was willing to take.

A chance she *had* to take.

It was as simple as that.

Ivory believed that life was a series of calculated risks. Nothing really came without risk. You could get hit by a car crossing the street, you could slip in the shower and hit your head, or you could choke on your food. Okay, so what she did with her life was a lot riskier than the average person, but still, someone had to do what she and Prey did. Someone had to fight for those who couldn't fight for themselves.

It was what she had been trained to do since she was two years old only instead of being used by a man with more money than morals as his own personal assassin, she brought down men like the one who had hurt her.

Irony at its finest.

The car bumped over something, and she was tossed up into the air, where it felt like she was suspended for a moment before she slammed back down.

"Ow," she muttered. At least she *could* mutter. Roman had said there was no way he was putting the ball gag back in, and Ivory hadn't felt like arguing about it. She hated the thing, hated the way it made her drool all over her chin, hated how it made her feel less than human. Plus, it wasn't like she could ask questions of any of the girls or the woman if she had it in.

Another bump sent her careening once more up into the lid of the trunk then slamming back down. She and Roman had gone back and forth over whether he would have hit her for her perceived shortcomings before returning her. He had been flat-out adamant that laying a hand on her was going too far and that he wouldn't do it.

Understanding it was asking him to cross a moral code he

37

couldn't give in to in the game he was playing, she'd let it go. Now it hardly seemed to matter, she'd be covered in bruises by the time they got there.

When the car stopped moving, Ivory focused all her attention and allowed her eyes to grow misty. She wasn't one for shedding tears often, that had been beaten out of her before she learned to read, but she had perfected the art of crying on command. More than once tears had helped her out of a tricky situation.

"Bouquet?" Roman roared as he got out of the car and slammed his door behind him.

The rain had stopped, and she could hear his footsteps pounding across the gravel to get to the trunk. When he popped it open and reached for her, Ivory found that if she didn't know they were playing roles she would have been terrified of this man.

There was a darkness inside him she recognized because it was the same darkness that had been inside the Master. Only unlike that evil man, Roman's wasn't born from a place of wickedness, it was born from dealing with the wickedness of others.

It was a weary darkness.

He was trapped in an ocean of pain, and he was drowning. What he needed was someone to throw him a life ring. She'd be that life ring for him if he let her, but she suspected he wouldn't.

Snatching her up, his hand clamped around her bicep with a grip so hard it would likely leave bruises. He dragged her with him toward the door just as it was opened.

"Senor Lennox?" Richard asked as he stepped onto the grand porch. "Is there a problem?"

Roman threw her to the ground at Richard's feet, and the

hiss of pain that escaped her lips was a real one. At least he accepted his role with gusto even if he didn't like it.

"Is there a problem?" Roman repeated mockingly.

Richard's eyes narrowed. "Well, is there? We told you the girl was not trained."

"It's not that she's not trained, I have no problem undertaking that task myself, it's her skin," Roman growled.

"Her skin?" Richard repeated, eyeing her naked flesh with a hunger that told her she wouldn't like to be alone in a room with him.

"It has scars. I wanted a blank canvas. I don't want some other man's work staring me in the face when I'm looking at a woman I paid good money for," Roman snarled.

"You are returning her?" Richard nodded to one of his bodyguards who was quick to step forward and yank her back to her feet.

"I have little use for her," Roman said as though that were glaringly obvious.

With another nod, the man holding her dragged her into the house and back toward a staircase that led down to a dank, dark basement. There were chains, whips, and other implements of torture. Some she'd had used on her before when she'd played this game, but she barely spared them a glance as her eyes scanned the space to see if anyone else was down here.

Luck was on her side.

The other adult woman from yesterday was there, chained to the wall, a thin blanket spread over her lap.

"Richard will be down to deal with you shortly," the guard told her as he tossed her down to the floor beside the woman and clamped a metal cuff around her ankle. Ivory was so sick of being thrown about like an unwanted piece of clothing, but she kept her mouth shut, her eyes down, and her thoughts to herself.

Delivering a swift kick to her hip, she couldn't help but cry out even though she knew better. Men like this got off on pain, but he'd caught her by surprise with the hard blow.

The man snickered at her then disappeared back up the stairs, and Ivory focused on the other woman. She wanted to reassure her that her ordeal would be over soon, but she also didn't want the woman to tip off the fact that a raid was coming. Letting the woman know what was coming would change how she acted and that could alert these men that something was about to happen. If that happened not only could the DEA lose their shot at El Compradores, but also, she and her sisters might lose their shot at the Master.

Given it was Christmastime, she hadn't expected to be sold yesterday, hoped that the girls might still be here, and hoped that the woman would be safe until the raid tomorrow.

Knowing she didn't have much time she whispered, "The man who came in after me, did he take the children?" Terrified brown eyes looked back at her. Of course the woman was scared, but Ivory needed information. "Please, it's important. Did he take the girls?"

The woman nodded.

"Did he say anything at all? Please, think, anything he said is really important."

"Who are you?" the woman whispered.

"Someone who has a job to do."

Hope lit in the woman's eyes as she obviously inferred that some sort of help was going to come. "He said something about the girls would go well with the fish."

Fish?

Ivory had no idea what that meant.

Before she could ponder it, the door at the top of the stairs opened again, and three men came down.

Time to face the music.

Two of them came to her, removed the cuff, and pulled her into the middle of the room. Then the one who had kicked her gave her a vicious snarl. "Girls who don't please their master deserve what they get," he said as he threw his fist into her stomach, knocking the air from her lungs.

* * *

December 25th

3:13 A.M.

This was hell.

Roman shouldn't care about what was happening to Ivory. Whatever she got was what she wanted, this was her plan, she'd been fully prepared to take whatever punishment she got for a chance at getting her information. The woman had guts, he'd give her that, but she was also crazy, he really couldn't think of another word to describe someone who would do what Ivory did, and risk what she did.

There hadn't even been a glimmer of doubt in her eyes, she was fully committed to her plan.

Guts.

Quite possibly the bravest person—man or woman—he'd ever met.

Pretty too …

"Oh, you're still here," Richard said as he reentered the study where they'd talked business earlier, and he'd received a refund for his purchase of Ivory.

"Well?" he snapped with equal irritation.

"Well, what?" Richard asked as he poured himself a drink.

"Did you find another woman who matches my requirements?"

"I'm sorry, we don't have another blue-eyed woman in storage."

Storage. Roman very nearly lost control of himself at the term the man used. Ivory had mentioned that was why she and her team couldn't swoop right in and shut the compound down. They had to make sure Richard didn't have the other half of the shipment of girls at one of his "storage" locations. The way the man talked about living, breathing women was sickening.

Sighing long sufferingly Roman said, "Fine, then I'll buy back the one I had, but I'm not paying full price."

Richard's eyes narrowed. "You returned her because you didn't like her scars. I refunded you even though the woman was naked and you had the chance to peruse her body. If you didn't like what you saw, you shouldn't have purchased her."

"These scars were hidden under the manacles," he growled. "I don't care about the other ones but these ones are on her wrists, it's not like I won't see them every time I'm with her."

With a disinterested shrug, Richard said, "Then keep her chained up, that way you won't have to see them."

That was likely how Ivory had gotten the scars in the first place, being chained up for long periods of time. "Look, it's been a long day, and I need to leave in the afternoon so I don't have time to wait for you to find what I'm after. I'll buy the girl back for half of what I paid since she has scars."

"She's not in the same condition as when you brought her here," Richard warned.

It took everything in him not to wince. "That's fine. I'm returning to my family today anyway so I won't have much time to spend with her until I leave on my next business trip. By then she should be healed. Half of what I paid you before."

"Fine, half," Richard agreed although his irritation was clear.

Pulling out his cell phone he transferred the money to the man's account and then snapped his fingers, communicating his own irritation. "Get the girl. I'd like to get at least a little sleep before I have to leave for the airport."

Richard nodded and left the room, and Roman waited as patiently as he could, aware that he couldn't pace the room as it was likely fitted with cameras and the last thing he wanted to do was communicate anxiety.

Ten minutes later Ivory was dragged into the room.

The only way not to let his anger explode was to bite down on his tongue until he tasted blood.

Ivory hung limply between two men, her chin on her chest. Already the red marks on her pale skin were beginning to bruise, and he could see smudges of blood all over her.

What he wouldn't give for five minutes alone with the men who had beaten a helpless woman to a bloody pulp.

"I hope I'm not going to need to take her to the hospital," he tutted disapprovingly.

"Relax. The girl will heal. I can't let my merchandise die, then I don't make anything off them," Richard said.

So, Ivory had been right about that at least, she hadn't been in danger of being killed, just badly beaten. He hoped it was worth it.

"Carry her out to my car. I don't want to get blood on me," he ordered then turned and stalked through the house, ready to be out of there.

Once they were outside, he opened the back door of his car. No way was he going to put Ivory in the trunk to be tossed about while she was unconscious. If the men thought there was anything odd about that, too bad, he wasn't going to let the woman be hurt again, and the backseat would be more comfortable than the trunk.

"Put her in," he ordered, and the men laid her out.

He was sure Ivory was unconscious, but when he leaned in to buckle the seatbelts around her so she wouldn't be thrown onto the floor the first time they hit a bump, he found her eyes open. They locked on his, and when one corner of her mouth curled up in an attempt to let him know she was okay, he felt something deep inside him. He didn't know what it was or quite understand its significance, but it felt like a door inside his heart had just been unlocked.

The drive back to his rental took half the time it should have, and it wasn't long before he pulled back into the garage. When he'd come back here earlier with Ivory in the trunk, he'd been concerned about dealing with a hysterical, traumatized victim, now he was concerned only with doing whatever it took to ease her pain.

"Hey, we're here," he said with uncharacteristic gentleness as he unbuckled her seatbelts.

"I'm okay, Roman," she assured him. Of course she wasn't, couldn't be, but he respected her need to try to make him feel better.

Not only was the woman brave and determined, but she cared about others, and put herself in horrific situations to save others. Her selflessness was an example to everyone.

Certainly to him.

Being selfish was the only way he had managed to survive his hellish childhood. Nobody had cared about him, whether he was successful in life or not, whether he built a life for himself or wound up in prison. If he wanted more than his family had given him, he had to work for it, put himself first, and not allow the complications of emotion and entanglements get in the way.

"Sorry," he muttered as he lifted her and she sucked in a pained breath.

"Told you, I'm fine," she gritted out.

"Sure you are." He gave one of Ivory's characteristic eye rolls as he bumped the car door closed with his hip and carried her into the house where he laid her out carefully on the couch.

Snagging a soft, fleece blanket from the back of the armchair, he covered her then started a fire. She was hurt badly, the last thing he needed was her going into shock. Once flames were roaring in the fireplace, he retrieved the first aid kit and a couple of bottles of pills from the bathroom cabinet. Ivory probably wouldn't appreciate it, but she needed sleep, real sleep, and he suspected the only way she was going to get any was to sedate her.

Roman paused in the kitchen on the way back to fill a glass with water before returning to kneel beside the couch. Ivory's eyes were closed, and he took a moment to categorize the injuries he could see. She had a split lip, one of her eyes was swelling closed, and her cheekbone under the other eye had a cut that looked as though it might need stitches.

The need to touch her, offer her comfort was overwhelming and he reached out a hand, pausing just shy of touching her before giving in to the need and sweeping a knuckle across her temple. "Hey, can you tell me your pain level on a scale of one to ten?"

Her eyes opened slowly, her pupils looked equal, and she focused on him without trouble, so he doubted she had another head injury. "I can handle the pain."

"No doubt about it, Wonder Woman, but I need to know

if you might have internal injuries I need to be worried about."

"I don't think so."

"Broken bones?"

"No."

"Ribs?"

She hesitated a moment before answering. "They might be cracked a little."

"Do you always downplay your own pain?" he asked, but his voice was mild and the question was more genuine curiosity than anger.

Ivory looked surprised by the question, and he was surprised by the honesty in her response. "Yeah, usually."

Not sure what to say to that, he slipped an arm around her shoulders and helped her sit. "You need to take something for the pain."

When she opened her mouth he put the pills—one a painkiller the other a sedative—on her tongue then held the glass of water to her lips so she could drink. Once the pills were down, he fluffed a pillow behind her and rested her head and shoulders on it.

With gentle, efficient strokes he began to clean the blood from her face, much too aware that Ivory was watching his every move with heavy-lidded eyes. After tending to her face, he'd make his way down her body. It didn't escape his notice that he'd seen Ivory naked more times than any other woman. When he bothered with women at all it was always a one and done kind of thing, yet he hadn't done anything with Ivory and had already memorized every inch of creamy white skin, every curve, and every smooth plane.

"Did you get what you wanted?" he asked.

Ivory yawned. "He took the girls, said they'd go well with

the fish. I don't know what that means," she told him as her eyes fluttered closed. "Did you drug me?"

"You need the rest," he replied unapologetically.

"You're a tricky one, Roman Morales." Her lips curved into a tired smile, and he found his own wanting to echo it.

"And you're a crazy one, Ivory Smith."

One of her hands moved out from under the blanket, circling his wrist and stilling his hand mid-swipe at a trail of blood on her neck. "Roman?"

"Yeah?"

"Thank you," she whispered before her hand dropped to her stomach and she passed out.

With more affection than he'd ever shown another human being, Roman picked up her hand and touched his lips to the inside of her wrist before tucking it back under the blankets and resuming his task.

"You're welcome," he whispered back even though she was already unconscious.

CHAPTER FIVE

December 25th
    5:35 P.M.

IVORY YAWNED AND STRETCHED, then immediately winced and sucked in a pained breath as her battered body protested the movement.

Immediately, a face appeared above her. "You all right?"

"Just stiff," she assured Roman, touched by his concern. It wasn't that she'd ever been lacking in people to be concerned about her. Ivory couldn't remember a time when her sisters hadn't been around, but she'd never had a man fuss over her before. After being rescued by Prey, Eagle had practically adopted them all, so her surrogate big brothers Eagle, Falcon, and Hawk had fussed over her, well not Falcon so much, he rarely fussed over anyone who wasn't his wife, and she was sure his baby when it came in a few weeks. And the former SEALs who managed her team had been known to fuss a little, but that was different, she wasn't attracted to any of those men. While they were all uber good-looking, with bodies that melted panties, they were like brothers to her.

Roman on the other hand, she definitely had no brotherly feelings when it came to him.

She was crazily attracted to him.

Even now, tired and in pain as she was, if he offered her sex, she was pretty sure she would jump at the chance.

All right, she was more than pretty sure, she would *absolutely* jump at the chance.

"Ivory?"

"Huh?" Had she zoned out? Roman had looked at her from behind the couch a second ago, but now he was standing in front of her.

Shirtless.

His dark jeans were slung low on his hips, his feet were bare, his hair damp as though he'd recently gotten out of the shower, and he looked so delicious she very nearly started licking him all over.

"Ivory?"

"Yeah?" She blinked and slowly lifted her gaze from his washboard abs to meet his worried eyes. They were so dark they reminded her of black holes, ones that could quite easily draw her in and she'd never be seen or heard from again.

"You keep zoning out, I didn't think you had a concussion, but maybe I was wrong."

"I'm okay, no concussion. Promise." Delicious aromas caught her attention, and she sniffed and turned toward the kitchen. "What's that amazing smell?"

"Dinner."

"What are you making?" She would have thought after the beating she'd taken eating would be the last thing on her mind, but her stomach rumbled, and she realized in fact she was starved.

"Turkey, stuffing, mashed potatoes, roast vegetables, and apple pie and whipped cream for dessert."

"Wow, you're really making all of that? You're like a real chef. Did you go shopping while I was sleeping?" Ivory was prepared to let the fact he'd slipped her a sedative without telling her slide because he was right, she had needed the rest.

Roman shifted uncomfortably for a moment. "No, I already had the ingredients in the house."

"You were going to have Christmas dinner all alone?" That made her so sad. Roman seemed like a good guy, okay, he was a little hard and maybe he could work on being a little more charming, but he'd helped her when he hadn't had to, and it was obvious he was worried about her injuries. Why didn't he have anyone in his life to spend the holidays with? Maybe it was her injuries and the emotional toll of the last few days, but her eyes misted at the picture of him eating alone in a house in Colombia with no decorations, no gifts, no laughter, and no companionship on a day that was all about love and family.

"Yes," he said shortly, turning his back on her and returning to the kitchen.

"What about your family?" Ivory asked as she planted her hands on the couch cushions and levered herself so she was standing. Pain stabbed viciously at her from all sides, but since there was nothing she could do about it she drew in a slow, controlled breath and did her best to compartmentalize it.

"Don't have any."

"I'm sorry."

"Nothing to be sorry about." He was fussing around the kitchen now although she could tell by his somewhat jerky movements that he was merely trying to appear busy so she would shut her mouth.

Only she'd never been one to let things slide when she could see someone was hurting.

"Well, I think it's sad you would have spent the holidays alone, but now you don't have to because you have me."

Roman's only response was a grunt. Which she didn't take personally because she knew how she'd feel if she didn't have her sisters. While not blood-related, they were bonded by something much stronger. Trauma and having to depend on one another for their very lives had made their bond unbreakable, and she couldn't imagine truly being alone in the world.

"I'll try not to take offense at your lack of enthusiasm," she chuckled as she turned to head for the bathroom.

A little unsteady on her feet, Ivory swayed, throwing up a hand to reach for the nearest stable object so she didn't wind up flat on her face.

Suddenly, an arm was around her waist, and she was steadied against a rock-hard chest. Her hands were still moving and landed totally by accident on the sleek planes of Roman's bare chest.

"I just got a little dizzy," she said breathily as her fingertips moved of their own volition, stroking across his smooth skin. It felt so good, and her stomach turned delightful little cartwheels. When had she ever had such an intense physical reaction to a man?

Short answer was never.

Mostly she'd had sexual relationships with men because she thought it was something she was supposed to do. Grownups had sex, so sporadically she dated and did just that, but while pleasant enough it had never been anything she really cared about.

Until now.

Now all she wanted was for Roman to pick her up, carry her through to the bedroom, and lay her out beneath him. He'd kiss her and touch her, she'd get her fill of every inch of him, then they'd make beautiful, sweet love.

"Ivory."

"Hmm?"

"Do you need help getting to the bathroom?"

Since she could feel his muscles twitching beneath her, hear his ragged breathing, and see the raw need in his eyes, she knew he was as hungry for her as she was for him, but if he didn't want this then she wouldn't push it.

"No, I can make it."

Taking her time, moving carefully, she went to the bathroom, did her business, avoided looking at her reflection in the mirror, and headed back for the kitchen. She passed a desk on the way and an idea sparked. Grabbing a sheet of crisp white paper, she carried it back with her to the living room and sat down at the breakfast bar.

"How long till dinner?" she asked.

"Should be ready in about five minutes," Roman replied. He wouldn't look at her, and she wondered if he was scared by whatever he felt for her.

Ivory was under no illusion. Things between her and Roman weren't going anywhere, once his team came in tomorrow, he'd go off on his mission and she'd go back to hers with her team, but she also couldn't deny that she wouldn't forget about the man anytime soon. Maybe he'd think about her too, she hoped so, and she wanted to give him something to remember her by.

While he moved about the kitchen, she worked on a little Christmas gift for him. He'd done so much for her it seemed only fair she return the favor and give him a little something.

"Dinner is ready," Roman announced just as she finished up.

"I have a little Christmas gift for you," she announced as she slid off the stool, bracing an arm under her ribs as she crossed to the table.

His eyebrows slanted into a V. "A gift? How could you possibly have a gift to give me? You wrangle up something out of thin air?"

"Kind of." She grinned as she handed him the small origami dragon she'd just made.

"You made this?" He took the dragon and looked at it in awe.

"Learned origami to cope with my anxiety after my sisters and I were rescued by Prey."

"You, anxiety? I didn't think you got anxious about anything."

"I get anxious about plenty, just can't let it cripple me, you know? Life is to be lived, and I try to remind myself that so many people are worse off than me. It helps. You've done so much for me, and I wanted to give you something to remember me by once this is over." The thought of never seeing Roman again wasn't a happy one, but he'd made it clear enough he wasn't really interested in pursuing anything with her, not even a fling while they were here together, and she didn't throw herself at men.

"It's amazing. Thank you." Roman dipped his head, touching a kiss to her cheek.

Knowing it was a bad idea but wanting just one more taste of him, Ivory turned her head just enough that the corner of her mouth brushed the corner of his.

She felt a sigh ripple through him, and then he curled an arm around her waist and pulled her up against him.

"I can't seem to resist you," he murmured, more to himself

than to her she suspected, then his lips claimed hers in a kiss that was fiery and bright, like a mass of Christmas lights had flickered on above them.

Too bad Roman didn't seem to want to see if there could be something between them because, shockingly, Ivory found that she did.

Since you didn't always get what you wanted, she decided to take whatever Roman was offering for the next few hours, so she splayed her palms on his chest and kissed him like it might be the last time she ever got to do it.

Because it probably was.

* * *

DECEMBER 26ᵀᴴ
  6:00 A.M.

As ALWAYS, Roman woke before his alarm and reached over to shut off his phone before the sound could wake Ivory.

Yesterday had been so very different than the Christmas he had envisioned.

After dinner last night—a dinner he had enjoyed a whole lot more than he should have—Ivory had crashed again, falling asleep about two minutes into the movie she'd chosen, some overly sweet, wholesome Christmas romance. Not wanting her to spend the night on the couch, he'd sat beside her until the movie finished before carrying her up to bed. He couldn't recall a single thing from the movie, his attention had been hijacked by the gorgeous blonde, but he also couldn't turn it off because the sound of it in the background had made everything so normal.

He'd felt normal.

For the first time ever.

Ivory had done that. He wasn't even sure how. She was braver than he could ever hope to be, been sweet enough to make him that origami dragon, and chattered away over dinner, not caring that he hadn't contributed much to the conversation. Roman might not have said a lot but he'd been feeling plenty. Weird emotions he had no experience with.

She hadn't woken as he'd cradled her in his arms, and she'd seen so small, so fragile, completely vulnerable to him. If he'd wanted to hurt her, he could quite easily, and yet she'd had complete faith in him. Trusted that he would take care of her and hadn't even stirred as he tucked her into bed. Nor had she stirred when he'd checked on her a couple of times throughout the night.

He would check on her again in a bit, but he usually started his day with a workout. But before he got to that he needed to make a call. It was time for a check-in with his boss.

Throwing back the covers, he grabbed his jeans from the chair beside the bed and quickly stepped into them, he couldn't sleep with clothes on, but he could hardly walk around the house naked. That would be all but asking himself to take what Ivory had offered.

Resisting temptation had been difficult, in fact he'd done it only because he liked and respected Ivory. If he hadn't, he would have accepted the sex she would have freely given him and walked away with a clean conscience.

But sex with Ivory would mean something, which meant when he walked away there would be no clean conscience.

The house was quiet as he grabbed his cell phone and headed downstairs, but it was a nice quiet, a peaceful quiet. Had there ever been a time when he'd actually felt peace? The answer to that was a depressing no.

Once he'd gotten coffee going, he dialed his boss. As he waited for the call to go through, Roman realized this was the first time he actually wished he didn't have to check in, that he didn't have to work.

For most of his life, work had been all there was, but this brief reprise had shown him what he could have if only he wasn't too disillusioned to reach out and take it.

"Morales?"

His boss' voice snapped him out of dreamland. While he wished nothing but the best for Ivory, hoped she could get her happy ending, move away from the pain she'd endured to find what he knew she wanted, that wasn't in the cards for him. Did he really want to tie anyone else to the addictive personality that lived inside him?

No one in his family had escaped that particular curse.

Not even him.

Roman had just made sure his addiction was one that helped humanity rather than hurt it. His addiction was his job, which was where his focus should be right now, not on the blonde asleep upstairs.

"Yes, just checking in, sir," he said. Jesse Masters was only a couple of years older than him, and while good at his job, had a chip on his shoulder the size of a meteoroid. Roman didn't like the man, but Jesse was his boss and had let him work this assignment even though it was personal to him so he tried to at least be civil.

"Anything new to report?" There was something in Jesse's tone that hinted he was angry with Roman, but he couldn't figure out a reason why his boss would be. Finding Ivory at the compound was a twist, but it didn't have anything to do with the mission. Tonight he'd be meeting up with the team raiding the compound, working in a support role since he didn't want to risk his cover being blown, and she'd be meeting up with her team. They'd both go their separate ways, return to their individual ops, and that would be that. All he'd be left with was the memory of a few kisses and a paper dragon that meant far too much to him. Ivory didn't know it, but it was the first gift he'd ever received.

"The raid of El Compradores still scheduled for tonight?"

"You're not going to mention the fact that you nearly blew this op wide open by returning to Bouquet's place?"

Roman stiffened. Anger burned inside him. This op was personal to him. It was vengeance for his sister's murder, possibly a way to relieve some of the guilt he carried, no way would he do *anything* to risk it. "Returning had nothing to do with this case, and it didn't jeopardize it. If anything, it reinforced the fact that Holdon Lennox is a serious buyer, that can only work in my favor."

"You weren't thinking about the case when you went back, you were thinking about the woman." The sneer in Jesse's voice rubbed him the wrong way. It implied that Ivory was truly nothing more than a whore to be used for sex. While sex with Ivory had been practically all he could think about once he realized she wasn't a traumatized trafficking victim, it wouldn't have been cheap and dirty like Jesse was implying.

"That woman is a highly trained, elite operator who works for the best security company in the world. Prey is unrivaled, and you know it. We're just lucky that the girls they were looking for weren't all there or they would have taken down El Compradores already. You should have made contact with them before we came to Colombia. Prey is an asset, they could have helped us." While Prey often did black ops work for the government, they also sometimes worked in conjunction with one of the alphabet agencies on joint taskforces. They were the best of the best and seemed to have eyes everywhere. Working with them would have been better than working against them.

"Prey should keep their noses out of other people's cases," Jesse spat.

"They didn't know we were working a case. If they had, chances are they would have reached out and made sure that neither of our investigations interfered with the other. If Ivory was snatched earlier, Prey would have already dismantled El Compradores' operation leaving us to start over." It wasn't like human traffickers ran Facebook ads. It took months of meticulous searching to potentially get a lead on a trafficker, then several more months' worth of work to make contact and be able to get a location. If they'd lost their chance at Richard Bouquet because Prey had gotten to him first it would have set the DEA's investigation back months, possibly a year or more. How many more women would have died in that time?

"The woman had no right to demand you take her back there and jeopardize everything we've worked for."

"Her name is Ivory," he ground out.

"I don't care what her name is, she's lucky I don't have her arrested for interfering with a federal investigation."

They both knew that wouldn't do any good. Charges would never stick, and Eagle Oswald would have her out of custody as soon as her feet hit the ground in the US. All it would do was strain relationships between the government and Prey which would hamper future investigations and cost lives.

"Since when do you have an ax to grind with Prey?" Granted, Roman had only joined the DEA a year ago and had pretty much jumped straight into working this case, but he'd never even heard Jesse mention Prey let alone let on he didn't like them. Personally, he'd never given the security firm much thought at all, but nobody could deny the world would be a worse place without Prey in it. They'd done a lot of good, rescued countless people from death or a fate worse than death, and taken down hundreds of high-value targets.

"Since always," he said bitterly. "And I won't have them interfering in my case. Cut the woman loose and focus on the job. You begged to be part of this case, and I let you even though you have a personal stake in it. Don't make me regret that, Morales."

With that, the line went dead leaving him with the clear threat hanging over his head.

Get rid of Ivory and focus on his case. It was what he wanted, what he should do, and yet a tiny piece of his heart revolted at the idea of Ivory leaving.

CHAPTER SIX

December 26th
  6:41 A.M.

CAREFULLY SHE TURNED, intending to slip away before he realized she was there—she was surprised he hadn't already realized he was being watched—but a floorboard creaked under one of her bare feet, and Roman spun around, weapon raised and aimed at her head.

"Oops, sorry." Ivory shot him her sweetest smile.

"How much did you hear?" he asked as he slowly lowered the weapon.

"Not a lot," she hedged. "Just that whoever you were talking to has an ax to grind with Prey." It wasn't the first time she'd encountered someone who hated Prey. Unless it was the obvious and they were someone who Prey had taken down, it was usually someone who wanted to work for the world-renowned company but hadn't been offered a job on one of the teams.

"You know it's not polite to eavesdrop," Roman snapped

as he stalked off toward the coffee pot and poured himself a cup.

"Sorry, sneaking around is a hard habit to break. I should of course, curiosity shot the cat and all that." Truly, she hadn't meant to eavesdrop. She'd woken up, felt a little better than yesterday, gone to the bathroom, and then come down in need of coffee. When she'd heard Roman talking, she couldn't stop herself from creeping closer and listening in, even as she knew she should go back upstairs and give him privacy, or at the very least, announce her presence.

Roman's lips curled into a half smile. "It's curiosity *killed* the cat."

"Hmm," she agreed, "certainly seemed like the cat was going to get shot for its curiosity." She nodded in the direction of the weapon he'd placed on the kitchen table. "You know it's also not polite to hoard all the coffee."

His smile grew just a little, and Ivory found herself wondering what it would be like to see him smile properly, freely and joyfully, no doubt it would transform his entire face. Probably better if she didn't see that, he was handsome enough as it was without her seeing him at his best. Already it was going to be hard to walk away, she liked this surly man a lot. There was a heart under there he was trying really hard to conceal.

"Here," he grumbled, thrusting a coffee cup at her. Despite his agitated demeanor, his hand was gentle when it clasped her elbow and guided her to the table, pulling out a chair for her. "How are you feeling this morning?"

"Better," she assured him. While he wasn't much of a talker while she'd been babbling away over Christmas dinner, he hadn't seemed uncomfortable, just content to let her do most of the talking. He'd gone along with the movie idea even when she'd chosen a chick flick, and he must have carried her up to bed at some point because she knew she'd fallen asleep on the couch. Roman had done a lot for her, risked a lot, she wanted to do something to pay him back. "So ...?"

"So, what?" His arched brow said he was truly confused about what she was asking.

Stifling a giggle, she asked, "So who do you know who hates Prey?"

"My boss apparently. Although I didn't know until just now and he didn't say why."

"He angry that you took me back to the house yesterday?"

"Yes."

Not deterred by his short answers, Ivory asked, "You going to tell me about your case? I haven't really asked you anything about it, and yet, you know all about mine. Since you know I have a problem with curiosity, I'm sure you don't want me to get shot or killed." Ivory winked, meaning it as a joke, but for a split second there was a moment of panic in Roman's eyes that told her he actually would be upset if something happened to her. Gentling her tone, she said, "Why don't you tell me who you're after. Prey has a lot of resources and contacts the government don't, and I promise we won't try to take over if that's what your boss is worried about. Let me help you."

"Help me?" He looked surprised by the very notion.

"You've done so much for me, including risking your own op to take me back to Richard's, and taking such good care of me, and cooking me the most delicious Christmas dinner I've ever had the pleasure of eating. I'd love a chance to at least partially pay you back if I can."

It was clear from the expression on his face that the idea of anyone wanting to do something nice for him was completely foreign. It was also clear he was debating with himself on whether or not he could bring her in on his case. While Ivory hoped that he trusted her enough to do so, they hadn't known each other very long so she could hardly blame him if he didn't.

When he stalked across the kitchen and began pulling eggs, milk, and bread from the fridge she assumed he'd decided not to open up. Disappointment flowed inside her. If she had time, she'd prove he could trust her, but they were splitting up tonight, each going back to the ops that had brought them to Colombia.

"My sister was an addict."

The cold, hard, emotionless voice caught her by surprise, and it took a second to register that Roman was talking to her. Opening up. Trusting her. As though she was dealing with an animal that might spook and flee at the tiniest of provocations, Ivory kept completely still.

"Started when she was in junior high, and she dropped out of school when she was a sophomore. Lived on the streets, prostituted herself to pay for her habit. Eventually turned to dealing as well. She was in and out of prison for possession, prostitution, and dealing."

Ivory clamped her hands together in her lap so she didn't go to him. Not only was she afraid of breaking whatever spell had him talking, but she was afraid he would reject her offer of comfort because he didn't believe it was real. Roman Morales didn't believe people truly cared about others, she was sure it was in part because of his sister's addiction, but she knew that it was only through the support of those who loved her that she was still here. Still alive, still standing, still fighting, and still smiling.

"I'm going after Albert Hendricks."

At his announcement time seemed to pause and the Earth stopped spinning. He was going after Albert Hendricks?

The well-known drug trafficker had wealth to rival the Oswald family and arrogance that had him all but flaunting his crimes. He had a team of lawyers on retainer and bought and threatened his way out of legal trouble.

While she wasn't surprised that the DEA was after the notorious trafficker, the story Roman had just told her about his sister had her putting two and two together and coming up with an answer she didn't like one bit.

"Is your sister one of the lost girls?" she asked, voice strained.

Roman whipped around, turning off the gas on the stove where he'd been making French toast. "What do you know about the lost girls?" he asked, his voice close to a snarl as he crossed the kitchen to stand above her.

"I know they're supposedly drug mules bringing drugs up from South America to Hendricks' dealers in the US. I know they're found with their heads and hands cut off. I know the cops think they're removed to hinder the bodies from being identified. I know their stomachs are cut open as though the bags they were carrying inside them burst, killing them, and were later removed. I also know what really happened to those women," she finished in a whisper.

A chair scraping across the floor captured her attention, drawing her out of a memory that had the power to consume her if she let it. Roman was sitting in front of her, waiting expectantly for her to tell him what else she knew about a man they both believed killed his sister.

"I know they were really brutally raped before being purposefully overdosed. I know that their hands and heads were kept as trophies. And I know for a fact that as well as being a drug trafficker, Albert Hendricks is a serial killer."

"How do you know all of that?" Roman asked, but the

anger had bled out of his tone, and now there was desperation.

"Because I was very nearly one of his victims. Case gone bad, he found the tracker and cut it out of me so my team couldn't get to me before he'd whisked me away. They found me before he killed me." Ivory shivered as memories of those four days she'd spent as Hendricks' prisoner filtered through her mind. It had come down to a matter of minutes. Hendricks had grown tired of raping her and taunting her, bragging about himself and how powerful he was. He'd been in the process of cutting off her hands before flooding her system with heroin and then cutting off her head.

When Roman's hands captured hers in a gentle hold, Ivory realized she'd been convulsively stroking the scars on her wrists. "Is that where you got these?" he asked as his thumb traced across the ugly red marks with a featherlight touch.

"Yes," she murmured.

"He was going to cut your hands off while you were still alive?" The anger was back in his tone, but his touch as he continued to sweep his thumbs across the scars was soft.

Ivory gulped. "Yes. Sirens rang out when Prey breached the property and he fled. I was in bad shape for a while after. When we tried to go after him again, he claimed I was an unreliable witness because I was so badly traumatized. His security is top-notch, he only hires skilled and bloodthirsty men to protect him, and he's been off-grid for the last year. He's not going to be easy to get to but if you have a plan I want in." Determination built within her, pushing away the memories of those horrific days before they had enough power to hurt her. "Let me help you, Roman, please. I owe you, and I want that man almost as much as I want the Master."

* * *

December 26th
  12:33 P.M.

Why had he agreed to this?

Roman looked around the room that was now full of Ivory's team. The four women lounged on the couches in the living room, laptops set up because the team of former SEALs they worked with would be video conferencing soon.

Ivory's team had arrived about thirty minutes ago, she'd filled them in on his case, and they'd been concerned about her. Worried that old wounds would be reopened, that she wouldn't be able to cope with assisting on this case. He could have told them not to worry, if ever there was a woman who could cope with whatever life threw at her and actually come out the other side stronger, it was Ivory Smith.

She handled her teammates' concerns with grace and a little bit of self-deprecating humor. It didn't seem to bother her that her team was doubting her competence, it was clear she didn't see their worry as a manifestation of doubt about her abilities, but just as an expression of their love for her.

These women weren't her teammates they were her family.

Pearl still watched him with thinly veiled distrust, borderline anger. Opal had fussed over him like a mother hen when she learned he'd lost his sister. Lacey had been flirty only through their greeting, he wasn't sure if Ivory had told her about their kisses or if the woman had sensed there was ... something between him and Ivory, but it was obvious she'd backed off.

Part of him wished she wouldn't. Lacey was exactly the

kind of woman he usually gravitated to. Gorgeous, flirty, fun, no-strings sex written all over her pretty face. They'd hit the sheets, he'd work off his sexual needs, and then he could walk away without feeling like he'd used the woman because she'd gotten exactly what she wanted too.

So why couldn't he stop thinking about Ivory?

"You okay?"

He looked up from the chicken he was thinly slicing ready to go into the Caesar salad. Ivory's team hadn't shown up with lunch claiming they'd loved the dinner he'd made for them all the first night and wanted him to make something for lunch. Roman had never cooked for anyone else before, he didn't date, didn't have friends, he was and always had been a loner. In fact, that meal was the first time anyone had ever tried his food, and he couldn't help but be a little pleased that Ivory and her family enjoyed it.

"Fine. Why?" he asked, aiming for nonchalance as he added the chicken to the other ingredients.

Ivory just smiled at him like she thought it was cute he pretended not to know what she was asking. "I know you don't like to be around people, and this case is personal to you. I just wanted to make sure you were doing all right."

This would be so much easier if she didn't seem to genuinely care about him.

He had no idea why, it wasn't like he'd been Mr. Charming since they met. If she was looking for a hero on a white horse, he was hardly the best candidate, although he doubted Ivory needed anyone to rescue her. Maybe that was why he couldn't get her out of his head. She was every bit as tough as he was on the outside, and yet inside her heart was warm and soft and big while his barely existed.

"Lunch is ready," he announced, feeling a shard of guilt in his dead little heart when he saw the disappointment on

Ivory's face. He knew she wanted him to open up to her but that wasn't going to happen. Roman didn't let people in. Ever. And he wasn't changing that, not even for a pretty blonde who would soon be nothing but a memory.

Despite the fact he knew he'd hurt her, you wouldn't have been able to tell it from Ivory's face. She helped him carry bowls and cutlery over to the table, the tightness around her mouth the only indication she was in any pain at all.

At least he could do something about her physical pain.

While the women dished up the salad into bowls, Roman went back to the kitchen to grab a couple of pills from the bottle of painkillers he'd left there. Ivory had refused any this morning saying she needed to keep a clear head, but he didn't like seeing her in pain.

"Here," he said gruffly as he set the pills and a bottle of water beside her cup of coffee.

The smile she shot him was nothing short of sunshine bright, and although he wanted to deny it, Roman felt it shine in and smooth away a few of the cobwebs inside him. What would it be like to spend more time with her? Could she clear away all the cobwebs if he let her?

It was almost a tempting idea, but the knowledge of the destructive genes inside him and the possibility that he could break this seemingly unbreakable woman was enough to have him shutting down this line of thought before it went any further.

When the phone alerted them to the incoming call, Roman almost sighed in relief. This hanging around with a group of women who were family was making him think about how much he had missed out on. His family had never sat down to meals together like this, nobody had ever worried over him the way Ivory's sisters worried about her.

Every laugh, every teasing word, every carefree smile was like a nail into his already bruised and battered soul.

Just because he looked normal on the outside, it didn't mean his soul wasn't as badly damaged as Ivory's body currently was.

"Hey, Fox," Opal said as she accepted the call and a man with brown hair and brown eyes appeared on the screen.

"That's Owen," Ivory whispered beside him. "He's married to Evie. They divorced for a while but got back together. They have a five-year-old son Sullivan and a daughter Sally who's three."

"Sorry we're late, but Chaos has decided now that Blake is two he's old enough to learn how to be a prankster like his dad," Fox explained with an eye roll, but there was a smile on the man's face.

"Chaos is Grayson, he and his wife Juliet have Blake and they're having another boy in a couple of months," Ivory explained.

"What did Chaos do this time?" Lacey asked, looking amused.

"Used a skipping rope to tie two door handles together. We were stuck in the living room at his house when we all caught up this morning to exchange Christmas gifts," a man with black hair and blue eyes explained as he appeared onscreen and dropped down into a chair at the table.

"That's Ryder, his nickname is Spider. He's married to Abby, and after two false starts they finally got their happy ending and now have two kids, RJ is six, and Talia is four," Ivory told him.

"I swear he's getting worse the older he gets, and now we have Chaos 2.0 who is already almost as bad as his daddy," a man with brown hair and silvery grey eyes said with an exasperated sigh.

"Night is just in a bad mood because his daughter has a boyfriend," Chaos taunted, his green eyes twinkling merrily.

"She does not," Night muttered, his silver eyes shooting arrows at the jokester.

"Isn't Anastasia six?" Opal asked with a laugh. "I didn't know kids started dating in first grade."

"She's not dating anyone," Night growled.

"Night is Eric, and he and his wife Lavender also have a four-year-old son, Christian," Ivory told him.

"You're not going to be laughing when Indy starts dating," Night said to another man who was stifling a laugh.

"Whoa, hey man, Indigo is one, she's not dating till she's forty, so I don't have to worry about that for a long time," the man protested.

"Charlie and his wife Faith just celebrated their daughter's first birthday about a month ago," Ivory added.

"At least you don't have twins," a huge man who had been sitting quietly listening to his teammates said with a groan. "I told Claire they're not dating. Ever. No man will ever be good enough for my girls."

"Maya and Mia are three and already have Shark—Logan —wrapped around their little fingers. They're not going to be pleased if he scares away the boys when they're old enough to date," Ivory said with a giggle like the idea of the huge man and his twin teenage daughters refusing to let him keep the boys away was already amusing to her.

Although Roman had been in Delta and these were SEALs, he had worked an op with the team before they retired and went to work with Eagle at Prey. He remembered their faces, although not their names until Ivory had told him. While he shouldn't care that they were all happily married with families, he hadn't been able to tell Ivory to stop with her little updates. He'd needed the reminders of why he could never let anything happen with Ivory even if each comment she made about how happy these men were was like another thorn piercing the tough skin he'd developed out of necessity.

"So, catch us up," Fox ordered. "I understand things haven't gone as planned."

The women looked to Ivory who nodded and answered. "I was bought by Roman Morales. He's former Delta and now works for the DEA. He's posing as Holdon Lennox, a mid-level dealer of prescription drugs, and he's after Albert Hendricks."

From the expressions on their faces, it was clear that Fox and his team weren't expecting to hear that news. "What was your plan?" Fox asked him.

"We learned of a resort in the Caribbean that Albert frequents, mostly wealthy businessmen like himself who enjoy coloring outside the lines. The plan was for me to infiltrate as Holdon, a chemist who has a reputation for making his own prescription drugs and selling them. Since Albert and his friends are into the whole sex slave thing, I was going to buy a woman, have her returned to the States, then another DEA agent would come in and play my slave. Hopefully, word will spread, and I'll get an invite to the resort. Once I make contact with Albert, I'll form a friendship with him and gather enough intel so the DEA can move in to take him down," Roman explained.

"Ivory, I take it you now want to stay and play the sex slave role," Fox said, turning an assessing gaze on Ivory who he felt stiffen beside him.

"Yes," she said firmly. "I'm sure the others told you that I saw the Master at Bouquet's place, I want him, but I want Hendricks too. DEA is raiding Bouquet's tonight, so no more leads will be gathered there. Only half the shipload of girls

71

was there, we don't know if Bouquet was keeping them at another location or if they're already gone to someone else, but that's a dead end now. Lacey tracked the Master to a hospital in the city, but he must have changed vehicles because we lost him. Lacey, Opal, and Pearl can keep tracking the girls, and I'll come in if we get a lead, but until then, I thought I could help Roman bring down Hendricks. If you give the okay," she added.

There was tension swirling inside her. She was obviously afraid she would be told no, that she was too close to Hendricks, and Roman almost hoped that she was denied. The idea of her putting herself back on the radar of a man who had almost murdered her made him feel sick. But the idea of putting a free spirit like Ivory in a cage, stifling her and her need to save others also made him feel sick.

One put her in more immediate danger, but the other would merely bring about a long, slow death. Roman found he couldn't stomach either option.

CHAPTER SEVEN

December 26th
    4:56 P.M.

THE HOUSE WAS QUIET AGAIN. Her sisters had left to go back to their hotel after she'd gotten what she wanted, permission to play Roman's sex slave as he went after Albert Hendricks. Eagle would be talking to the DEA and getting her official permission to be on the case, and in the meantime, Roman would help with her search for the missing shipload of girls and the Master.

Everything had worked out the way she wanted, so why did she feel so tense?

Ivory hadn't been able to settle to anything since the video conference call ended an hour ago and her team packed up and left. Roman had disappeared to go for a run, she would have loved to go for one too, let her mind take a break from constantly whirling in a hundred different directions all at once, but she wasn't up to running.

So, she'd been stuck at the house trying to do her own

workout and refusing to give in to her body's need for rest because rest meant her brain would completely go into overdrive.

She was a thinker, she considered everything carefully, ran scenarios in her head, considered all angles, and took every piece of information—no matter how small—into account. It was one of the things that made her good at what she did, but it was also one of the things that had the potential to break her. The world was a dark place, she knew that far too intimately, so allowing herself to get lost in the vastness of the evil that roamed free and the somewhat pointless task of tackling it, would only wind up destroying her.

It almost had destroyed her after she was rescued by Prey, and again after she was barely saved from a horrific death by her team and Prey.

The need to play out what could have happened, the million different things that could have gone differently resulting in her death, the mistakes she had made and how she could have—and would in the future—done things differently, had forced her into a deep hole and she hadn't known how to get out. If it wasn't for the love and support of the people closest to her, their encouragement, and gentle prodding for her to get her game face back and do what she did best, she might have succumbed to the pressure.

Ivory was aware of the fact that Roman thought she was this sweet, somewhat innocent no matter how incongruous that was with her past, sunshiny woman who only saw good, was always happy, and looked at everything that happened to her as though it were no big deal.

But that wasn't true.

Not at all.

She'd been to the dark place, felt the temptation to give in and give up, and managed to find a way to fight through and come back.

Without her support system, she would never have been able to do that, and she believed that was what Roman was missing. She knew there was more to his past, maybe even a darkness to rival her own horrific childhood, the only difference between them was Roman hadn't had anyone there to support him, watch his back, and hold him up while he found his way. So while she'd managed to turn her pain outward using it as fuel to help her grow stronger, help more people, and destroy what evil she could, he had turned his inward, letting it slowly eat away at him until he was nothing but an empty shell.

If he let her, she'd be that support person for him.

She wouldn't ask for anything in return. Not his body, not his affection, not his love, not even his friendship, not a single thing.

Ivory had long ago learned that the best things in life were those you offered freely to another person in need. When you wanted things for yourself, when all you focused on was yourself, all you ended up with were things that didn't last. Sure, they might feel good in the moment, but that feeling was gone before you knew it, and all you were left with was the desire to fill that void with more stuff.

When you helped someone in need, you got something that couldn't be taken away from you, something that lasted forever. Something that filled you with a joy that couldn't be explained. It gave you a sense of purpose, a reason for being, and it made you feel good about yourself.

Carefully, Ivory eased herself onto the floor to lie on her stomach. She'd stretched and gone through a controlled yoga routine. She needed to keep her muscles moving because she was working two cases more important to her than all the others she'd ever worked put together. While she couldn't pretend she was even close to the top of her game, she at least had to remain limber and keep her strength up.

Placing her hands on the smooth floorboards she locked her legs, straightened her back, and pushed up.

Pain flared through her body, centered around her ribs, but no part of her had been left unscathed from El Compradores' brutal beating. Her entire body was a kaleidoscope of black, blue, and purple bruises, and she had the aches and pains to go with them.

Still, nothing in life was easy.

There was no gain without pain.

The idea of an easy way and a hard way was a nice one, but sometimes life didn't present you with an easy way, only hard, harder, and hardest.

No matter what you got, you had to make the most of it, and that was what she was doing right now. The opportunity to go after the two men who had hurt her the worst was a dream come true, and it sucked that she would have to go up against two powerful men while she was injured, but at least she had this chance.

With slow control, she lowered her body down.

It screamed a vicious protest, but she ignored it and pushed back up until her elbows locked. Her arms were shaking badly, and she was pretty sure she wasn't going to make her usual hundred push-ups, but each one she did would strengthen her just a little more and in no time at all she would be back to her usual self.

Up.

Down.

Up.

Down.

Each motion weakened her just a little more. Sweat was

pouring off her even though the temperature in the room was only mild, her entire body was shaking now, but she wasn't going to give up.

Not ever.

Up.

Down.

Up.

Do—

"What do you think you're doing?"

The voice caught her by surprise, and what little control she had been clinging to vanished as she dropped down, landing awkwardly and causing a spike of agony to shoot down her body.

"Roman," she groaned, "you scared me to death."

"You're doing push-ups? Did you forget that not even forty-eight hours ago you were beaten?" he snapped as he strode across the room until he was standing above her.

Ivory rolled over onto her back so she could look up at him, both irritated by him treating her like an invalid as well as amused by it. He looked so glorious standing there, hands planted on his hips, dressed in black sweatpants and a white t-shirt that clung to his muscled frame. His dark eyes seemed to burn a hole right through her.

"No, Roman, I didn't forget," she said on a painful chuckle. Her ribs protested the small laugh, and she had to close her eyes and brace an arm across them to breathe through the pain.

Strong arms circled her, gathering her up. Roman carried her up the stairs, and the idea of fighting him on it never even occurred to her. It felt so good right where she was.

"Roman?"

"Hmm?"

"You're a little intense, you know that?" she teased, tucking her face against his neck.

"And you're a little crazy, you know that?" he shot back.

She smiled and somehow that helped to ease the pain assaulting her body. "You may have mentioned it a thousand times already."

"There's a simple answer to that, you know." He opened a door and set her down on what she saw was the bathroom vanity when she opened her eyes.

"Yeah?"

"Stop doing crazy things." His hand reached out, palming her cheek in a gentle caress. But then like he realized what he was doing, he quickly snatched it back. "I'm going to run you a bath. I don't want you to get out till I come up to tell you that dinner is ready." He walked over to the walk in shower, turned on the faucets, and moved back so the spray didn't hit him. "Don't overdo things like that again. Your body isn't up to a workout yet and forcing it is only going to set you back. I don't want to have to pull you out of the shower because you pass out from pain and exhaustion."

An image of Roman's hands on her naked body flashed into her mind, and almost absently, she trailed a hand from one shoulder, over one of her breasts, and let it settle on her thigh, her fingertips mere millimeters from the part of her that wept for Roman's touch.

"Ivory," he warned as heat and desire flared in his dark eyes.

"Yeah?" she asked innocently. She never flirted with men, didn't even think she could. Lacey always told her she was hopelessly useless when it came to flirting with the opposite sex, but now she felt like her entire body throbbed with a need that only this particular man could satisfy.

"I'm going downstairs now." Although he said the words

he didn't move. Just watched her with the same hunger she felt.

"Okay."

"I need to start on dinner."

"I'm not stopping you."

"You're impossible," he snapped, making her laugh.

As he finally turned away, she called out, "Roman, you can trust me, you know. I won't hurt you and I won't let you down."

Ivory could have sworn she saw his shoulders sag, the weight of the world heavy around his neck, his pain made so much worse because it had never been acknowledged before now. Nobody had ever cared about this man, she knew that as certainly as she knew her own name, only that wasn't true anymore.

She cared.

He didn't want it, she could tell that too, in fact he almost seemed to resent her for it, but it was what it was.

Her heart cracked just a tiny bit as he left without a word.

* * *

DECEMBER 27TH

7:22 A.M.

WHY DID he always seem to be picturing Ivory naked?

Yesterday in the bath, and now as she was upstairs taking a shower, it was hard not to think about her soft curves, her delectable skin, her sweet mouth, how delicious it would be to bury himself in her tight, wet heat and maybe steal a little of her light for himself.

The more time Roman spent around her, the harder it

was to resist temptation. And now to make matters worse, she had permission from Prey and the DEA to play his slave when the time came to go after Albert Hendricks, and he was to help with her case in the meantime. That hadn't been part of the original plan, but Eagle Oswald must have convinced the higher-ups at the DEA to loan him to Prey to help with their search for the Master and the missing girls.

For sure Jesse would have thrown a fit when he learned about it because no way would the man voluntarily loan him to Prey. If it was up to his boss, he'd be back Stateside tonight and assigned something else to work on until his alias Holdon Lennox got an invite to the resort.

Upstairs the water shut off, and Roman had to adjust his pants because he'd grown almost painfully hard picturing her under the water spray, her hands running all over every inch of that creamy skin as she washed. Okay, so the fact that her beautiful body was currently a mess of cuts and bruises should dampen his arousal, but he couldn't seem to not think of Ivory and sex in the same sentence.

Her phone rang, startling him out of his sex stupor, and he stalked to the kitchen table and snatched it up. "Hello?"

"Roman?" It was Pearl and she didn't sound amused.

The woman clearly didn't like him, but he didn't care why or to do anything about it. He might be working with these women for the time being, but once they wrapped up both their cases, they could all move on. Hopefully, with the closure they all needed to move on with their lives.

"What do you want, Pearl?" he asked.

"Where's Ivory?"

"Upstairs taking a shower."

"Should she be upstairs in the shower on her own? She's a mess, I don't want her to get dizzy, lose her balance, fall, and hit her head."

The implication that he was to blame for Ivory's present condition, and that he wasn't doing enough to take care of her irked. He was doing the best he could. She was the one who wanted to go back to El Compradores, it wasn't his fault she'd been beaten. Roman didn't take care of people, and he'd never had anyone to tend to him when he was sick. He had no idea what he was doing, but he was keeping her wounds clean, making sure she rested, and remained hydrated. What more could he do?

"What do you want, Pearl?" he asked, a sudden weariness weighing him down.

"Lacey found what might be a lead on the Master. There're rumors of a man who lives on the Texas border who owns a gun range. Talk is that he has a large aquarium, only not a normal one."

Not in the mood for a game of twenty questions, he asked, "Doesn't sound like it has anything to do with us. What's going on."

Pearl sighed, and he had to remember that this case was as personal for her as it was for Ivory. This man had abducted them, kept them prisoner, trained them to become killers, no doubt done horrific things to them, he really ought to cut her a break.

"Maybe it doesn't, but the man with the gun range has an odd fetish. Fish. Mermaids. Dolphins. It's rumored that he has girls and women that he keeps in an aquarium that he made himself somewhere on his property. From what Lacey could gather, he keeps the girls and women in water permanently. As you can imagine this breaks down their skin and they don't live very long, so he needs a steady supply of women. Living on the border he has access to people trying to cross illegally, but he also likes to buy women on occasion. This is all supposition and rumor, no one has any proof, so the cops have never been able to raid his property."

"If it's true, what does this have to do with the man who kidnapped all of you?" While this man absolutely needed to be stopped, he wasn't seeing a connection between him and the man Ivory called the Master.

"What's going on?" Ivory asked as she limped into the kitchen. He knew she was still in pain although she'd never admit it.

"Sit," Roman ordered as he pulled out a chair for her. She rolled her eyes at him but crossed to the table and sat. Fresh from her shower her wet hair was braided, hanging in a thick rope down her back. Her skin was rosy from being freshly scrubbed, and not even the mottled display of bruises could diminish her beauty.

"Pearl?" Ivory asked, taking the phone and putting it on speaker. "You guys find something?"

"Maybe. We're not sure yet," Pearl replied.

"Possibly a link to the Master," he added.

Ivory's eyes lit up at that. "You think you got a lead on him?"

"There's a man in Texas who likes fish, made his own human aquarium," Pearl explained. "Since the woman from El Compradores mentioned fish, we decided to look into him."

"It's weird that the Master took the girls, they're older, he took all of us when we were babies or toddlers. Older girls would be harder to train, harder to mold into what he wants, and not as easily controlled," Ivory said.

"We're thinking that the Master took the girls to the man in Texas and made a trade," Pearl told them.

"This fish man has access to babies and toddlers?" Roman asked.

"If he's mostly abducting people trying to cross the border illegally, chances are that some of them had little ones with them," Pearl said. "From what we know, Douglas Chayter—or the *fish man* as you called him," she added, sounding uncharacteristically amused, "he doesn't like babies or small children. They're too young and they cry. Apparently, he has a thing about crying, it makes him lose his temper. It's also rumored that he never leaves his property. Ever."

"Where would the Master meet up with this guy?" Ivory asked.

"Who knows where these monsters make friends, but we know it's a tight-knit community. Traffickers can't allow many people into the fold, it increases the chances they'll get caught," Pearl said.

"He's been underground for so long, why has he come back now?" Ivory asked. There was a thread of pain in her voice, and he felt the unnatural urge to reach out and take her hand. Comfort her.

Only what did he know about offering comfort?

Never before had Roman felt inadequate. He had always accepted his shortcomings and focused on what he was good at. He was driven and determined, it made him a good Delta operative. He had a high threshold for pain, he was calm under pressure, he wasn't afraid to get his hands dirty, all those things made him a good Delta operative as well.

But Ivory didn't need a trained operative right now, she needed a friend. Someone who knew the right thing to say to reassure her that they'd get this man, to console her if she needed to let go and cry, to care about her.

That was something he couldn't afford to give her.

Caring about her would wind up getting them both hurt.

"I don't know. But he is back, you saw him with your own eyes. This time we won't let him get away," Pearl said fiercely.

"So, we go to the fish man—Douglas Chayter," Ivory corrected with one of her trademark grins, and Roman had to admire the way she managed to pull herself back from the brink when he was sure she was going to fall apart. "And hope we get a lead on the Master before he goes underground again."

"That's the plan. You two are going to Texas. Fox organized for one of Prey's jets to pick you up, and the rest of us are going to follow up a few leads here before we leave," Pearl told them. "Gear will be on the jet. Stay safe."

"You too," Ivory said before Pearl hung up. Then she turned and looked up at him, a smile on her lips, a twinkle in her eye, no fear, no concern that her injuries might slow her down, hamper her ability to protect herself, and watch his back. "Looks like we're going on a road trip. Well, a jet trip," she said with a laugh at her own joke.

Her laughter was like magic. It did funny things to his soul, softened his edges just a tiny bit, cracked the walls he had in place for a reason, made him weak, susceptible, and allowed everything he'd worked so hard to achieve to hang precariously in the balance.

Yeah, a road trip with the woman who could be his undoing, that was exactly what he needed.

CHAPTER EIGHT

December 27ᵗʰ
   10:38 A.M.

THREE HOURS LATER, Ivory studied Roman with open curiosity as they sat side by side on Prey's jet on their way to Texas.

The man was a puzzle, and one she found herself getting more and more invested in figuring out.

What would it take to get him to open up to her?

Was it even possible?

Should she care?

Ivory knew she was treading a thin line. Allowing herself to get any more attached to the strong, silent man was basi cally asking to wind up hurt. They were working on separate missions even if they were temporarily helping each other. When their missions were wrapped up, they would both go back to their separate lives. She was under no illusion that even if she could persuade Roman to start something with her while they were spending time together it would end the second the ops did.

Did she even want there to be more?

She hadn't been looking for a relationship. Didn't even think that she wanted one, yet she couldn't deny that Roman was growing on her far too quickly for her brain to be able to keep up.

It was probably for the best that she let the infatuation go. There was nothing wrong with being attracted to him, nothing wrong with liking him either, but she needed to be smart and not let things go any further. Roman wasn't looking for anything permanent, and she didn't even know what she wanted, certainly not the basis to build anything real.

Still, despite her acknowledgment that the thing to do was to keep things professional between them, that wasn't what came out when she opened her mouth. "Do you have any questions about the Master?"

Roman's eyes widened as he turned in his seat to look at her. If he was surprised she had offered to talk about the man who had caused her so much pain then he could join the club. Ivory had no idea what possessed her to make that offer.

Her past wasn't something she talked about very often. Sometimes she and her sisters would discuss it, but there wasn't really anything new to add, anything they hadn't already talked through when they'd been rescued and were adjusting to their new lives. It wasn't that she was ashamed about the things that had been done to her, none of them were her fault, it just wasn't something that was easy to talk about.

It involved a level of trust she'd never experienced with

anyone outside her sisters and her Prey family, and even most of them didn't know the details.

But she trusted Roman.

She had no idea why she had trusted him so quickly. Perhaps it was the genuine concern in his eyes when he'd first brought her into the rental house in Colombia when he thought she was a trafficking victim. Or the way he'd taken her back to El Compradores so she had a chance to find more information on the Master even though it went against his instincts. Or the way he had been so very gentle when he tended to her wounds, making sure to keep his touch soft.

Whatever the reason, she trusted him enough to bare her still healing wounds.

With a nod of respect that conveyed he knew this wasn't easy for her and that she was taking a leap of faith in trusting him, he shifted in his seat so he was facing her properly. "Where did he keep you and your sisters?"

"On a small farm deep in the Alaskan woods."

"That's a harsh climate."

"It is," she acknowledged, although she would much rather face the Alaskan wilds than the harsh treatment she'd received in the Master's house.

"Were there only ever the four of you or were there other girls?"

"There was just the four of us. Although once we were rescued, we did wonder if he would take more girls, but Raven was never able to find anything on him. Until I saw him the other night there's been nothing from him in five years."

"Five years? That's when you were rescued?"

"Yes."

"You're what, twenty? So you were fifteen when you were rescued?"

"Are you trying to butter me up, Mr. Morales?" she teased. "I'm twenty-three. I was seventeen almost eighteen when I was rescued. I wasn't quite two when he took me, so I was with him for more than fifteen years." That was the only life she had known, hadn't even realized that normal people didn't live that way. Hadn't even known there was another way to live. She'd had nothing to compare her life to, so she just assumed that all parents treated their children the way the Master treated her and her sisters.

"How old were you when he started training you?"

"Two. He started basically right away. The first lessons were that he was the master, the boss, the one in charge. He controlled what and when we ate, when we slept and where, he controlled everything."

"What's your earliest memory?"

"Being in the dark in a small room, not a closet but about that size, only completely empty. It was pitch black, you couldn't even see your hand in front of your face. I remember being locked in there for what felt like forever. I was terrified and sobbed until I exhausted myself and fell asleep. I think I was probably two and a half, or maybe three."

"How old were you when he started training you as an assassin?"

"Maybe four or five? I think before that it was mostly gaining our complete compliance. There were punishments for everything. Wetting the bed, not cleaning the house properly, being too slow completing a chore, and slight hesitations when given an order. We were chained up and left to sleep in the doghouse for days on end, starved, had our clothes taken away, locked in the closet, left out in the snow, blindfolded, gagged, then as we got older, beaten, whipped, burned, whatever he thought would hurt us. He was good at inflicting pain," she said softly. As horrific as her childhood had been, at least it had given her the skills to withstand torture and humiliation which meant she was able to save other girls like her.

There was a slight hesitation when he asked, a hint of apology in his dark eyes. "When did the sexual abuse start?"

"When I was ten. He said I was old enough then to learn a skill I'd be able to use to complete my missions. He told us that men lose their minds when they start thinking with their other head, that they become dazed with need. They don't pay attention to their surroundings, forget about safety, become weak and that was our opportunity to strike." Although she did her best to block it out, memories of the night she'd lost whatever innocence she'd had left filtered into her mind. The fear, the tears, the pain as it felt like her body was being ripped in two. The blood that came afterward and the inability to walk or even stand the next day.

A hand closed around hers, which she found were curled into tight fists on her lap. When she looked up, she saw there was compassion in his eyes. A deep compassion that confirmed her belief that he had also been badly hurt as a child.

"What was his plan for you and your sisters? Do you know who he wanted you to kill or why?" Roman asked.

"No," she replied softly. "I don't even know if he had a specific goal in mind. I much suspect it was more to do with a power trip than to achieve any particular goal. Wasn't like he saw himself as some sort of one-man CIA and intended to use us to take down evil men and high-value targets," she said wryly. "Maybe he had plans we were unaware of, but all I know is that he was training us to be sent in to seduce and kill whoever he wanted us to. Perhaps he had aspirations of taking out political targets, maybe wealthy businessmen who bought and sold politicians for their own reasons. I honestly don't know, but he must have had a plan, he put a lot of time and effort into teaching us how to shoot, use knives, and explosives. We were even trained in chemistry to make and administer poisons."

The hand holding hers squeezed before withdrawing. "I'd say I'm sorry, but I don't think that's an adequate response for all you were subjected to. The best I can do is promise that we'll get this man and he'll pay for what he did."

Ivory hoped that was true, prayed it was, but she was realistic enough to know that not all evil was punished or stopped.

The Master might well be one of those who remained free. Still, she appreciated Roman's attempts at comfort. Although she suspected he believed he was not well acquainted with the notion or perhaps rusty at it, he'd provided exactly the comfort she needed these last few days. With Roman she felt safe and protected, even though she could take care of herself it was a nice feeling.

"Thank you for sharing with me," Roman said as he returned his gaze to the window.

As she watched him, she realized she was disappointed that he didn't seem inclined to share anything of himself with her. Had she opened up with him in the hope he would do the same with her?

Ivory wasn't usually one to be manipulative, and she didn't like that subconsciously she had talked about her past to try to get him to do the same. That wasn't like her at all, and yet when she was around Roman, she found herself doing a lot of uncharacteristic things.

Did she really want to know why that was?

Or was it better to feign ignorance?

* * *

December 27th
12:03 P.M.

Thankfully they had reached Douglas Chayter's property.

Roman had come dangerously close to spilling his guts on the plane.

It was Ivory's plan, he'd known that, and while he hadn't been upset about her manipulation because he'd sensed it was somewhat innocent, he'd still felt himself falling for it.

She'd spoken honestly about the horrors she'd lived through even though he knew it had been difficult for her. How could he not want to open up to her when she wasn't holding anything back?

But, somehow, he'd managed to keep his head on straight, not an easy thing to do with a beautiful woman trusting him with her deepest pain.

The right thing to do though.

The only thing he could do.

There was no other option. Roman didn't want a relationship, would never inflict what biology had cursed him with on another person. Especially not one who had already been through so much.

"Roman?"

"Yeah?"

"Do you think we should wait until dark?" Ivory asked.

They sat side by side in the SUV they'd rented once they got off the private jet at the small airfield. They'd gone back and forth on a plan. Ivory had wanted to pretend that he was a trafficker, and she was his victim, and he was bringing her into the country. His plan had been for them both to pretend to be attempting to sneak into the country, but Ivory had argued that while he had Hispanic blood in him, making him easily passable as a Mexican fleeing into the USA, with her pale skin, white hair, and blue eyes it would be less believable that she was trying to sneak into the country from Mexico.

Hopefully, it would be a moot point, they only needed a cover story if they were caught, but Roman was hoping they could gather intel without alerting anyone to their presence. Once they knew what they were up against, they could decide how best to proceed. For now though, this was nothing more than a recon mission, and hopefully one that wouldn't involve them coming into contact with anyone.

While Roman trusted his skills and his instincts, and Ivory was trained probably as well as—if not better than—he was, she was also injured, which meant her reaction times would be slower, and if she had to fight one on one she wasn't going to come out on top. His attention would be split between watching out for her and watching out for anyone coming after them.

Waiting for dark might be a smart idea, but it could also mean that the man would be more on alert. "Let's go now. If you're not up to it …"

"I'm up to it," she interrupted, shooting him a glare that only made her cuter. The woman was a delicious mix of sexy, sweet, adorable, and strong. No wonder he was finding himself drawn into her web.

"All right, let's go then."

Each holding a weapon, they slipped out of the vehicle, which was hidden behind a clump of shrubs. There wasn't a lot of cover out here, the property was extensive, a couple of acres, and the shooting range was toward the opposite end from where they were. The house was also toward the front of the property, but from the aerial images they had there were at least another half a dozen buildings. Plenty of space to hide trafficked girls.

There was a large building not far from where they'd left the car, may as well start there.

Watching each other's backs, they made their way toward the structure. It felt like they were sitting ducks and given this was a shooting range and everyone here would be armed, he expected they would shoot first and ask questions later. Prey had a lot of sway, and he'd been assigned to work Ivory's op as well as his own, so they had the authority to make an arrest if need be, but anyone who saw them would immediately tag them as trespassers.

They made it to the closest building without incident, and Roman held up a hand to stop Ivory as he carefully eased open the door. The space inside was one large open room, an entire wall taken up with a fifteen-foot-high aquarium.

Although his attention was of course automatically drawn to the gruesome sight, his life—and more importantly Ivory's life—depended on him playing smart. Smart meant clearing the room first.

As he stepped inside, he felt Ivory behind him, and he kind of liked the idea of her there, watching his back, even as he was afraid for her safety. Letting himself get attached to her was ridiculous and yet he couldn't seem to help himself.

The rest of the room consisted of a staircase at the far end beside the aquarium, leading up to the top. There was a huge bed on the opposite wall to the aquarium, a couple of couches grouped together, a dining table and six chairs, and a small kitchenette. There was a tiny room closed off behind the kitchenette, and he assumed it was a bathroom.

There was nobody in the room, but still they cleared every space. Under the bed, behind the couches, in the kitchen cabinets, and in what was indeed a luscious bathroom with a large screen TV above the jacuzzi tub.

Weapons in their hands, both he and Ivory made their way over to the wall of glass and stared into the water.

When she spoke, Ivory's voice trembled. "She can't be more than nine, ten at the most."

His shock and horror weren't far off hers. In his time in Delta, he'd seen a lot of horrible things. Men who treated women as less than human, women who used their own children as weapons, people who hurt and terrorized others just for having different beliefs, but this had to be the worst thing he'd ever seen one human being to do another.

Wordlessly, he reached out and took Ivory's free hand.

They stood like that, hand in hand, drawing silent strength from one another as they took in the horror before them.

The aquarium was fifteen feet high, ten feet wide, and ran twenty-five feet in length. The water was filled almost to the ceiling with a few feet of spare space. There were what looked like oxygen tanks attached to the ceiling above the water, and tubes ran from the tanks down to the bodies floating in the water.

Eleven women and girls were in the water.

Chains around their ankles or wrists kept them anchored there, not allowing them to swim to the surface. Oxygen masks on their faces were attached to the tubes that ran up to the oxygen tanks allowing them to be submerged for prolonged periods of time. All the women were naked, but none were malnourished meaning they were regularly brought to the surface and fed.

Hair wafted softly in the water giving the aquarium an air of life even though none of the women left inside were alive.

"How could he do that?" Ivory whispered in a broken voice and Roman ached to say something comforting, but what was there to say?

He had no idea what would possess a person to do this. Obviously, Douglas Chayter was a sick, twisted, evil monster who enjoyed sitting around and watching the woman he bought and abducted trapped underwater with no hope of escape. It was obvious the man spent a lot of time in here and given that there were six chairs at the table and three couches it didn't look like he came here alone.

Did other members of the gun range come here after shooting at targets to get their rocks off watching women suffer? Was this how Douglas had met the man Ivory called the Master?

"Roman?"

"What?"

"That girl." Ivory pointed to a girl toward the back of the aquarium. "She's one of the girls from El Compradores."

"Are you sure?" The girl had long brown locks and wide brown eyes, but it was hard to tell if he'd seen her before. That night he hadn't been paying a lot of attention to the girls. He'd known that he couldn't pretend to buy one of them, they wouldn't have fitted in with his plan to make contact with Albert Hendricks. Unable to stomach the thought of the girls being harmed, he'd tried not to pay too much attention to them. If he'd known someone was coming to look at the kids after he'd left, he would have bought them and to hell with the mission, no matter how much it meant to him. But he'd been under the impression that Richard was fitting him in on Christmas Eve at the last minute and that the raid would happen before those kids were sold.

He'd been wrong.

One of the girls had paid a high price for that mistake and who knows what had happened to the other five who had been bought by the Master.

"I'm positive," Ivory replied. "Someone tipped him off. No

way he would have killed all his women without having replacements. We have to …"

Ivory broke off as the door to the building opened, and Roman tackled her to the ground a second before a bullet whizzed by their heads.

CHAPTER NINE

December 27th
    12:39 P.M.

BRUTAL PAIN SHOT through her as her body slammed into the hard tile floor.

Made worse by the fact that Roman's huge body pressed down on her.

Ivory knew he was protecting her, using his own body as a human shield to stop any bullets flying toward them from hitting her, but the pressure of his large frame shoving her ruthlessly into the floor was agony on her cracked ribs.

After what felt like forever but couldn't possibly have been more than a few seconds Roman shifted, propping himself on his elbows so his weight no longer crushed her. His dark eyes were glittering only this time, not with the lust she had become accustomed to seeing, but with something dark and dangerous she didn't quite understand.

"You okay?" he asked as he stood, taking her hand and pulling her up along with him.

"Yeah." The word wheezed out of her on a pained breath, and she cursed the fact that she was hurt and a burden. Pulling her own weight had been drilled into her since she was two years old and knowing that right now she was putting Roman's life in jeopardy because of her injuries was an almost crippling blow to her sense of self.

If she wasn't strong, tough, and capable then who was she?

This was the only life she'd ever known.

Fighting, working her body past its limits, getting better, faster, stronger, improving her aim, perfecting her knife technique, and running training drills was all she'd done in her life. After being rescued by Prey, Eagle had offered them the opportunity to do whatever they wanted with their lives, be whomever they wanted to be. Yes, he'd offered them a job if they wanted it, but it had been their decision to use the skills the Master had taught them to do good.

Now when she needed those skills her body wasn't cooperating.

"I hurt you. I'm sorry." There was genuine remorse in his tone, and it made her smile. This man pretended not to care about anything, but maybe his problem was he was afraid of feeling too much.

"You saved me." From the trail of red on his cheek he'd been nicked in the process. "And you got shot for me."

"It's nothing." He took a step back, releasing his hold on her hand as though he needed to put some space between them.

Or she was reading way too much into it.

After all, they did have way bigger problems than the giant elephant in the room which was the sexual tension between them that neither seemed inclined to address.

"Did you get him?" Ivory thought she remembered him firing off a shot as he kept her body pressed against the floor.

"Yes," he answered shortly, pulling the keys to their rental from his pocket. "I want you to go to the car and get someplace safe."

"Are you insane? I'm not leaving you here alone."

"You're hurt. You'll slow me down, divide my attention." His voice was hard, borderline harsh, and she tried not to take offense because he was right. But she'd been part of a team all her life, and a team watched each other's backs. Right now, she and Roman were a team, which meant she wasn't leaving him alone.

"We don't know how many more of them there are," she reminded him. Gunshots out here where there weren't supposed to be any would bring anyone else in the area running.

"You're a liability."

The cold words were supposed to upset her, maybe make her break down, but instead she laughed. If that was the worst thing he'd ever do to her, insult her to try to keep her safe, then it was close to one of the nicest things anyone had done to her.

"Something funny, sweetheart," he ground out.

It was the first time he'd used an endearment with her, and even though it was said almost mockingly, her heart did a funny little flutter. "Yes, actually. If you think I abandon a teammate for any reason then you really are insane. I can still shoot, still watch your back. And the longer we spend standing around discussing it the greater the chance that Chayter's men can plan something."

From the abrupt way Roman turned and stalked toward the man he'd killed, she knew he agreed with her, he just didn't like it.

Fighting a smile, she followed.

Smiling certainly beat crying. Ivory had shed enough tears to last a lifetime, if it was up to her, she'd never shed another, instead spending her days laughing. But her life was more often than not plunged into darkness by choice, but still smiling and laughing were her way of finding the light.

Roman crouched and confirmed the man—not Douglas Chayter—was deceased, then secured his weapon and reluctantly motioned for her to follow him to the door.

No sooner had he opened it than more shots fired toward them.

"They probably have us surrounded," she said as she moved toward the other door.

"But they don't know there are two of us. If they knew we were in here they would have come in together, outnumbered us. They came when they heard the shooting, they're waiting for us to come out."

"So, we wait them out," she said, glancing around the room. "If they don't know there are two of us then I'll go up there." Ivory pointed to the top of the ladder that led to the water. "When they come in between the two of us we can pick them off, one by one. Or all at the same time. Their choice."

Still looking like he wanted to argue, Roman nodded and pulled over the table to the aquarium's glass wall, turning it on its side and climbing behind it. She climbed the ladder and had no sooner positioned herself up the top of it than the door was flung open.

Roman took out the first four to come through the door, but when two men came through the back door Ivory quickly eliminated them with efficient headshots that dropped them immediately.

It would be preferable to take at least one alive, they

needed to know where Douglas Chayter had gone, where the rest of the girls from the shipment she'd been tracking had been taken, and what they knew about the Master, but it was more important they both stay alive. More leads could always be found, but once they were dead, they were dead, no way to fix that.

When no one else entered the room, Ivory slowly made her way back down the ladder while Roman checked all six of the men were dead and procured their weapons. The men weren't dressed in fatigues or any gear, just jeans and shirts, and she suspected they weren't really men who worked for Chayter, but men who used the range and were aware of the owner's unusual kinks.

"We need to find Chayter," she said as they made their way to the door. "And call Prey to tell them we left a body trail."

"I should call my boss too," Roman said as he grabbed her elbow and maneuvered her behind him as he opened the door.

No more bullets, so they both slipped out and back-tracked toward where they'd left the car. When they were both safely buckled in, Ivory pulled out her phone and sent off texts to her team and then to Fox, who would then alert Eagle. Roman called his boss, who would likely be unhappy that they'd killed seven men, and she was sure it would be Prey's fault in his mind.

"Jesse wants us to drive around to the main entrance and go and ask after Chayter," Roman told her when he ended his call and turned on the engine.

"If he knows what went down in the aquarium just now he'll be long gone."

"Then let's hope he doesn't know yet."

"Roman look," she said, pointing behind them. A big black

SUV was approaching, t she was pretty sure it wasn't the FBI or any of the other alphabet agencies. "Could it be Chayter?"

"Or one of his men," Roman said, ramming the car into reverse and approaching the other vehicle. Ivory had to admire his skills. He maneuvered over the dirt and sand, around the shrubs and few trees, with absolute ease. Driving wasn't one of her strong suits, it wasn't a skill the Master thought was necessary, and while she'd been seventeen when she'd been rescued and learned, she still wasn't particularly comfortable behind the wheel.

Whoever was driving the other car must have been distracted because they didn't notice them until they were practically on them.

Once the other driver did realize they weren't alone, they began shooting.

"I'm sick of people shooting at you," Roman muttered and sped up, forcing the other driver to put down their weapon and move their vehicle if they didn't want to be hit.

"Shooting at both of us," Ivory corrected as she shifted in her seat and pulled out her weapon. She wanted this one alive, needed answers, she had to find the rest of those girls before they met the same fate as the one in the aquarium. If they never found the Master, would she ever be able to put her past behind her?

Aiming at the tires she fired, the driver lost control, and the car went skidding off the road and down a small embankment.

But not before the driver got off a couple more shots, taking out their tires too, and soon they were sliding backward down the same embankment.

* * *

DECEMBER 27TH

1:04 P.M.

"I CAN'T WAKE HIM UP."

The panicked words were the first thing to slide into his consciousness.

The voice was familiar, but for the moment, he couldn't place it.

What he could place was the hammering inside his head.

Roman groaned and tried to blink open eyes that seemed to be glued closed.

"Yeah, I checked, he's unconscious too. I took his weapon and tied him up, but I can't wake Roman."

There was a wobble in the voice, and he felt an unusual urge to soothe it away.

"Wait, his eyes are opening." A gentle hand touched his shoulder. "Roman, can you hear me?"

He wanted to assure the sweet voice that he could and would be fine as soon as someone stopped using his head for hammering nails, but he couldn't seem to control himself quite yet.

"I thought he was waking up, but he's not saying anything." There was a pause and then, "I'm not panicking, I'm just concerned."

Despite the woman's words, her tone had a definite thread of panic.

Again, the urge to comfort her, reassure her, hit him hard. It was an unexpected feeling. Roman always watched his teammates' backs. He cared if they were hurt. He grieved in silence when he lost a brother in arms, but always in silence. His pain and his feelings were his own, not something he ever cared to share, and he expected—right or wrong—for others to behave the same way.

He didn't want to feel their pain, yet he felt this woman's as though it were his own.

"Maybe I should try to see if I can drive out of here. I feel like we're sitting ducks out here in the open. I can get the man into the car and drive into town, meet up with you guys there. I could so move the body from that car to ours," the voice huffed obviously offended.

Roman felt a small smile curl his lips up.

Ivory.

No one else could make him smile like she could. No one else could bring out fiercely protective instincts he hadn't even known he possessed.

"Could not," he ground out through his dry throat.

At his teasing, he felt lips touch his cheek, and his eyes opened to meet Ivory's, which were watery with unshed tears as she looked over at him from the passenger seat.

"Don't scare me like that again," she huffed. Then a brilliant smile lit her face. "And I could too get the man into our car."

"Maybe if he was ten," he said just to tease her, and the dramatic pout she gave made him want to kiss those plump lips, forget about where they were and what they were doing, forget everything but this driving need he felt to claim this woman.

"Are you guys laughing at me?" Ivory asked into the phone she held to her ear. "So now you think Roman's funny? I know, I didn't know he could make jokes either." Her eyes twinkled at him like gorgeous icy blue stars. His teasing had eased away the concern and worry in her voice, and he was proud he'd done that. "We'll see what we can get out of the man and then hand him over to whoever is going to work this case, we still have to find those girls."

There was pain in her voice as she mentioned the girls she was looking for, and Roman knew they were her priority. As badly as she wanted to catch the Master and Albert Hendricks, she saw herself in those little girls and she wouldn't stop until she'd found them.

It was an admirable quality, being able to set aside your own needs to meet someone else's, and one that wasn't nearly as common as it should be, and Roman found his respect for her growing again. He'd never met a woman like Ivory Smith, and he had to wonder if she was perhaps strong enough to handle the demons biology had handed him.

Quickly, he shoved away that thought and winced as he unbuckled his seatbelt and shoved open the car door to climb out. They'd gone backward down the embankment but must have turned at some point because they were now facing the way they'd come. He must have hit his head as the car spun. Despite the fact he'd lost consciousness there was no dizziness, no nausea, just a pounding headache, so he didn't think he had a concussion.

"I don't think you should be standing," Ivory said as she hurried around to join him, slipping an arm around his waist as though she could help him stand even though she was a tiny little thing.

"I'm fine," he assured her, then his eyes narrowed as he saw the way she was holding one of her arms somewhat protectively against her stomach. "Ribs or shoulder?"

"Huh?" She looked up at him confused.

"You already had cracked ribs. Did you hurt them again in the crash, or did you hurt your shoulder?" The last thing they needed was for her to have broken her ribs, a broken rib could puncture a lung or even her heart.

When he continued to stare at her, and she realized he wasn't moving on until he got a response, she rolled her eyes. "I popped my shoulder out in the crash. It's an old injury. I was able to pop it back in, it's just a little sore."

"Let me see." Without waiting for her permission, he gently took her wrist then placed his other hand on her shoulder. Ivory didn't pull away and he was humbled by the trust she once again placed in him. Carefully, he manipulated her shoulder until he felt another small shift. "Wasn't quite all the way in."

Ivory winced, then rotated the joint when he released her and smiled at him. "You're right, that feels much better."

"You were going to try to get our prisoner into our vehicle with a dislocated shoulder, cracked ribs, and all your bruises?"

She arched a challenging brow. "You saying I couldn't have done it."

Roman laughed, surprising himself. "No way, darlin'. I guarantee you can do anything you set your mind to."

Pleased with his response, she smiled back before sobering. "I was worried about you, I couldn't wake you up." Her fingers smoothed along his forehead just above where his pain was centered.

Her genuine concern soothed a deep hurt inside him. The pain of never having had anyone care about him was something he'd buried deep, but it was always still there. The knowledge that his parents had chosen addiction over him, even when presented with opportunities to get help had left him feeling unworthy and unlovable. Somehow Ivory managed to make him feel like he could be both.

Not willing to allow himself to take a step down that path —or at least not a step further down it since he already found himself on it—he stepped back and turned rather abruptly and stalked toward the other vehicle. The driver's door was open. Ivory had pulled the man out, cuffed his hands behind his back and his ankles, and then hogtied him.

"We need answers from him," he said as he knelt beside the man. Focusing on why they were here was what was important, and they weren't here for personal growth and healing. They were here to catch a dangerous man who bought and imprisoned women, and to find leads on the missing girls and the Master.

If she was upset by his sudden change in demeanor, Ivory didn't mention it as she stood beside him. "I'm not great at interrogations," she said, her voice hinting that she believed this to be a fault on her part. But one could hardly call not being able to hurt another person—even if they were evil—to get information out of them a fault. Although he was sure that wasn't what the Master had instilled in her.

"That's okay, I'll do it," he said with a hint of weariness. Over the years he'd perfected the art of being cold and remote. It was the only way he had been able to survive. When your only family was the ones trying their best to drag you down with them, you weren't left with a lot of choices.

Roman had done what was necessary not to succumb to addiction like everyone else in his family had. In doing that, he'd become a man who felt nothing. Locking down his emotions meant that addiction couldn't use them to lure him in.

For years he had been content with the life he had chosen. Not happy per se, you couldn't really be happy when you lived never allowing yourself to form real attachments, not even with yourself, but you could be content. Content was better than wasting away addicted to drugs, alcohol, and sex.

Content was what he'd wanted.

Until Ivory came along, making him want things he could never have.

With another wave of weariness, he hoisted the man into his arms and carried him over to their SUV. Content was no long what it had been, no longer what he wanted, but it was his only option.

CHAPTER TEN

December 27th
3:32 P.M.

ROMAN WAS GIVING HER WHIPLASH.

One second he was almost sweet, and the next he was right back to hard and cold again. The Roman who had teased her, touched her so gently, even made jokes had quickly disappeared, and the Roman who barely spoke, who seemed to wear a constant glare, and who rarely even glanced in her direction seemed to be back to stay.

Whatever he'd been through had made him so cold inside, and as much as Ivory wanted to thaw out his heart, if he didn't want to let her there was nothing she could do to change that. The more time they spent together, the more she found herself confused by him. He seemed to care for her, or at least sometimes he did. But at other times he seemed like he couldn't get far enough away from her.

Did whatever he felt for her scare him?

What she was beginning to feel for him certainly scared her.

Maybe Roman's attitude was the right one, after all. Whatever this thing between them was couldn't really go anywhere. Roman worked for the DEA, often undercover, she worked with Prey, often undercover. How would they even go about making a relationship work? Then there were her sisters, they were everything to her. How could she walk away from them and give her heart to a man?

Work.

They were both here for work. Albert Hendricks and the Master were dangerous men. Now they'd thrown Douglas Chayter into the mix, there was more than enough to keep them busy and keep her mind occupied. So why did it keep wandering to Roman?

"You think Chayter is already gone?" she asked as they stood side by side by an abandoned factory Prey had found for them to use to interrogate the man at the shooting range.

"No."

His answer surprised her. "No?"

"He doesn't leave the property. That's no doubt why the Master picked up those girls and brought them to him. He's still there. Somewhere. It's a large property and he no doubt was prepared for the day a raid came. Stupid not to be."

"The FBI has been trying to get him for years, but there was never enough for a search warrant, and any undercover guys they tried to send in never got an invite to the aquarium."

"Right. Chayter is smart. He can obviously pick out a plant, there's no way he's not prepared for what happens if someone ever gets onto his property."

"Prey and FBI are doing a joint raid tonight." According to what her sisters had told her on the phone, Chayter had been on everyone's radar for a long time, but the problem was there were so many bad guys out there, and Prey only had six active teams. Between jobs they were hired privately for, or government black ops missions, they just didn't have the time to hunt down every criminal in the world.

"Which means we need to get what answers we can out of him now about the Master and those other girls before we have to hand him over to the FBI."

Twelve girls had been snatched and placed in that shipping container. Six of them had never made it to El Compradores. Whether they were already dead, had been sold to someone else, or were in one of the ring's storage facilities they didn't know. Richard Bouquet was now in custody, but he hadn't talked. None of them expected that he would.

Six girls had been taken, presumably by the Master, to Douglas Chayter, but only one of those girls had been in the aquarium. Where were the other five? Had the Master taken them with him, selling or trading them along the way to other twisted perverts? Were they hidden somewhere on Chayter's land?

The only way to get answers was from the man bound and gagged and waiting for them.

"Why don't you go find us a hotel?" Roman suggested in one of his rare and seemingly uncharacteristically sweet moments. There was genuine concern in his dark eyes, and if nothing else, at least she knew she wasn't alone in feeling this invisible pull between them.

"No. I'll stay."

"It's not necessary."

"I know."

"Things could get ... messy."

"I know."

"You're not comfortable with that."

There was no judgment in his tone, but still, she flinched at the words. The Master had always been angry that she was squeamish when it came to torture. In his mind, it made her a bad operative in whatever his plans had been. She could—and had—killed when she had to, but it was always a swift bullet between the eyes, an effective and quick kill shot. That she could do, but this …

"I'm staying."

Assessing eyes searched her face, but he merely gave a nod and turned to head into the large, partially dilapidated building. Ivory had no idea how Prey found this place, if it was a location they'd used before or one they'd found specifically for this purpose. All she knew was that GPS coordinates had been given to her, and Bravo team would be picking up their prisoner after they interrogated him.

Inside was surprisingly bright, probably because the building was mostly empty and large portion of the ceiling was missing, allowing the winter sunlight to stream in. They'd left their prisoner tied to a chair and gagged. The man had regained consciousness in the car on the way here and had fought them as they'd brought him in. Overweight and at least sixty, the man hadn't been any match for Roman's size and strength. It was clear that while he might know how to shoot, the man didn't know how to fight and likely wouldn't hold out long before spilling whatever he knew.

Scared hazel eyes with a hint of defiance watched them approach. The gag was more to keep the man off-balance than because they were afraid his screams would be heard. There was no one around, while Roman had secured their prisoner, she'd conducted a sweep of the property.

"This can be done the easy way or the hard way," Roman

said as he reached out and removed the tape over the man's mouth. There was a coldness to Roman's voice that hadn't been there before. She had known he could be hard, and scary—although she'd never personally felt afraid of him—but this was like a whole other level. Their prisoner flinched at the unyielding tone, apparently correctly determining this was a man who would do whatever it took to get what he wanted.

Defiance won out in the end and the man just stared sullenly at them.

Wrong move.

Roman didn't give him another opportunity to speak, just slammed a fist into the man's gut, shoving the air from his lungs.

Their prisoner cried out in pain as air wheezed in and out of his chest.

Like some sort of shell of a man Roman merely stood and watched, no emotion on his face, not even a flicker of something in his eyes. It was in this moment that Ivory realized that it might not actually be possible to gain Roman's trust, let alone his heart. She still wasn't even sure if she knew what she wanted, but she recognized the signs of a man who hadn't just learned to shut his emotions down but remove them entirely and knew it might not be possible to reach him.

"We'll start with an easy question. Name?" Roman demanded in that dead voice that made the hairs on the back of her neck stand on end.

The man hesitated, and Ivory resisted the urge to ask him if he was an idiot. Didn't he know Roman would do whatever was necessary to get the information they needed to find Chayter, the Master, and the five missing girls?

Roman pulled a large knife from a sheath on his calf and

pressed the tip of the blade against his forefinger as he watched their prisoner. The man's eyes widened as he looked at the sharp knife and swallowed convulsively.

"Dale," he muttered. "Dale Drake. Everyone calls me Double D."

With an approving nod, Roman pulled up a chair. They'd found both the chairs, along with a couple of others here at the abandoned factory. They were both in bad condition, and both she and Roman could quite easily have broken them and gotten free if their positions were reversed, but Dale was older, out of shape, and didn't seem to have any real skills to get himself out of this situation.

Good for them, bad for him.

"Where were you going today, Dale?"

"I wasn't going nowhere," Dale replied somewhat petulantly.

"No?" Roman arched a brow in exaggerated confusion. "Why'd you shoot at us then?"

"Didn't know who you were."

"Why would you think just because you didn't know who we were, we were someone you needed to shoot at?"

"Thought you might be illegals."

"You don't like immigrants, Dale?"

"Got no feelings either way, just thought you were up to no good." Despite what he'd said, Ivory could clearly see his contempt for immigrants written into his expression.

"You know who owns that land, Dale?" Roman asked.

Knowing they wouldn't believe him if he said no, he obviously decided this was something he had to admit to. "It's a shooting range."

"It is. You were a long way from the range though. What were you doing?" If it was possible, Roman's voice hardened even further.

Dale's gaze flitted around the room as though help might be hidden somewhere and if he could just find it he'd be out of there.

Roman's hand flicked out, the knife slicing through one of Dale's fingers, severing the digit.

The man squealed like a pig as the finger hit the ground and bounced, then promptly threw up all over himself.

The strong metallic smell of blood mixed with vomit, and Dale's fear had her own stomach churning, but Ivory willed herself not to be sick. Roman was doing this for her, to help her find the missing girls and the Master. The least she could do was stand beside him.

"Won't ask again, Dale." The threat in Roman's voice, the promise to cut off more fingers, toes, an ear, an eye, whatever it took, was clear, and Dale began to sob.

"Th-the a-aquarium," the man said as his body shook.

"You've been to the aquarium?"

When Dale hesitated, Roman moved the knife, pressing the tip of the blade beside the man's left eye, drawing a circle around it just hard enough to draw blood. "No! Don't! Please. I've been. Just a couple of times. My wife left me. At feeding time, Douglas sometimes lets them out. They'll do anything to stay out of the water for as long as they can."

Ivory shuddered in revulsion, imagining the terror of those women trapped in the water, with no way out, their skin slowly breaking down, their only reprieve another nightmare, forced to perform sexual acts on perverts.

"One of those girls was just a child. Little girls turn you on, Dale?" Roman moved the knife until it hovered just above the man's crotch.

"Please!" Dale squealed. "I never touched the little ones. I swear."

"Does he often have little girls as his pets?"

"Sometimes."

"When did that one arrive?"

"Yesterday, just yesterday." Now that he'd started and realized the seriousness of his situation, it seemed Dale was only too happy to talk.

"Were there more little girls with her?"

"There were six of them. I stopped by just as they arrived. Douglas only kept one though. Gave the man a baby in exchange for the kid."

"Where did the baby come from?"

"Douglas found a family, husband, wife, and two little boys. They were crossing the border on his land. He killed the man and boys, but the woman was pregnant. Said he could get a lot for a baby, so kept the woman till she gave birth, that was just before Christmas."

"The man with whom he traded the baby for the girl, what do you know about him?"

Eager to please now, Dale nodded as he spoke. "I seen him around only once before, about six months ago, he did another trade. He's in his fifties, completely bald, not even got any eyebrows. His voice is real quiet, and he always looks angry. Don't know his full name, but I heard Douglas call him Bart."

Bart.

A name.

That was more than they'd ever had.

It wasn't a lot, but at least it was something. They knew the Master had been here, knew he'd had the other five girls on him when he left, and knew he was likely ready to build another army of girls. Why he'd been gone so long didn't matter, all that did was finding him and stopping him before he ruined more innocent girls' lives.

"You gonna let me go now?" Dale asked hopefully.

Roman barked out a humorless laugh, then swung his fist at the man's head, knocking him out.

Without a word, Roman stood and stalked out of the room, and she knew her emotionless warrior wasn't quite as emotionless as he wanted her to believe. His feelings were in there somewhere, but he was determined not to let them out. Was she deluding herself in thinking it was possible she could help him?

* * *

DECEMBER 28TH
6:26 A.M.

ROMAN STOPPED mid stomach crunch as he saw Ivory emerge from the bedroom.

She was dressed in black leggings that clung to her legs like a second skin, and a fitted t-shirt that immediately drew his attention to her breasts.

Breasts had always been his favorite part of a woman's body. When he bothered to spend time with a woman, he always chose one well-endowed in that area. Ivory's breasts were much smaller than he usually liked. In fact, if he'd met her in a bar because of their size he would never have given her a second glance, and yet for some reason he'd never in his life wanted to touch and taste a pair of breasts more.

They would fit perfectly in his hands, her nipples would pebble between his fingers, and they'd taste like sweet perfection when he took them in his mouth. She would moan in delight when he scraped his teeth over the hard little buds and thrust her chest forward, shoving them deeper into the wet heat of his mouth.

"I said good morning."

When he blinked, he saw Ivory was giving him a bemused smile, and because he was painfully hard but couldn't do anything about it, his temper snapped. "Morning," he muttered.

"Aren't you a little ray of sunshine today," she said as she rolled out a mat on the floor beside where he was working out.

Great.

Because that was just what he needed, watching her do her own workout, dressed in those skintight clothes.

As if he wasn't already insanely attracted to her.

There wasn't a single thing that he didn't like about her. Her strength, her beauty, her bravery, her compassion, her warm heart, her delectable lips, her perfect body. There wasn't a single thing he liked about her either because every one of those qualities only served as a painful reminder that he couldn't ever have her.

His desire to claim her would forever go unfulfilled, and that only added to the anger inside him.

Ivory eased down to sit on the floor, and although he knew she tried to hide it, she winced at the pull in her cracked ribs. The car accident yesterday had aggravated them and given her a new layer of bruises on top of the ones that had yet to heal, but at least she hadn't broken anything. And they'd gotten the information they needed from Dale Drake, now they knew the Master's real name, or at least the name he went buy. It wasn't a lot, but it was better than nothing and more than they'd had before.

She sucked in a pained breath as she lay down on her back, her knees bent, and started doing sit-ups.

"What do you think you're doing?" he demanded. The

sight of her in pain at least managed to douse his raging hard-on. He ought to be thankful for small mercies.

"What does it look like?" Ivory asked with a chuckle.

"It looks like you're doing crunches."

"Bingo," she said with another laugh that turned into a wince as she did another sit-up.

"You really are crazy," he growled. Why was she deliberately causing herself pain? Didn't she know that seeing her hurting pierced his cold, dead heart?

"You know you really ought to stop calling me crazy," she said mildly, although it didn't seem like she was particularly upset about it.

"Then maybe you should stop doing crazy things," he growled. Really, he should leave well enough alone. If she wanted to do insane things, constantly put herself in danger, and cause herself pain, then that was her decision. It wasn't any of his business, they were nothing but temporary partners, her life choices were nothing to do with him.

Yeah, maybe if he kept telling himself that for long enough, he might actually convince himself that it was true, that he really didn't care what happened to her.

"I don't do anything you don't do," she said. Some of the humor had left her voice, but she was still talking to him patiently like one might to a toddler who wasn't understanding what you were trying to explain.

That was true.

Yet it was different, he just didn't know how to explain that without sounding like a sexist jerk.

It wasn't that Ivory was a woman, it was that she was *his* woman.

Well, not his woman, but he ... hell, he didn't even understand, he just knew the thought of her in danger gutted him.

"No snappy comeback for that, huh, little ray of sunshine?"

He ignored her because anything he said would have only been mean and snarky and while he was in a bad mood today, he didn't want to argue with her.

Side by side they did sit-ups, and although he hadn't done anywhere close to his usual hundred, he knew she wasn't stopping until he did, so he stopped and got to his feet. As predicted, Ivory clambered to her feet beside him. Roman knew he should have offered her a hand and helped her up, but if he touched her, he wouldn't be able to resist tasting her, and there could be no more kisses.

He was only halfway through his workout, but he may as well call it quits. Things were tense enough between them, had been ever since they'd dropped off Dale Drake and come to the hotel, and spending more time than necessary with each other was only going to make it worse.

"You stopping already?" Ivory asked when he headed for the bathroom to take a shower. "I know you aren't finished."

"Well, you are," he said without turning around.

"Believe it or not, I've had worse. And we're working two cases here. While we're waiting for leads on where the Master is, we need to start connecting with your contacts so we can try to get into the resort where Albert goes."

Something strange happened.

His chest tightened, and he felt a tingly feeling in his extremities. For one horrifying second it felt like the world spun in a slow circle around him.

Ivory was going to be playing his slave. That meant he'd have to take her with him to the resort. The resort wouldn't know that it was a ruse, they'd expect him to treat her like a slave. Other men might want to touch her, hurt her, and he'd have to let them. The most important thing was to keep their cover and get what they needed to bring Albert Hendricks down.

Ivory's words echoed in his head.

I don't do anything you don't do.

No, she didn't.

And she attacked each of her ops with the same determination he did. She would do anything, sacrifice anything, to get their guy. Yes, this case meant everything to him. He'd thought he would be willing to make any sacrifice to get the man who killed his sister. Now he wasn't so sure. How could he make Ivory a sacrifice?

"We need to rethink the plan," he said.

"What? Why? I've done more undercover work than you have, and you need someone to go in as your slave, that's your cover, your in." Her pretty face was crinkled in confusion, and all he could think about were the bruises marring her otherwise perfect skin.

He couldn't allow her to be hurt.

"I don't want you going in as a slave," he gritted out.

"Why? I don't understand why you're acting so weird all of a sudden. It's like you're angry with me about something, but I don't have any idea what I could have done to make you mad."

"Why are you so determined to do this? Why do you always have to put yourself in danger?"

"Is that what this is about? I do what I have to do to make the world a safer place. Same as you do."

No. Her reasons for joining Prey were a lot more selfless than his for joining the military and then the DEA. Joining the military was about saving himself, and joining the DEA was about revenge.

Ivory, on the other hand, was about as selfless as a person could be.

Fueled by an anger born out of fear, he threw a snarl at her. She was doing this, in part, for him because of what had happened to his sister as well as because this same man had almost killed her. If this was anyone else, he would believe it was purely for herself, but this was Ivory, and he knew she wanted to give him peace by getting justice for his sister.

If she was hurt or killed on this op it would be partly his fault.

"You're doing this because you have a death wish," he growled as he turned and stalked toward the bedroom.

"I'm doing it because I have a live wish," she said softly.

As he slammed the bedroom door behind him, Roman sank against it, Ivory's softly spoken words seeping into him. He'd spent his whole life waiting for death to come for him, either at the hands of his parents, grandparents, aunts, uncles, cousins, or one of their associates. Ivory, on the other hand, had fought to live. While she put herself in dangerous situations it wasn't to taunt death, dare it, like he did, it was to give others the same second chance at life that she had been given.

If anyone had a death wish it was him.

CHAPTER ELEVEN

December 28th
    12:46 P.M.

PICKING AT HER LUNCH, Ivory cast a glance at the closed door to Roman's room. He'd been in there pretty much constantly since their argument earlier.

An argument she didn't even really understand.

She thought they'd already settled the plan. He was helping her look for the missing girls and the Master until they got an invite to the resort. When one of his contacts got them access to the island resort to see Hendricks, she was going to play his slave. That had all been decided, so why was he freaking out about it all of a sudden?

What had changed?

Her phone rang, and she smiled when she saw Pearl's name on the screen. This was exactly what she needed right now. It might have only been a couple of days since she'd last seen her sisters, but they rarely went long periods of time apart. They were more than just her family. When they'd been in the Master's clutches their very survival had depended on one another. As the youngest, there had been many times when one of her sisters had stepped in to protect her as best they could from a punishment, particularly when she'd been very young. Once she was older, she hadn't allowed them to do that anymore, but they all still looked out for each other.

Now she couldn't imagine her life without them, which made any relationship she might have had pretty much pointless. What guy would want to be with a woman who couldn't go more than a day or so without needing to see her sisters?

With a glance at the closed bedroom door, she picked up the phone and accepted the call. "Hey."

"Hey, girl, how are you?" Pearl asked.

"Sore but okay," she answered honestly. Long ago the four of them had decided that they always had to be honest with each other. With everything they had to endure they needed to support one another, there was no other way they could have survived. So, when they'd been rescued, they had all made a vow that no matter what they would continue to be honest. They still needed that support system even if their lives were different.

"You don't sound okay," Opal said in her soft gentle way. Despite the fact they had grown up in the same environment, they were all wildly different people, which made sense given that none of them were biologically related, but still made her smile. She liked they all had different strengths and weaknesses it was what made them such a great team.

"I *am* okay, I'm just … confused," she admitted. It was kind of a hard admission to make because she was tough, strong, and competent in so many ways. But not in this. Not when it came to men.

"What are you confused about?" Pearl asked.

"I know," Lacey said confidently. "A certain grumpy, kinda rude but amazing cook, muscle mountain of a delicious man."

Ivory experienced a strange rush of jealousy as she heard the mostly buried desire in her sister's voice. Lacey never missed an opportunity for sex with a hot man. Of the four of them, she was the only one who was completely comfortable with sex after what the Master had done to them.

Would Lacey go after Roman? Make a move on him?

If she did, would he accept what she offered?

No-strings sex seemed more Roman's thing, and she wasn't sure that was something she could give him.

"Ivory?" Opal said. "Talk to us. Why are you confused about Roman? Has he done something to hurt you?"

No.

Well, not physically.

Although his freak out earlier and his resistance to giving her a chance did hurt a little even as she knew she was being ridiculously oversensitive.

"No, he hasn't hurt me," she said.

"But you like him, right?" Lacey asked, clear delight in her tone.

There was no real point in denying it. Given her little meltdown yesterday when she couldn't wake Roman up after the car crash it was pretty obvious that she did in fact care for the DEA agent. "Yeah, I like him. I'm just so confused about the whole thing. I don't even know if he likes me, and I don't even know if I want him to like me."

"Of course you don't want him to like you," Pearl said. "We made a deal. It was the four of us sticking together. We said we would never let a man break us up."

That was true.

It was a deal they had made shortly after Prey had rescued them. They were all each other had ever had, and they had made a promise that it would always be the four of them. So far no one had even come close to falling for a man. Lacey enjoyed sex with as many hot guys as she could find. Pearl seemed to hate men and avoided any who weren't part of the Prey family like the plague. Opal had a friends-with-benefits thing going on with a man they'd met on their first op, and she rarely felt the urge to indulge in anything physical with a man.

Had anything really changed?

Did she want it to?

"If Ivory met someone she likes she should go for it," Lacey said. "Who says that has to change anything about our deal? We promised that we would stick together and never let a man come between us, but that doesn't mean we all have to stay single for the rest of our lives. Ivory can be with Roman and still be our sister, and I don't think he's the kind of man who would resent us being close. I mean, he knows about our pasts, he has to expect it."

Thank goodness for the sudden voice of reason in their little team. Of all her sisters, she had expected Opal to be the most vocally supportive. She'd expected Lacey to tell her to enjoy as much sex with Roman as she could before he cut her loose. Instead, it seemed like Lacey was in fact her best ally right now.

"She doesn't even know if he likes her back," Pearl pointed out. "And having met the man, I can't see him liking anyone let alone wanting anything permanent. Besides, if she gets together with him things will change, no way they won't."

All of that was true.

Roman didn't seem like the kind of guy who would be

interested in marriage, but that was because he was afraid to let himself feel anything. If he would give her a chance, he would find out that she knew all about pain and would always do her best not to inflict it on anyone.

But if by some miracle he did give her a chance, it would invariably change things. That was inevitable.

"Change doesn't mean bad though," Opal said.

"Of course it doesn't," Lacey added. "I definitely think you should go for it. At least give it a chance, see where it goes. If he's not interested in anything at least you'll know and you won't live with regrets."

"I think you should give him a chance too," Opal said. "After all, the worst that can happen is a broken heart and you've survived much more."

"We don't even know if her heart is already involved, all she said was that she liked him," Pearl said, somewhat sullenly.

Ivory found her heart breaking for her sister. She'd never been in love before and could hardly call what she felt for Roman love, but it was something, and her heart was involved. Lacey and Opal were both open to the possibility of one day letting someone else into their hearts, but Pearl was so closed off, so angry. Was her sister's heart already as hard and cold as Roman's?

The thought of Pearl and Roman never knowing what it was to love and be loved made her almost sadder than she could bear.

It also showed her the truth of her feelings.

"My heart is already involved," she told her sisters. Saying the words felt good and gave her power. It certainly didn't mean anything would work out with Roman, but it showed her that she was ready to take the risk.

After all, she was nothing if not a fighter. When had she ever been presented with a challenge and turned it down?

Never.

"That's great, Ives. I'm so happy for you," Lacey said.

"You know we're here for you no matter what. You have our full support. All of ours," Opal added, and Ivory could picture her oldest sister shooting Pearl a frown that dared her to disagree.

"Whatever," Pearl muttered. "I still think this is a mistake."

"Maybe," Ivory acknowledged. "But if it is it's my mistake to make. I'm a big girl, and I can take it if Roman shoots me down."

No longer confused, Ivory knew she could run away with her tail between her legs, pretend there was nothing between her and Roman and just work with him then leave. Or she could fight for her feelings, for what could be her future, and pray that she had enough strength to heal her heart if Roman was too scared to face his own fears.

* * *

DECEMBER 28ᵀᴴ
6:38 P.M.

THE KNOCK at the hotel suite door told him room service had arrived.

Roman had been a coward, hiding out in the bedroom all day. Yeah, he'd worked the entire time—well in between obsessing over the gorgeous blonde in the other room— putting out feelers, getting in touch with every contact he had. The quicker he got Albert Hendricks, the quicker he could get Ivory out of his life before he did something they would both live to regret.

It was getting harder to resist her.

Harder not to touch her, taste her, claim her.

Worse than that, it was getting harder not to open up to her and let her in.

The fact that she was completely happy and willing to put her life in danger to help him get the man who killed his sister was his undoing. Even though he knew she was doing it partly for him and partly for herself, he couldn't deny it felt so good to have someone do something for him for a change.

No one had ever done anything for him before.

"Roman?" Ivory's voice called out as she knocked on the bedroom door.

He should ignore her.

Going out there would only make things worse.

Weaken his resolve.

Instead, he stood from the chair at the desk and crossed the room to open the door. They'd taken a two-bedroom suite. He couldn't trust himself alone with her if there was only one bed, no other room to flee to escape her presence.

The second he opened the door and saw her sweet face smiling up at him that resolve he'd spent the day shoring up vanished as though it had never existed.

"Leave, Ivory," he snarled. If she didn't, he couldn't be responsible for what would happen next.

She didn't.

Instead, the softest smile touched her lips, and she reached up to cup his cheek, her gentle fingers caressing his skin. "It's okay, Roman. You're safe here with me. You're safe to let go."

Let go?

Did she know what she was asking?

129

As much as her willingness to sacrifice for him touched him it also made him angry. In his world, people didn't do something nice for another person unless they wanted something in return.

So, what did Ivory want?

"Why?" he growled.

Her hand didn't move. Her blue eyes met his, and held them in a grip he couldn't seem to break. Wasn't even sure he wanted to break. "Why what?"

"Why are you doing this?"

"For you."

Her answer was so simple it nearly broke him. Did she know he wasn't worth it? That if he tried to give her what he thought she wanted, he would destroy everything good that lived inside her?

"I'm not worth it," he whispered brokenly.

Ivory stood on tiptoes and touched her lips to his in a featherlight kiss. "Everyone is worth it."

Roman wanted to argue and convince her she was wrong when it came to him. She didn't know him, didn't know the family he'd come from, didn't know that addiction was his family motto and that sooner or later, he would succumb to it and destroy her along with himself. He wanted to push her away before he broke her.

But instead, he did what he always did.

Selfishly, he grabbed her hips and lifted her feet off the floor, then spun around and pushed her roughly up against the nearest wall.

His mouth came crashing down against hers, his tongue plunging into her mouth.

It wasn't enough.

Bracing her against the wall, he tangled one of his hands

in her hair as he kissed her like a dying man while his other shoved her t-shirt up, baring her breasts.

She wasn't wearing a bra.

When his fingers grazed her nipple, she moaned into his mouth. When he took one of her nipples between his thumb and forefinger and tweaked it, she ground her center against the growing bulge in his jeans.

Tearing his mouth from hers, he hefted her higher, so her breasts were right in front of his mouth and closed his lips around one of her pebbled nipples and sucked hard.

"Roman," Ivory moaned as her fingers tangled in his hair, holding his head to her breast as though he had any inclination of moving it.

He sucked and licked until Ivory was squirming against him. At the back of his mind, he thought he should stop and take her to the bed where he could make love to her properly. But he wasn't ready to acknowledge that this was anything more than sex. Quite possibly the hottest sex of his life, but nothing more.

No intimacy.

No promises.

No strings.

He'd blow her mind, she'd blow his, and then they'd go back to being partners, and he'd do his best not to think of sex and Ivory in the same sentence ever again.

One taste was all he could allow himself, so he better make it last.

"Put your legs over my shoulders," he ordered as he grasped her hips and lifted her higher. Once Ivory complied, he pulled her leggings down, shoving them behind his head, then grasped her panties. "These have to go."

Ivory giggled when he ripped them off her. "I've never

had anyone do that before. I didn't even know you could literally rip off a pair of panties."

"Babe, I don't want to think about another man this close to you." It was bad enough knowing what the Master had done to her and that this was a one-off, that there was no way he could keep her in his life. The last thing he needed to think about was that other men had touched her in the past and other men would touch her again in the future.

"Sorry." Ivory winced, but when his tongue darted out to spear her it morphed into a moan and her fingers once again tangled in his hair, holding his head in place while he ate at her.

There were no words to describe her intoxicating taste as his tongue slid deep into her before sweeping up to tease her hard little bud. His lips closed around it and he suckled hard. Ivory's hips thrust forward, wordlessly begging for more as her breathing grew ragged.

Roman slipped a finger into her tight heat, then another, stretching her, then opening her so his tongue could delve deeper.

When he had to let her go, he wanted to ruin her for other men, wanted it to be his fingers, his mouth, his hard length that was imprinted on her soul. Selfish of him, he knew that, but he couldn't help it, there would never be another woman who even came close to Ivory Smith.

None that ever meant something to him.

This woman did.

Denying it would be lying.

"Roman, please," she begged. "Please. I need to come. Please."

"I got you, darlin'," he assured her. Pumping his fingers in and out, he closed his lips around her bundle of nerves once more and swirled his tongue along the quivering bud before sucking hard, and she fell apart.

His name fell from her lips as her internal muscles clamped around his fingers. He didn't let up, licking and sucking until he felt her wave of pleasure begin to ebb. Then he unbuckled his jeans, his length springing free the second he shoved his boxers out of the way.

As aftershocks continued to ripple through her body and her eyes were still dazed with pleasure, he slid on the condom he'd grabbed from his wallet and buried himself inside her in one thrust. He was already achingly hard, and the second her heat surrounded him he felt himself losing control.

Claiming one of her breasts again he licked and nipped. One of his hands touched her where their bodies joined, working her sensitive bud again, and when he felt a second orgasm rip through her he finally allowed himself to find his own relief.

It felt like he left Earth. Entered another universe where anything was possible, even love.

But as he slowly drifted down from the high, he realized nothing had changed.

This woman was too good, too pure, to be defiled by the hand nature had dealt him. Roman didn't have a single relative who hadn't been plagued by addiction. Why should he believe he would be any different?

What happened if he couldn't get revenge for his sister's death?

What happened if he lost his job at the DEA and he had no purpose?

What happened if he let himself fall for Ivory and then he lost her?

Sooner or later one of those what-ifs would become a

reality, and when it did, he feared that was when addiction would claim him too.

Pulling out of her, Roman regretted the loss of her heat as soon as he left it. He set her on her feet, removed the condom, and stuffed his semi-hard length back into his boxers, then buckled his jeans and stepped out of the bedroom, closing the door behind him.

Effectively closing the door on anything that could have been between him and Ivory and breaking his own heart in the process.

CHAPTER TWELVE

December 28th
    11:05 P.M.

SHE WAS ALMOST surprised Roman hadn't just walked out of the hotel suite without telling her he'd made contact with one of his sources who had a connection to Albert Hendricks and would hopefully be able to get them into the resort.

After they'd had sex, he'd retreated back to his room and slammed the door effectively cutting off anything they might have had.

Ivory liked Roman and would love to help him if he'd let her, but he'd made it pretty clear that it wasn't what he wanted, and she wasn't stupid. There was no way she was going to throw herself at a man who obviously didn't want her.

It hurt, but it was what it was. From now on, she was going to do what Roman was and pretend there was nothing but work between them. She could do that, even if it felt like the bottom had dropped out of her world. Ivory had never really believed she would ever find a man she could see herself having a future with, not after everything she'd been through in her life and what she did for a living.

Then along came Roman and everything changed.

Twenty-three was a little old to have her heart broken for the first time, but that was exactly how she felt as she sat silently in the passenger seat of the SUV as they drove toward a seedy bar.

But it was something she was going to have to get over.

And quick.

Distractions on a mission caused mistakes, and the last thing she wanted was her broken heart to get Roman hurt or killed.

"Remember we're going in as Holdon Lennox and the woman he bought," Roman finally said, breaking the tense silence.

"I know. It's why I died my hair, put in contacts, and did my makeup." If this played out the way they hoped it would, they might be heading straight to the Caribbean from the bar in Florida. Albert Hendricks would never know that the woman Holdon Lennox had bought had white hair and blue eyes, and because she shared a past with the man, she had to make sure he wouldn't recognize her. With her new dark brown locks and dark eyes, she looked more like Snow White than her usual Elsa from Frozen. There was no way he would recognize her now, not that he was likely to pay much attention to a slave anyway.

Roman grunted, and Ivory fought the urge to roll her eyes again. At least no one would question the fact he was treating a slave too nicely because he barely seemed to be civil with her.

Part of her wanted to ignore it, let it go, it was obvious all Roman had been interested in was sex. No, that was her wounded pride talking, he had been sweet and gentle with her, and she believed he liked her. He was just afraid, and she couldn't fault him for that.

"I won't mess up, Roman. I've done more undercover work than you have, you can trust me. I'm not going to let you down. I know how important this is to you, I want you to get justice for your sister," she said softly.

Parking the car in the dark lot, he shifted in his seat to look at her. There was a softness in his eyes now, and she was glad that she hadn't let her hurt feelings lead her to say something they'd both regret.

Patience.

It hadn't always been her strong suit, but she'd learned how to be patient when working an op. All she had to do was treat this like an op. Not all missions were successful, and she might not be now, but it was better to try and not succeed than to give up.

Ivory was no quitter.

"Let's go do this," she said.

When he'd told her that one of his contacts had reached out, they'd gone through a few basics of their plan while they got on a plane and flew to Florida. The man they were meeting was a high-level drug dealer, who wanted to talk to Holdon about expanding his business. News that Holdon Lennox had made the move to dabble in human trafficking must have already spread because the man they would be meeting with had told Roman to bring his slave with him.

The plan was for Roman to focus on getting as much information as he could out of the dealer. Because nobody would pay much attention to her. After all, she was just a slave, nothing of value, she could scope out the place, take notes on faces, possibly even listen in on other conversations, and gather any other intel she could.

"Ivory, I …"

"It's okay," she assured him. She knew that he was battling something major and she was sure he thought keeping his distance was for the best, but she'd seen the truth in his eyes when they'd had sex.

He cared.

So while, yes, she was hurt by how he'd shut her out immediately afterward, she was prepared to set that aside both for their case and because she knew her feelings for him were growing. There was no way he could have hurt her so badly by storming off as soon as he pulled out of her if she didn't care.

"Come on, partner, let's go get ourselves an invite to the resort," she said, offering him a smile that she hoped told him she understood he was scared, but if he let her, she could be his safe place.

Roman gave her one of his uncharacteristic smiles, it was brief, but it made her heart flutter and soar. Patience, understanding, and gentle encouragement, maybe with a combination of that she could make some progress.

Then his face hardened into his Holdon Lennox expression, the same one he'd worn when she first met him, and she let her face go blank as she slipped into her role. Roman got out of the car, and she waited till he came and opened her door before getting out. The bar they were going to was heavy on the kink and she'd dressed accordingly. Black boots that stopped just above her knees, a black leather mini skirt that barely covered everything, a hot pink halter top that was little more than a strip of material, and lace panties in the same shade of pink. Her hair hung in soft waves down her back, her makeup was understated, and she wore a pink collar around her neck with a chain attached to it so Holdon Lennox could lead around his new slave.

Both in character now, she kept her gaze fixed on the ground as she followed where Roman led her. Although to anyone watching Roman looked like a cocky, arrogant, smarmy drug dealer, she could feel the tension inside him.

He didn't want to be doing this.

Not the going after Albert Hendricks part, but the including her part.

Her ego wanted to argue that she had more undercover experience than he did, and she could handle herself, but the part of her that was all swoony over Roman recognized it as his need to try to protect her. He might not want to care about her, but he did, and that had to be a small victory in and of itself.

Ivory let thoughts of her and Roman fade from her mind. For the next couple of hours, she had to be a woman who'd been kidnapped and sold, nothing more and nothing less. If she thought too much about Roman, she'd worry too much, and that would mean she'd be more focused on him than on playing her part and gathering her intel.

They stopped at a door where a bouncer dressed all in black was waiting for them. The man was huge and looked like he was a weightlifter when he wasn't on bouncer duties.

"Name?" the man asked, sounding bored.

"Holdon Lennox, here to see Zeke MacAvoy," Roman replied. With his dark jeans, black leather jacket, and shades, he looked sinfully sexy, but for Ivory it wasn't just about his looks. With a dark past she was sure rivaled hers, he brought out her protective side, her need to heal, and he stirred her heart in a way nothing and no one ever had.

"You're on the list," the bouncer said as he opened the door.

Pulling on the chain attached to her collar, Roman led her

through the door and into a long, dark walkway with a white door at the other end.

It sounded like the door behind them was closing, but then something cold touched her temple.

The barrel of the gun.

The other door opened and two more men with guns approached.

A trap?

Did Zeke MacAvoy know Roman was really a DEA agent?

What had they just walked into, and how were they going to get out of it alive?

* * *

DECEMBER 29TH
   2:02 A.M.

AS CONSCIOUSNESS RETURNED, the first thing that Roman felt was panic.

Not for himself but for the beautiful, sweet woman he had allowed to walk into the bowels of hell with him.

Now they were trapped.

With a gun pressed against Ivory's temple, there had been no way he could avoid putting down his weapon and allowing himself to be captured. He could have taken out all three of the men but not before the bouncer put a bullet in Ivory's brain.

Her life was more important.

With horrifying realization, Roman accepted that was true. In his mind, her life was more important than this mission. The most personal op he'd ever been on. Revenge for his sister's murder had been all he could think about since he got the news that she had been found dead from a supposed drug overdose while trafficking drugs into the country.

He'd known it was a lie.

Alexa had finally gotten clean about a year before she was murdered. When she'd reached out to him to tell him he hadn't believed her, had thought he was the only family member who had managed to stay away from drugs and alcohol. His arrogance had played a part in getting her killed. The signs that she had turned her life around were all there. She was proud of herself but also cautiously optimistic and realistic about the fact she would always battle her addiction. She'd looked healthier than he'd ever seen her, her skin smooth and rosy, a spark to her eyes that he couldn't remember ever seeing before. She'd gone back to school, had a job and a little apartment, and had told him she'd been seeing a therapist.

She had overcome their past and was prepared to battle the odds and remain clean. Instead of congratulating her and offering his support, he'd told her she was no better than the rest of their family and would be back in the gutter on drugs within the month.

Then he'd turned his back and walked away. It had been mission after mission, and he'd ignored her attempts to keep reaching out, and then he got the news she was dead.

How could he not wonder that if he'd accepted her olive branch, she might still be alive?

"I know you're awake, Lennox," said a voice he recognized as belonging to Zeke MacAvoy. So, the man had lured them to the bar, he just didn't know whether it was because his cover had been blown or because he'd actually managed to garner enough credibility to get himself and Ivory an invite to the resort.

From what they knew of MacAvoy, the man was ruthless, and although he didn't traffic women himself, he was well known for his love of sex and slaves. Although he'd never admitted he'd bought the women he had a lot of kinks, most of which involved torturing the women he bought. Besides that, he was a drug trafficker who was constantly traveling from country to country making it difficult for any government to do much about him, although he was on Interpol's radar and had been for many years.

"Your new pet is a beautiful one, I wouldn't mind spending a little time with her," MacAvoy taunted.

Even though he knew he was being goaded into revealing he had regained consciousness he didn't even kid himself into pretending he would ignore it. "I don't share, MacAvoy," he growled as he opened his eyes to find himself sitting in a leather seat in a private jet similar to Prey's. He wasn't restrained, his weapon sat on the seat beside him, and he had to take that as a sign that things were looking promising.

Sitting across from him was Ivory. Her eyes were open, her hands tied together with the lead she'd been wearing, her hair was a little mussed, and her lipstick was smudged.

Someone had kissed her.

Was that all they'd done?

She was staring at the floor and seemed otherwise uninjured, but when MacAvoy, who was sitting beside her, reached over and placed his hand on her thigh, his fingers brushing just across her center, Roman didn't think. He just acted.

Launching out of his seat, he slammed his fist into MacAvoy's face. While that move was all him, the sight of another man putting his hands on his woman filled him with red hot rage, it was also in character with his alias Holdon Lennox. Lennox's cover was a man who retaliated brutally and immediately when someone encroached on his territory. Anyone trying to sell drugs on his turf had an eye and a tooth removed, to go with the saying from the book of Exodus in the Bible. Roman thought that Lennox would extend that philosophy to a woman he owned.

"Said I don't share," he snapped as he dropped back into his seat.

Two bodyguards stood and moved toward him, but MacAvoy merely grinned and waved them back down. "I like your attitude, Lennox. Told the others you had what it took to play with the big boys. I mean, anyone who buys a woman and then goes to return her because they didn't like her scars, and then manages to buy her back at a discount isn't lacking in the confidence department."

"Take your hand off her leg," he gritted out. It was clear he had what he'd gone to Colombia for; an in to the circle Albert Hendricks ran in, and yet all he could think of was that he didn't know what had been done to Ivory while he'd been unconscious. If MacAvoy had raped her, he would kill the man himself once this case was over.

MacAvoy grinned but removed his hand. Picking up a glass of scotch instead, he swirled the amber liquid and glanced out the jet window. Apparently noticing the man's attention wasn't on them, Ivory lifted her gaze just enough that she could meet his. Her eyes were red-rimmed and watery, but he knew she could cry on cue, and the spark in the now brown depths told him all he needed to know.

She was okay.

Dragging in a breath, Roman shoved away his anger at himself that Ivory was here and in danger, there was no point in wishing that he had refused to let her work with him on this. She was here, and he wouldn't let anything else happen to her. Now he had to focus on what came next. He had to assume they were on their way to the resort in the Caribbean. Who would have guessed that Ivory's need to go back and gather any other intel she could on the Master before Richard Bouquet's house was raided was actually what had gotten him access to this dark circle.

"This is not how I usually conduct business," he said haughtily.

"I'm sure you understand that complete discretion is needed in meetings such as these," MacAvoy said with a smile as he turned back to face Roman.

"I don't understand," he snapped. "I don't know where we're going."

MacAvoy's grin grew. "You're about to arrive at an island that is about nothing but pleasure. Anything you could ever want, everything you always wanted to do, nothing is off limits, and the supply is limitless so there is no need to be careful if that's not your thing." Casting a sly glance at Ivory, who was once again staring at her lap, he added, "Oh, and don't worry, if you tell everyone your woman is off-limits no one else will touch her."

Relaxing into his chair, he nodded at MacAvoy's drink. "Scotch?"

"Neat or on the rocks?"

"Neat."

MacAvoy nodded at one of the bodyguards who immediately stood and fixed a drink. He didn't bother asking for anything for Ivory even though he knew she was likely thirsty after being drugged. Not wanting anyone to touch what belonged to him was one thing, but Holdon Lennox wouldn't care about his slave's comfort.

Since he didn't want to impair his judgment by getting

drunk, he took a sip, lowered his glass, and fixed MacAvoy with a hard stare. "Tell me more about this island."

"It's paradise in paradise. No rules, anything goes. Well, there is one rule, what happens on the island stays on the island, you don't talk about it with anyone. But given the business you're in I suspect you're not going to have a problem keeping it a secret. We've had our eye on you for a while now, your practices, and the way you run your business. With proper funding you could do so much more. Then when we got word you were looking to make a purchase," his gaze slid to Ivory again, and it was clear he wouldn't mind getting his hands on her, "we knew you were one of us. Going back and getting yourself a discount only sealed the deal. There are a couple of very wealthy men willing to invest in you. Play your cards right, and you could walk away from this trip a very lucky man."

Roman intended to.

He intended to get his revenge on Albert Hendricks and hopefully get a lot of powerful perverts locked up.

First though he had to keep himself and Ivory alive long enough to achieve all of that.

CHAPTER THIRTEEN

December 29th
  9:47 A.M.

IVORY DID her best to surreptitiously glance around as the boat approached the island.

She could hardly believe that it worked and they were actually being brought to the island resort where wealthy men did whatever they pleased without anyone there to stop them.

As the boat pulled up to the dock, she realized they could achieve so much more than they had planned.

How many major players in human trafficking could they take out now that they knew about this place? The tiny tracker implanted inside her would show Prey where she was. Ivory had to fight not to let her excitement show on her face.

So far, she hadn't been treated too badly. She'd regained consciousness first, and Zeke MacAvoy had taken great pleasure in sticking his tongue down her throat and his hand between her legs. Knowing he was doing it to get a rise out of Roman when he woke, she had maintained her cover as a terrified new slave. Roman had reacted exactly as she thought he would, regardless of his wanting to deny this thing between them he was protective of her, and he wouldn't be able to help himself. Hitting MacAvoy was within Roman's Holdon Lennox character and appeared to be exactly what MacAvoy had expected.

Right now, no one suspected anything, but they would have to be careful to make sure that didn't change.

"I'm sure you understand that until you're vetted you won't be able to spend the night, but you can stay for a few hours, network, then I'll see you back to the boat, and you can head back to Florida," MacAvoy said as he and his body-guards stood.

Roman stood too, pulling on her lead to indicate she should follow him, so she did. Ivory hated the way these men talked about buying, selling, and abusing women like it was nothing. The word network really irked her too, but she stowed her anger, it wasn't useful right now and kept her gaze down as she climbed out of the boat.

MacAvoy was chatting away to Roman, telling him who he should make contact with, who to schmooze, who he had to impress if he wanted an invite to come and stay here, but Ivory didn't bother to pay attention. Roman's job was to gather information from the men. Hers was to see what she could get from the other slaves. Just because the men here treated them like toys they weren't, they were living women with eyes and ears, and they likely had a wealth of knowledge that could destroy the powerful men who had bought them.

"You can leave the girl over there if you want, or you can bring her inside with you," MacAvoy said, gesturing to a grassy space where half a dozen women were standing bound to a post, much like old-fashioned hitching posts where men left their horses.

"We can leave her there," Roman said dismissively, his gaze locked on the large building as though he were much more interested in the connections he might be able to make inside than in where she was kept while he did so.

Walking her over to the post, he looped the lead around it, sparing her only the briefest of glances. That second was all it took for her to know what he needed though. Reassurance. He didn't like the idea of treating her like property because he was a good man who would always treat a woman with respect. But they were playing roles right now, she knew that and didn't think any worse of him for doing this. Like she'd told him, she'd gone undercover plenty of times and had to do a lot worse than let a man kiss her and be tied up in the sunshine.

Her nod wouldn't be noticeable to anyone else, and MacAvoy was already chatting to a man who had wandered out of the hotel and then excitedly waved Roman over. Obviously, the Holdon Lennox cover had attracted a lot of attention. She had no doubt Roman had been meticulous in building it. Not only was he intelligent and paid attention to details, but this case meant something to him.

That was why she was so determined to help him.

Yes, she wanted Albert Hendricks caught for what he'd done to her, but she cared more about getting Roman justice for his sister than anything else.

Roman wandered off, and all three men plus the body-guards disappeared inside the building. Ivory wasn't afraid to be on her own in this, it was the way she usually worked, and she scanned the surroundings. The weather was warm, the sky blue, the sun shining, and other men were wandering along the beach and swimming in a nearby pool. There were also guards patrolling, but nobody spared a glance at her and the other women. To them, they were nothing more than the flowered bushes, birds chirping in the trees, or the waves crashing on the sand. They were nothing and certainly not a threat.

"Hey," she whispered softly to the girl beside her.

The woman startled as though the idea of someone talking to her was foreign.

"What's your name?" Ivory asked. The name she'd been using when she'd flaunted herself in El Compradores known trafficking area was Lilly, and she thought it best to stick with that in case Richard had shared her name with MacAvoy when they'd talked about Holdon Lennox. It wasn't likely but better safe than sorry. "Mine is Lilly."

"Shh," a woman on the other side of the post hissed. "You'll get us in trouble."

There were bruises on the woman's skin, no doubt put there by the monster who had bought her. Of course, she had good reason to be scared, she didn't know who Ivory was, and she couldn't tell them because that risked blowing their cover and ruining everything, but Ivory needed as much information out of them as she could get.

"No one is listening," she whispered. "The man who bought me is a drug dealer. His name is Holdon Lennox." Maybe if she shared her "story", the girls would feel more comfortable sharing theirs. The names they would give her would be instrumental in putting a major dent in the world human trafficking trade.

"Did he do that to you?" another woman asked, nodding at Ivory's bruises. She hadn't made any attempt to hide them because the whole point of Roman buying a slave was for word to get back to Albert Hendricks, which meant they would know the story of how she was bought.

"Kind of." Casting a glance around as though she was worried someone might approach, she lowered her voice further. "He bought me and took me to a house, but when he saw I had scars on my wrists he got angry. He took me back and the men who kidnapped me, who sold me, they were angry." She let tears tumble down her cheeks and her voice hitch. "I thought they were going to kill me, but then they took me back to him."

"You were kidnapped?" the woman she'd first asked her name asked.

"Yeah. I was on vacation in Mexico, and I was grabbed off the streets. I woke up in some house. He'd taken me to Colombia," she said, voice wavering.

"I was taken from Paris," the woman said, her French accent obvious.

"I was taken from London," another woman spoke up.

"I ... I was sold by my stepfather after my mom died," a young woman down the end said softly. The girl looked no more than mid-teens at most and as she always did Ivory was overcome by a flaming need to rid the world of every single sick, twisted pervert so things like this never happened to another woman.

If only that were possible.

No matter how hard she and her sisters worked, no matter how much good Prey did in the world, no matter how many strong, courageous men and women worked for the DEA, CIA, DHS, FBI, Interpol, and law enforcement agencies across the world, they could never completely eradicate evil.

It was here to stay, but that didn't mean you had to give up and accept it, do nothing to stop it. Ivory did what she could, played her part, and counted every victory for the win that it was. While she might not be able to stop every monster, she could stop Albert Hendricks and the other men who came to this resort to do unspeakably wicked things to innocent women.

As long as she and Roman stayed alive.

* * *

<small>DECEMBER 29TH</small>
7:35 P.M.

ROMAN LET OUT the first full breath it felt like he'd taken since he and Ivory were ambushed at the bar.

They were safely back in Florida inside their hotel room.

Ivory was standing before him, all in one piece with no injuries. He prayed nothing had been done to her when he hadn't been there.

Despite the fact he had vowed he would never touch her again in any way other than what was necessary to maintain their cover, he stalked toward her, grabbed her, and dragged her toward him, then crushed his mouth to hers.

There was no hesitation, even though he knew he'd hurt her when he'd stormed off straight after sex, her hands lifted to cover his and her mouth opened, inviting him in.

This woman was more than he deserved.

Which was the very crux of his problem.

She didn't know him. She seemed to be under the impression that because he had served in the military, joined the elite Delta Force, and then gone to work for the DEA to get justice—revenge—for his sister that he was some sort of heroic figure.

She couldn't be more wrong.

Even though it was the last thing he wanted to do, he couldn't be selfish again and take what Ivory would freely offer when he knew he had nothing to offer her in return—at least not until she knew the truth about who he really was—so Roman pulled back.

Big brown eyes stared questioningly up at him, but Ivory didn't say anything. Apparently, she was putting the ball in his court.

If he wanted anything to happen between them, he was going to have to make a move.

Walk away.

That was what he should do.

There could be nothing between them, no future, nothing besides more hot sex until their partnership was over, and they had the men they wanted in custody. There really was no point in telling her about his sordid past, and yet … she'd held nothing back. Shared her deepest pain, parts of herself she hadn't had to give him, parts he knew she'd given him because of what she felt for him.

Roman felt like he owed her the same.

"We need to talk," he announced.

"Uh oh, that sounds ominous," she teased to lighten the mood.

How did she do that?

How did she not let her past destroy her?

"You told me about your past. I owe you the same," he announced.

There was sadness in her eyes but also so much compassion. It was the compassion that made his heart crack and emotions start to seep through. It had been so long since he'd felt anything other than anger that he didn't know what to do with what he was feeling right now.

Life was so much easier when you felt nothing.

"Oh, Roman, you don't owe me anything." Ivory took his

hand and squeezed. "I told you because I wanted you to know. If you don't want me to know that's okay."

It was because she would never try to force him to tell her that made him want to do it. "I want to," he said gruffly as he led her over to the bed and sat her down, taking a seat beside her. "Can you …?" Roman hesitated, his request sounded silly, but he knew Ivory would do it if he asked.

"Can I what?" she asked gently.

"Can you take out the contacts?" He needed to see Ivory's real eyes as he told her about his past. It sounded stupid, but the only way he could do this was to allow himself to feel the connection between them. Draw on her strength.

"Of course." Ivory touched her fingers to her eyes, removed the contacts, and set them on the nightstand before shifting so she was sitting on the bed, propped up against the headboard. He knew that she'd done it to give him a little space, but the fact that her now bare feet—she'd removed the boots the second they got into the hotel room claiming they were killing her feet —touched his thigh said she was also offering her comfort.

The best of both worlds and he loved her for knowing exactly what he needed.

"My parents were addicts," he began. "Both came from parents who were addicts as well. My dad was one of nine kids. All of his siblings battled drug or alcohol addiction, some both. My mom was an only child whose parents died when she was young. She grew up in the system, met my dad when they were young teens, had me at fifteen, my sister two years later."

Ivory didn't say anything, but there was so much warmth and understanding in her face that he had to glance away, sure that if he didn't, he would succumb to the tears threatening to clog his throat.

Roman hadn't cried since he was three years old. He'd quickly learned, even as young as he was, that the only thing crying about his situation did was make it worse.

Tears led to punishments.

Starved, cold showers, locked in his bedroom.

Those were his punishments if he was lucky.

"My dad was an alcoholic, my mom loved drugs. She was also addicted to sex. I think I was about four the first time I remember seeing them having sex in front of me. My dad didn't care who she did it with as long as she brought home money he could use, so she spent her nights working as a prostitute, her days so high she didn't know who she was most of the time. There was no one to take care of me and my sister so I learned young how to take care of myself. Tried to take care of my sister too."

Only he had failed.

He hadn't stopped Alexa from turning to drugs and he hadn't stopped her from being brutally murdered.

Unable to sit still any longer, he stood and began to pace the length of the hotel room, feeling like his emotions—which he had spent a lifetime burying—were quickly finding a way to dig themselves back up, and were chasing after him, ready to smother him any second.

"First time we were put in foster care was when I was seven. Mom was out working and Dad had no money for booze, so he called a couple of friends around. Alexa had just turned five. They laughed while they raped her. I tried to fight them off, but my father threw me away and then asked if I thought it was only girls his friends were willing to pay to do. All I remember next is the pain and the smell of the alcohol on their breaths. Lex and I were in such bad shape my mom had no choice but to take us to the hospital when she came home and found us both bleeding on the floor. Dad did a few years in prison, we spent a while in foster care, then Mom got us back. I liked foster care. The family was nice, not warm or caring but they left me alone other than making sure I had food to eat and clean clothes to wear. Mom took Dad back when he got out of prison. I was twelve by then, but a big twelve, I hit him the first time he tried to come after me. He left me alone after that, Lex wasn't that lucky. She started using when she was thirteen. We did a couple of other stints in foster care, but it stopped mattering to me where I was. All I knew was that I wanted a better life for myself. I didn't want to wind up like the rest of my family."

For so long that was all that had mattered to him.

Getting out.

Away from his family.

"That's why I joined the Army. I didn't want to be like my parents, their parents, my aunts, uncles, and cousins. Didn't want to be like my sister. I couldn't afford college, and while I got good grades, they weren't good enough for a scholarship. I didn't know what I wanted to do with my life and couldn't see myself sitting in a classroom for several more years so the military seemed like the obvious choice. A way to get away from the life my family had chosen, a way to keep on the straight and narrow. I didn't join for noble purposes, Ivory. I didn't join to save the world or defend my country and its people. I joined for me, to channel my addictive personality into something that wouldn't destroy me."

Only in a way the choices he'd made had destroyed him.

He might not have ever touched drugs, didn't drink, and rarely had sex, but he was cold and hard and not a man anyone would ever be proud of.

Roman stopped pacing and swallowed hard. There he'd done it. Told her everything. It wasn't easy but it seemed only fair. "So now you know what kind of man I am. Why I can't ever give you more than this. Sex. Just sex. I don't know how to be intimate with a woman or let anyone in. Even if I did you know my history, my genetics. Addiction. I've avoided drugs and alcohol, but I'm addicted to my job.

"Oh, Roman." Ivory raced across the room and leaped off the floor, wrapping her arms around his neck and clinging to him, her wet face pressed against his neck.

It didn't seem to bother her that his arms hung limply by his sides. She wasn't there for him to hug her back she was just there for him, so he wouldn't be alone, so he would know that she still cared about him.

Why?

He wanted to grab her, shake her, and demand she explain why and how she saw anything even remotely desirable about him.

Instead, a sound perilously close to a sob ripped from his chest, and he lifted his arms, held Ivory close, and allowed her warmth, her goodness, her wide-open heart to ease a little of the pain that would destroy him if he let it.

CHAPTER FOURTEEN

December 29th
7:35 P.M.

HER HEART BROKE FOR HIM.

What he'd been through was truly horrific, and it was no wonder he didn't know how to let anyone get close to him. Cutting himself off from emotional connections was the only way he had survived.

Would he give her a chance?

Had telling her been a first step in letting her in or his way to convince her to run as far away from him as she could get?

Ivory hoped for the former while fearing it was the latter.

Understanding him better made her ache that much more to show him that while there were a lot of evil people in the world, there were also a lot of good ones. While she'd suffered the same sorts of horrors he had, she'd had something he hadn't. The love and support of her sisters.

Without them, she wouldn't have survived.

It killed her to know that through everything he'd had to endure, Roman hadn't had anyone there for him. No one to hold him when it felt like everything was too much, no one to encourage him when it felt like he wanted to give up, no one to get angry with him and rage against the unfairness of it all.

But not anymore.

"I'm here, Roman. You don't have to be alone anymore," she whispered and prayed he believed her. She couldn't make him, couldn't force him to give them a chance, but she hoped that he knew she would never hurt him on purpose.

Instead of saying anything, he reached for her wrists and unhooked them from around his neck so he could lift her up and crush his mouth to hers. The kiss was hot and fiery, full of passion, but she could also feel him holding back.

Her body responded to his almost instantaneously. Need pulsed through her, and her panties grew wet. As much as she wanted this, she couldn't have sex and have him walk away like he had last time.

Being there for Roman, offering him all of her, didn't mean allowing him to treat her as though she were just a tool in his efforts to forget.

Ivory knew her own strengths and weaknesses. Her strengths were her ability to see through the darkness that had cloaked her most of her life to find the specks of light that shone through like stars in the night, allowing her to still find beauty. Her weaknesses were her ability to have her heart turned against her. She couldn't let Roman do that to her because if she allowed it, not only would she wind up hurt but he would as well.

Despite his best attempts at convincing himself he no longer felt anything, he was a good man, one who could be as fiery and passionate as the kiss. If he used her, he would wind up regretting it.

"Roman, stop." With tremendous effort, Ivory pulled back. There was a second of confusion in his pitch-black eyes then a stark flash of pain before they blanked and went empty. "No, stop," she said again, pressing her mouth to his and kissing him, letting everything she felt flow through the kiss. "I care about you, maybe too much given we haven't known each other very long. My heart is breaking for everything that happened to you and what you think about yourself, but I don't judge you for it. Trauma cuts deep and changes everything. I want this." She reached between them and clasped his hard length straining against his jeans. "But you can't do what you did last time. I'm not asking you for promises, just an acknowledgment that there's something between us. I deserve better than sex against the wall then being ignored."

Having said what she needed to say, there was nothing to do but wait and see his response. If he couldn't give her that then there would be no sex today, but that didn't mean she would give up on him.

Ivory wasn't sure she could ever give up on Roman.

Already she was in too deep, her heart too entangled, the beginnings of love already planted inside her.

For what felt like an eternity, Roman stared into her eyes, obviously seeking an answer to a question he couldn't voice. She did her best to keep her gaze wide open, allowing him to see deep inside her, down to the very depths of her soul. There was nothing she would hide from him, but he had to be ready to accept that she cared before things could progress.

Then he carried her to the bed and very gently laid her down.

Her heart cracked.

He was going to walk away.

Unable to give her what she was asking for but unable to hurt her, he was going to leave, claiming it was for the best.

Then he reached out and traced a finger from her temple down her cheek and along her bottom lip. "I hate that you were hurt. I hate that you're in danger. I hate that I had to leave you alone today on the island knowing someone might touch you."

Ivory reached up and covered his hand with her own. "I know."

He studied her, his expression the most open it had been since they met. "I don't know how to give you what you want. I don't think I can be what you deserve."

This man. How desperately she wished he could see what she saw in him. The strength it took to overcome both nature and nurture and become a strong man with principles. Knowing the more she allowed herself to be vulnerable to him, the more comfortable he would become doing the same with her, she said honestly, "I'm not sure what I want. For a long time, I thought it was just to save others, but now I think maybe I want … maybe I *need* more. I just want to be … cherished. I think maybe that's what you want too."

"I've never made love before. I've only ever had sex."

"Me too. After what happened to both of us when we were young, I don't think it's a surprise that we have hangups about sex. But maybe we could learn together?"

"Maybe we can," he echoed somewhat thoughtfully as though the idea that he could learn to be something different hadn't yet occurred to him.

Reaching behind her, he undid the halter top and pulled it down, baring her breasts. When his mouth dipped and he took one of her nipples between his lips, his touch was soft, sweet, different than yesterday when he'd felt like a starving man.

Although she wanted to touch him, let her hands and mouth do their own exploring, she also didn't want to break the spell that seemed to have captured them both, cocooning them in a bubble she feared would pop far too soon. Ivory lay there and let him play with first one of her breasts and then the other. She'd never even known they were as sensitive as they were, but as Roman's tongue licked and swirled, the heat of his mouth pulsing around those little buds as he sucked, she felt herself growing wetter and needier.

"Roman," she pleaded, needing more.

All he did was shoot her a crooked smile and kiss his way down her stomach. When he got to the waistband of her mini skirt he lifted her hips, slid it and her panties down, then eased them down her legs and tossed them onto the floor. "You're so beautiful," he murmured as she stared down at her naked body.

"I have scars," she said, suddenly self-conscious of the marks. He'd seen her naked, she'd been wearing no clothes the first time he laid eyes on her, but things had shifted between them tonight, and she felt vulnerable and raw.

"You have evidence of your spirit etched onto your body," he corrected, touching a kiss to a scar on her hip.

The words soothed the hurt inside her. "I feel like things are a little unbalanced here." Ivory touched the bulge in his jeans. "I'm naked and you're completely dressed."

"I think we can fix that." Roman stripped out of his clothes and stood before her in all his muscled glory.

She couldn't look at him and not touch, so she let her fingers do a little exploring, tracing the lines of his muscles, then dipping lower to curl around his impressive length. If it hadn't been inside her already, and she didn't remember in perfect detail how amazing it felt, she wouldn't have thought it would fit in her.

Roman shifted, stretching out above her, and while her hand trailed lazily up and down his throbbing length, his hand dipped between her legs. His fingers filled her, stretching, stroking, while his thumb found her needy little bundle of nerves.

Ivory could feel it building inside her. A pleasure she'd never even known existed and feared she would never find for herself.

In this moment, there were no dark pasts, no fear of what the future held, there was nothing but a man and a woman who cared about one another. Nothing but the touching of lips, the bringing of pleasure, the joining of bodies.

"Roman, I need you inside me," she said as her hips began to thrust, bringing his fingers deeper inside her.

"All right, baby," he whispered as he grabbed a condom from the nightstand and rolled it on.

As he slid inside her, filling her, Ivory felt a deep understanding touch her soul.

This was the man she would fall in love with.

The man she would spend the rest of her life with if only he would give her a chance to show him what it was like to be loved.

That knowledge sent a wave of pleasure crashing through her as the dam broke and the most intense orgasm overloaded her senses. Vaguely she was aware of Roman finding his own release as he continued to thrust into her, forcing the orgasm to last until she felt like it had stripped her bare, revealing to her what she'd hidden from for so long.

What had happened to her hadn't broken anything inside her. Her fears that she could never truly love a man had been for nothing. She had been the one preventing herself from finding this level of happiness. It was easier to run from your fears than to face them, but she was done running.

Was Roman?

His forehead touched hers for a moment and he slid out of her, standing to roll off the condom. This was it. The moment of truth. Was he going to stay or was he going to run again?

He disappeared into the hotel's bathroom, returning a moment later with a warm cloth that he used to clean between her legs. She watched him, desperate to ask what he planned to do next, but she had to show him that while she had faith in him and wasn't giving up on him—on them—she also couldn't allow him to use her.

Once he'd cleaned her up, he returned the cloth to the bathroom and then he came back to her. Her heart soared. Roman had chosen her, not his fear. He lifted her, pulled back the covers, lay them both down, and tucked them in.

His arms were warm and strong around her as he tucked her against his side. "Just want to hold you," he whispered as his lips touched a soft kiss to her temple.

"Perfect, because I want you to hold me."

It might be a small one, but they'd just taken the first step toward building something real.

* * *

December 29th
10:47 P.M.

Roman never wanted this moment to end.

It was perfect.

After making love, he'd cleaned Ivory up, tucked them

both into bed and pulled her into his arms. Neither of them had slept, but they were still here, hours later, lying together, holding onto one another.

He never wanted to let her go.

A terrifying thought for a man who had known without a shadow of a doubt that there was no way he would inflict his bad genetics on another person.

Could he give Ivory the forever he knew she wanted?

Despite her words telling him she wasn't asking for a promise, he knew that wasn't quite true. While she would never demand that he tell her what she wanted to hear and make promises he wouldn't or couldn't keep, he also knew she hoped he would find a way to overcome his fears and give them a chance.

Maybe if he knew for sure that things would work out between them it would be easier to make a decision. Deciding to let go of his fears and knowing that he would be spending the rest of his life with Ivory was something he might be able to do. But even if he gave them a chance, there were no guarantees they would work as a couple. They could try and break up a few months down the road.

Where would that leave him?

Destroyed.

"You're thinking so loudly," Ivory said as her fingers began to trace small circles on his chest. So far, they hadn't exchanged words. He'd been content to just hold her, and she seemed content enough to let him.

"We should try to get some sleep. It was a long day, and we don't know when we'll hear from MacAvoy again." It wasn't really intentional, but it was almost a test of sorts. Not fair of him when Ivory had been nothing but supportive, but he wasn't ready to talk more tonight. Already he felt like he'd been flayed open, there was no way he was at the point where he was ready to admit out loud that he was falling for the sweet woman snuggled against him. If Ivory pushed now, he had an excuse to push back, walk away.

Was that what he wanted?

At this point, Roman truly didn't even know anymore.

"Okay," Ivory said, stifling a yawn. "Sleep does sound pretty nice about now. Nice to sleep in a bed tonight too, better than being drugged and tied up on a plane."

Roman found himself smiling despite himself and his mixed-up emotions. It might not be fair to test Ivory, but she certainly passed with flying colors. The woman had been nothing but open and honest with him, and he was glad he'd opened up tonight.

Imagine that.

Actually glad he'd shared the horror story of his childhood.

Maybe his subconscious mind knew something his conscious mind had yet to figure out. He could trust Ivory.

"Can't argue with that, darlin'."

A small sigh whooshed out against his chest and Ivory snuggled closer.

"What?" he asked.

"I just like when you call me darlin'," she said sleepily. "Night, Roman."

"Night. Darlin'," he added, suddenly filled with a need to make her smile.

She did. He felt her lips curl up and she rested one of her hands right above his heart.

It took a long time for his mind to drift toward sleep. His brain was in a battle to figure out if Ivory was too good to be true or whether he really had gotten this lucky when he'd walked into Richard Bouquet's house ready to purchase a woman, save her life, and build his cover.

Falling for the woman he bought had never even entered his mind.

The shrill ring of his phone jarred him from sleep. It felt like he'd only just drifted off and a glance at the clock on the nightstand confirmed it was only fifteen minutes since he last looked.

"Is that the Holdon Lennox phone?" Ivory asked as she sat and blinked sleepily.

He had two cell phones, his personal one and the one used for his cover as Holdon Lennox. "The Lennox one," he replied as he reached out and snagged a hold of it. He knew Ivory was experienced enough to make sure she was quiet. If Holdon Lennox was a real person, he wouldn't be snuggling with his slave in bed at close to midnight. "Lennox," he said into the phone as he answered.

"You did it," Zeke MacAvoy announced. "You impressed all the right people and got yourself invited into the inner circle."

Perfect.

Now all he needed was a sighting of Albert Hendricks. Although there had been several other high-profile men at the resort today, some he'd actually been surprised to see there, others he'd heard rumors they dabbled in a dark underworld, Hendricks hadn't been one of them.

As soon as Hendricks showed up on the island, Roman would find a way to tag the man with a tracker so they could finally take him down. Him and all the other monsters from the resort. They needed to move carefully, and make sure the men didn't have time to take out their slaves because without the women's testimonies, there was every chance the wealthy men and their lawyers would try to make it all look like a mutually beneficial scenario. That the women enjoyed playing at being slaves and were paid for their services.

Roman was confident that with the women's testimonies at least one of the men from the resort would flip on the others to make a deal, and then he could finally bring down the man responsible for his sister's murder.

"Didn't doubt that I would," he said in Holdon Lennox's smug voice. "What time tomorrow morning should I meet the boat?"

"Right now. We're en route to pick you up. By the time you check out of your hotel and make it to the marina, we'll be there to get you."

That wasn't what he'd been expecting, and there was a part of him that was disappointed not to be spending the night holding Ivory. But the quicker they got this case wrapped up, the quicker they could find the Master, and then … well, he wasn't completely sure, but he knew he actually wanted to figure it out.

"Perfect. I'll just untie my little flower, and we'll be there." Then he made his voice extra smarmy. "I'm sure now I'm in I'll have access to all the good stuff?" Today's trip to the island hadn't shown him much other than a few women tied up and the odd slave servicing her master. He needed proof of drugs, trafficking, and anything else he could get to bring these men down.

"You'll get everything," MacAvoy replied. "Anything you can think of we have. Drugs, weapons, women, even the little kind, you want something we have it, and if we don't, we'll get it."

"Perfect," he said again even as his stomach revolted. "We'll be at the marina in thirty minutes." With that, he ended the call to find Ivory's excited eyes watching him.

"We did it," she exclaimed.

"We did." While he couldn't deny he was pleased with the prompt progress they'd made, he also had to acknowledge that this time Ivory's position would be even more precarious. Last time they'd been testing him. This time they were welcoming him into the fold, which meant that nothing was off-limits. As much as he wanted Hendricks and all these other men brought down, he didn't want Ivory hurt in the process. "Remember your safety is our number one priority."

She merely smiled at him, kissed his cheek, and climbed out of bed. "I know what I'm doing."

Problem was, did he?

Was he putting the woman he was falling for in danger because of his own selfish need for revenge?

This was an amazing opportunity to put a huge dent in the trafficking world, but Roman knew he wouldn't feel any joy from either his revenge or what they'd achieved if Ivory was hurt in the process.

They both dressed, checked their gear, and headed down to the lobby to catch a cab to the marina. The second they stepped out of the hotel room they played their roles. He couldn't hold Ivory or touch her in anything more than the possessive way Holdon Lennox would touch his slave. There could be no whispered words of encouragement, no last-minute reminders not to take any risks, and no telling her how he felt about her.

As he gripped her arm as they got out of the cab and watched it drive away, Roman wished he'd taken an opportunity at the hotel to hold her one last time, kiss her one last time, and tell her before they walked into hell that he cared for her.

But he hadn't.

Because he was a coward.

Now there was a chance he might not get to.

Excruciating pain suddenly wracked his body, and he hit the ground hard.

Ivory cried out as she fell beside him.

Tasers.

The pain didn't stop as electrical currents raced through his body, lighting his every nerve on fire.

Gray spots danced in his vision.

Black boots walked closer.

Ivory disappeared from his view.

He tried to reach for her.

Couldn't let them take her.

Ignored the pain and his deadened limbs and tried to clamber to his feet.

Another shock jolted through his body.

This one took him out.

CHAPTER FIFTEEN

December 30th
   12:34 A.M.

As BAD AS the pain coursing through her body was, fear for Roman and what was happening to him overrode everything.

What had happened?

It was clear their cover had been blown. Maybe they'd even been lured into a trap by Zeke MacAvoy.

But that didn't quite make sense.

If they weren't confident in believing that Roman was really drug dealer Holdon Lennox and she was really a slave, then they never would have invited them to the island resort. And if there had been doubts once they got there, they wouldn't have been allowed to leave. Taking them on the docks where anyone might have stumbled upon the attack and abduction made no sense when they could have quite easily disposed of them from the resort and dumped their bodies in the ocean where they'd never be found.

Maybe only one of their covers had been blown.

It was more likely they would have realized Roman wasn't who he said he was than she was a Prey operative. With her brown hair and eyes, she looked nothing like her usual self. And while it certainly wasn't the first time she'd played at being a slave to take down a human trafficker, it was unlikely they would suspect that she would be here. This was definitely the largest sting Ivory had ever participated in and not one that would have come about without Roman and the DEA.

Whoever was carrying her dumped her onto something hard. She landed awkwardly on her back with her legs and arms sticking straight up in the air.

It took a second for her to realize that it was because whatever she'd been put on—or rather in—was too small to hold her.

Someone shifted her and folded her arms and legs so they were pressed up against her chest.

Ivory did her best to defend herself, but her limbs were weak and useless. Pain still zinged through them, and she wasn't sure whether it was best to keep pretending that she was Lilly the kidnapped and sold slave, or fight like the trained operative she was.

In the end, the fact she'd been tased and her body was still experiencing the aftereffects made the choice for her.

She couldn't fight back.

She was as weak as a kitten.

Which meant she was trapped.

Again, there was a tinge of panic, but this was by far not the worst situation she had ever been thrown into, and it was still fear for Roman that overrode everything else.

Something clunked down above her, and she heard what sounded like a key in a lock.

Box.

They'd locked her in a small box, barely big enough to hold her even as she was folded into the fetal position.

Was Roman here too?

Was he still at the marina?

Had he been taken somewhere else?

Or was he dead?

The last had tears welling up in her eyes. She couldn't bear anything to happen to him. He was a good man whether he believed it or not, and he was just starting to realize that he had locked himself in a prison of his own making. While his focus had been on not becoming like the rest of his family, he was merely existing not really living.

A slight rocking motion told her that they were on the move.

Ivory wasn't afraid, she had the trackers implanted in her. Prey would be watching her every move and they would come for her. Depending on who had taken her and why, there was always a chance that she would be dead before Prey could get to her but given that someone had bothered to take her and not kill her on the docks, she had to assume they didn't want her dead.

At least not yet.

And a chance was all she needed.

Even now her strength was returning. Hopefully, by the time they got where they were going it would be back completely. Of course, being trapped like this meant that if she was kept in here for too long, her limbs would be virtually useless.

But she was alive, she was being tracked, and she was armed. The chunky gold bracelets on her wrists—which they'd put on to cover the scars there given that was the reason Roman had "returned" her—both contained small blades as did the collar on her neck.

If whoever had taken her thought they had a helpless little slave then they would be sorely mistaken.

The mission had changed but not completely. It was still gathering whatever information she could, do what she had to keep herself alive, and wait for the cavalry to come.

Even though Ivory knew she had the skills and the determination to do whatever it took to keep herself alive, and to rescue herself, she also knew the value of a team. You were stronger together than you were on your own. She'd known that since she was a very little girl and wished Roman had been lucky enough to have the same. She prayed he realized he had that now. She was there for him, she would watch his back, do her best to protect him from pain, and care about him, if only he'd give her the chance.

They stopped moving, and she wondered if they were at the resort or perhaps a different island. Could this all be just some sort of bizarre initiation ritual?

Of course these men were secretive and wary. They knew what they were doing was wrong, and they used their money to try to hide it. Letting someone new in always involved a risk, and maybe this was their way of reminding Holdon Lennox that if they so chose, they could have him disposed of and there was no way he could stop it from happening.

Since she couldn't see or hear anything trapped in here, Ivory jerked in surprise when she felt the box lifted and carried. There had to be at least two men, between her weight and the wooden box there was no way one man could carry it alone.

Whatever information she could garner she had to. She couldn't allow fear over Roman to distract her from her job. He was well trained too, and would do whatever was necessary to keep himself alive, she would do the same.

Residual pain fired through her body when the box she

was trapped in was set down, and when the lid was opened she had to scrunch her eyes closed in protest to the sudden light.

Two men lifted her out, picking her up and carrying her like she was nothing but a ragdoll over to a large table in the middle of a small room. Since she didn't have enough information yet to know what was going on, she decided that keeping her cover was for the best.

So instead of fighting them off and taking them down like she longed to do, she whimpered and allowed tears to tumble down her cheeks as she was laid down on the table, her wrists, ankles, and neck secured with leather cuffs. The leather was good. It would be softer on her skin, and also afforded her the chance to cut through it if she needed to free the blades and get herself out of there. Thankfully the cuffs had been placed just above the bracelet she wore with her tiny blade hidden inside.

If they thought she was Lilly then they'd know she had been kept only a short time by El Compradores, not enough time to be trained, so they wouldn't be surprised if she spoke. "P-please," she sobbed, "why are you doing th-this? Who are y-you? That man, he b-bought me, I just w-want to go h-home."

The men ignored her, didn't even bother to glance at her, merely picked up the box she'd been transported in and left.

Alone, Ivory looked around, trying to gather every clue she could while she had the chance. It looked like they were on a boat, no doubt a luxury yacht of some sort, one big enough for the smaller vessel that had collected her from the mariner to dock in because she had simply been carried off it. That didn't do her any good though. They were in Florida and had been heading to one of the Caribbean islands. All the men at the resort were ridiculously wealthy, any one of them could be the owner of the yacht.

"Tears, my dear?"

At the sound of the soft, melodic voice, Ivory felt her blood turn to ice.

She knew that voice.

Heard it in her nightmares.

It belonged to the one man she thought might have destroyed her.

The Master had taught her the value of strength, of surviving no matter what was thrown at you, but it was Albert Hendricks who had cracked the iron shell she thought she'd encased herself in and shown her that she had vulnerabilities not tortured out of her as a child.

It was Albert Hendricks who stood before her now, watching her with a mixture of lust and fury.

"Last time you held out so well, didn't shed a single tear if I remember correctly."

He knew who she was.

She had no idea how. The disguise should have been enough, and she hadn't even seen him at the resort yesterday.

How did he know she was Ivory Smith and not Lilly?

"I see you have questions, my dear," Albert said as he came closer, running a finger across her neck, above where the leather strap held her in place. "All of them shall be answered, but first we have a lot of catching up to do."

Ivory knew how this would end. Her torture and death. Likely before Prey would be able to come and rescue her. Roman would likely be tortured and killed as well.

Because of her.

She hadn't saved him, instead she'd gotten him killed.

* * *

JANE BLYTHE

DECEMBER 30TH
12:40 A.M.

QUIET.

When Roman opened his eyes, he was alone on the marina's docks.

There was lingering pain in his limbs, but he shoved it aside and staggered to his feet. He had to find Ivory.

She'd been taken. Kidnapped.

But by who? And why did they leave him behind?

It didn't make any sense, but he was going to have to figure it out if he wanted to get the woman he was falling for back alive and in one piece.

They'd both known they were taking a crazy risk by attempting to pull this off, but everything seemed to be going so well. His meticulously crafted cover story had been bought, and it had got him exactly what he wanted. Access to the one place that he could get to Albert Hendricks. What had changed between his visit to the island and now?

Had Zeke MacAvoy's call been to lure him into a trap?

If it had they should both be gone, but he had been left behind. Did that mean someone didn't know who he really was but had recognized Ivory?

An approaching boat caught his attention, and he curled his hands into fists as he saw MacAvoy and his two goons sitting on board.

If the man had set him up, he was going to make him pay.

"Lennox, I'm sure you're …" MacAvoy started as he climbed off the boat.

He didn't finish his sentence because Roman grabbed the man and rammed him up against a nearby pole, his arm pressing against the drug dealer's neck. Roman barely registered the fact that both of MacAvoy's goons had their weapons aimed at his head. He knew he was overplaying his cards, but fear for Ivory was crawling over his skin, eating its way through him until he knew it would destroy him.

"Did you think you could trick me and get away with it?" he roared.

The man's face was already turning red. "I … don't … what …?" MacAvoy stuttered.

"We were ambushed. Tasered. They took my slave. She was mine. I bought her, she belonged to me. I don't do well with people messing with what's mine," he snarled.

"I didn't … wouldn't …." MacAvoy wheezed.

For some reason Roman believed the man. It didn't make sense that he was in on the ambush because if he had been, he would have approached more cautiously knowing that Holdon Lennox would be furious. Easing up on the man but not letting him go, he said, "We were ambushed. They were waiting for us, tasered us then took Lilly."

MacAvoy's eyes widened, and fear lurked in their blue-green depths. "I had nothing to do with that. *Nothing*. We were slightly delayed leaving. Someone misplaced the keys to the boat. I expected to find you both here waiting. I swear I did."

Someone from the island had intentionally misplaced those keys, Roman would bet his life on it. Which meant someone on that island knew who Ivory was. It was the only thing that made sense.

Obviously, they didn't know he was undercover with the DEA or he would have been taken as well. That or killed.

Could Albert Hendricks know Lilly was really Ivory?

The man already knew she went undercover as a slave because that was how he'd gotten his hands on her in the first place. Just because they hadn't seen him on the island yesterday didn't mean he hadn't been there. Didn't mean he didn't have eyes everywhere and had spotted Ivory and seen through her disguise.

He needed to call in help. They had the location of the resort and he was sure he could get Zeke MacAvoy to turn. It was time to send in a team and have them deal with that, he had to focus on getting Ivory back alive.

"Get out of here," he said, releasing MacAvoy. He didn't have time to waste on the man right now.

"You're not coming?"

"To the resort, after someone from there stole from me? No, but you can rest assured I'm going to find who did it."

MacAvoy shrugged. "She's just a slave. We have more you can purchase at the resort."

Good to know, but he still wasn't going there. "It's not a matter of replacing her. Of course I can do that, it's the principle of it. Someone that I would need to trust not to go to the cops stole from me. I won't tolerate that."

Not wanting to waste another second, he turned and stalked away, ignoring MacAvoy's calls for him to wait.

Waiting wasn't something he was going to do with Ivory's life hanging in the balance.

By the time he arrived at a different hotel thirty minutes later, he'd already sent texts out to Prey to update them on what was going on so they could set up a raid of the resort, and his old commander to find out if there was a Delta team in the area who could help him find Ivory. His old team was on a mission on the other side of the world, but a team nearby would meet him at his hotel in an hour.

An hour felt like an eternity.

What would happen to Ivory in those sixty minutes?

More than he could stomach.

Already she'd been gone long enough to have been beaten, raped, or even killed.

Her fate rested on who had taken her and why. If it was someone who was merely trying to make a statement to the new guy, then there was a chance they merely intended to keep her for themselves or sell her to someone else. Ivory would find a way to take them down, he knew that. She was smart and she was armed, she could get herself out.

But if whoever had taken her knew who she really was then they would anticipate that she had the skills to save herself and make sure she couldn't.

They would do whatever it took to disable her, physically or psychologically. Ivory had been through so much and always made it out the other side, but that didn't mean she couldn't be broken.

Especially by someone who knew too much about her.

Albert Hendricks.

His mind kept circling back to the man, and his gut was telling him that somehow Hendricks knew who she was and had decided to take the opportunity to get his revenge on her for almost taking him down.

He was pacing around the hotel room, feeling like a caged tiger who wanted to be free to hunt but was trapped by circumstance, when his phone rang. It was an unknown number, but praying it was the Delta team coming to work with him, he answered.

"Morales."

"It's Ghost. We're on our way up to your room," Keane "Ghost" Bryson said.

Roman had worked with Ghost and his team before. All of the men were highly skilled, they worked well together, and all of them had gone through something terrifying with the women they were now married to. He knew no one would work harder to help him get Ivory back alive than these men.

Not even five minutes later there was a knock on his door. Knowing it was the Delta team he still made himself check the peephole first to confirm, then threw open the door.

Eight large men filed into the room, and for the first time, Roman felt like maybe they stood a chance at doing this. Rescuing Ivory might actually be possible.

He prayed it was.

How badly he wished he hadn't allowed his fear to hold him back and he had admitted to her before they left the hotel earlier that he cared for her. He'd thought he had to figure everything out first, get all the answers before he did anything, he'd thought caring about something was an intellectual decision.

He'd been so wrong.

Caring came from the heart not the head, and he cared for Ivory, only she might never know that. There was a chance he would never get an opportunity to tell her, and he had no one to blame for that but himself.

A hand rested on his shoulder, and he looked over into Ghost's understanding eyes. "We will do whatever it takes to get your girl back."

Roman nodded. He had to believe that if he wanted to be able to function. "She has trackers in her, but something is blocking the signal. Last we know she was on the ocean somewhere." Again this was more proof that whoever had taken her knew who she was and that they would need to prevent a team from coming in and taking them down.

"You got a theory on who took her?" Beckett "Coach" Ralston asked.

"Oh yeah," Roman said, indicating that the guys should

sit. "Let's sit and I'll get you all up to speed." It was time to put his game face on, do what he'd been doing for a lifetime and stifle his emotions, so he could do whatever it took to bring Ivory home alive.

Only problem was, for the first time ever he wasn't sure his emotions could be turned off.

CHAPTER SIXTEEN

December 30th
1:15 A.M.

"ARE YOU READY, MY DEAR?" Albert asked as his finger stroked backward and forward across her neck. The caress would have been sensual if done by a lover, but Ivory felt his promise of pain in the man's touch.

She knew how this would play out. He would tell her whatever he wanted her to know, he'd torture her until he got bored, then he'd rape her and finish what he'd started two years ago.

Although she had no idea how he had figured it out, it was clear that Albert knew who she really was so there was no point in pretending otherwise. Her best bet at staying alive was to keep him talking as long as possible, wait until she was alone, get herself free, get hold of a gun, and kill the man herself.

Her goal should probably be to detain him, but she knew that Albert had already proved that he had what it took to pay off a team of lawyers to work for him and then disappear. For two years now the man had managed to avoid being caught by anyone. There was no way she could allow him to get away again.

"Still the strong silent type I see," Albert said as he took a step back and picked up a knife from a table beside them.

Ivory well remembered how much the man loved knives, and while she would love nothing more than to pull out one of the blades in her jewelry and give him a taste of his own medicine, she'd never get free in time to hurt him.

She'd just have to wait.

"Where are they?" Albert asked.

"Where are what?"

"Ah, so you do have a voice after all."

Albert smirked like he'd won a victory, but she had no intention of not speaking. Her goal was to gather as much intel as she could. If she didn't kill Hendricks, he was going to spend the rest of his life in prison, she would make sure of it.

"I won't let you ruin things for me again. Tell me where the tracking devices are." Albert held up the knife as though she would be intimidated into telling him with the threat of pain. Too bad for him she had grown up in a world where pain was the norm.

Ivory kept her lips sealed. Those trackers were the only thing that would tell her team where she was, she wasn't letting him remove them.

"If you think I won't cut open every inch of your body to find them then think again." With quick, efficient swipes of the knife he removed her clothes and tossed them aside. His gaze roamed her body, and although she knew sooner or later he would rape her, right now his expression was all business.

Never in her life had she been more thankful for her myriad of scars. Some were larger some small, there was no way Albert would be able to find the scars that covered the implanted tracking devices. The trackers were undetectable. If he wanted to find them, he really would have to cut open every inch of her body.

The first prick of the blade had her sucking in a breath, but her body quickly remembered the feel of steel slicing through flesh and tossed that pain into a locked box it had no hope of breaking out of. She could do this, endure whatever he dished out, she'd done it literally hundreds of times before.

"You think you can survive this, tough it out, but when you're bleeding from dozens of cuts let's see if you're still this tough girl," Albert sneered.

"How did you know it was me? I didn't see you at the resort," Ivory said. No way was she going to bring Roman into this. She was hoping that Albert believed she was playing the same undercover game with Roman as she had with him, and that he had no idea who she was and what she was doing.

Albert pulled the blade from her stomach and held it up, allowing her blood to drip down onto her chest while he watched in what she could only describe as fascination. "You met someone while you were there."

The only people she'd spoken to while there were half a dozen other slaves. One of them must have been Albert's.

"My favorite pet is quite the little information gatherer." Albert had an almost fond smile on his face as he spoke about her. "She always reports back to me. Everything she hears. Everything she sees. When she told me of a young woman tied up with the rest of the slaves who wanted to talk and was asking too many questions, I knew it had to be you. You just can't leave well enough alone, can you?" This time he buried the small knife in her thigh, twisting the blade inside her until she couldn't not cry out in pain.

Triumph lit his face, and she hated giving him anything.

"All I had to do was ask around about the new guy, found out where he was going to be, then delayed the boat so my men would arrive first," Albert explained.

"What did you do to him?"

Albert pulled the knife from her thigh slowly and walked around her to stand on her other side. "You care about what happened to him?"

"Of course I do," she answered honestly. Then because she had to keep Roman's cover added, "I want him to be punished."

"He's alive. My men left him at the marina. I am sure that when he finds out you were using him and weren't some poor kidnapped woman after all, he'll be pleased to know I took care of his problem before you could bring him down."

Ivory almost laughed at that one. The last thing Roman would ever be was pleased with Albert Hendricks. He'd be furious that the man had kidnapped her and tortured her, and he wanted nothing more than the man's head on a platter for what Albert had done to Roman's sister Alexa.

"Although, you wanted more than just him, didn't you?" Albert pressed the knife to the side of her neck where he knew he would miss all major arteries when he broke her skin. "You wanted all of the men at the resort, you wanted me."

"I won't stop until you're dead or in prison," she warned.

He merely laughed as he dug the blade into her neck. "And how do you propose you'll do that, Ivory Smith?"

If he thought she cared that he knew her real name, she

didn't. She'd known he did, he would have done his research into her and Prey just like they had done theirs.

"There's a device jamming all transmissions which means wherever your tracking device is hidden it won't do you any good." The knife pressed into her side this time, deep enough that it hurt like crazy, but he was being careful not to hurt her too badly. He didn't want her to bleed out until he was ready for her to die.

Her momentary panic at the thought that she was out here alone, without Prey watching over her was quickly washed away by the fact that he wasn't completely sure that she couldn't be tracked. If he was confident in his jammer, he wouldn't care where her tracking devices were.

"My team will come," she said confidently as Albert circled around her.

"You really believe that?"

"One hundred percent." And she did. No way would Prey and her sisters ever give up on her. Roman wouldn't either. He was likely out of his mind with worry, and while she was eternally grateful he was safe, she wished there was a way for her to assure him that she would be okay. She had survived everything else life had thrown at her, and she could survive this too.

"Then I'm disappointed in you, my dear. Perhaps I underestimated you as an opponent. You have to know that I won't let you live. I'll keep you alive until you're begging me for death, and then I'll keep you alive longer."

His threats didn't bother her, she'd known ever since she saw him walk into the room that was what he was going to do, and Ivory had faith in her team, in Prey, and in Roman. No one was giving up on her, and she wasn't giving up on the people she cared about.

That was what she had been trying to show Roman. He'd

been in Delta, he must have trusted his team with his life, but he didn't know how to trust anyone with his heart. She trusted her sisters with both her life and her heart. If she made it out of this alive, she would show Roman what it was like to have someone care enough about him to treasure his heart, to protect it from pain, and to help it grow strong.

Albert slid the blade of his knife into her ankle, not too deep, but the promise was there, she could see it in his eyes. He could slit her Achilles tendons and render her unable to walk. He could slit the tendons in her shoulders and leave her arms useless. He could sever her spinal cord if he wanted and have her completely at his mercy.

"I'll let you get a little rest, my dear. You're going to need your strength for what I have planned next."

With that, he turned and left her alone in the room to figure out just how she was going to survive and get back to her man.

* * *

December 30ᵀᴴ
1:26 A.M.

"So, what's your theory?" Cormac "Fletch" Fletcher asked as they all took seats.

Roman was the only one who remained standing. There was no way he could control himself if he sat down, he needed movement as an outlet for his emotions. Already he was struggling to keep it together. It was only through so many years of practice denying his emotions that he hadn't fallen apart yet.

Now more than ever it was imperative that he keep it

together. Ivory was depending on him, and he wasn't going to let her down, not after everything she'd done for him. She was in this mess because she was helping him with his personal mission of revenge.

This was exactly why you should never let anything get that personal.

His guilt over not making things right with his sister had led him to this point. He had been prepared to sacrifice anything, do whatever it took, but now that the price he might have to pay was Ivory it no longer seemed acceptable.

"You've heard of Albert Hendricks? Wealthy drug dealer and dabbler in human trafficking?" he asked, sure the Delta team had.

Graham "Hollywood" Caverly whistled. "Yeah, man, everyone has. He almost got taken down a couple of years ago but tried to ruin the only witness. Has a whole team of lawyers on retainer and doesn't go anywhere without a dozen armed bodyguards. After he got the charges dropped he disappeared. Managed to stay off the radar completely, nobody knows where he's been staying."

"Your girl the witness Hendricks claimed was unreliable?" Ghost asked.

"She works for Prey, right?" Dane "Fish" Munroe asked.

"Yes, and yes. Prey was trying to take him down but her cover got blown. He kept her for four days, raped and tortured her, apparently it came down to seconds, but her team got to her in time. She has proof that the lost girls aren't drug mules. She knows Hendricks is a serial killer as well as a drug dealer. He overdoses them after he's raped them and cut off their hands and heads. Then he cuts their stomachs open and dumps them near the border, making them look like mules. He keeps their heads and hands as trophies."

Hollywood whistled again. "And your girl is the only one with proof of this. No wonder he tried to make her look crazy."

"She's far from crazy," Roman said, feeling the need to defend Ivory even though he knew it was unnecessary.

"No one's saying she is," Ghost soothed. "But she is in a whole lot of trouble."

"Like I don't know that," he snapped.

"You sure that's who has her?" Troy "Beatle" Lennon asked.

"No, but it makes sense. I've been building a cover for over a year trying to get access to Albert Hendricks. I managed to build enough contacts to hear about a resort in the Caribbean frequented by wealthy men who are into human trafficking. Anything goes, no limits. I needed a slave to get access so I managed to get contact details for El Compradores. Ended up buying Ivory who was there under-cover looking for some missing girls. Instead of bringing in another DEA agent, Ivory stayed on to play my slave, and we got an invite to the resort. I thought everything was going well, I made contacts, played up how much my cover Holdon Lennox was enjoying having a slave, and we got a call just before midnight to say I was in. Then we were ambushed. Don't know who else it could have been. Somehow, he knows who Ivory really is and he took her." Roman tried really hard not to imagine what Hendricks was doing to Ivory right at this moment.

"You were tased, right?" Aspen "Blade" Carlisle asked.

"We both were. When I saw someone grabbing Ivory, I tried to get to her, got tased again, and passed out for a moment."

"You got an idea?" Ford "Truck" Laughlin asked his teammate.

"Maybe," Blade said slowly. "I was just thinking that since you were at the marina it's a fairly likely scenario that Ivory was taken in a boat."

"Last time her trackers pinged before they went dark was on the ocean," Roman agreed. "Prey will have to search all islands in the vicinity and check out all flights leaving the area after Ivory was taken." It would be a grueling search and one that would take much too long. Hendricks was out for revenge. He might keep her alive for a while, but not indefinitely. And unless they could get access to her trackers again it would take days at least to search the area, and by then they could be anywhere in the world.

"I think we need to start searching boats in the area," Blade said.

"You think he's been living on a boat?" Beatle asked.

Blade shrugged. "No one was looking for him on a yacht. All he has to do is stay in international waters, move around a lot, and he keeps himself off the radar."

It was a great suggestion and one he was sorry he hadn't thought of himself. So simple and yet what a great way of preventing anyone from finding him. "We need access to the footage of the marina. I know what time she was taken, we need to know what craft she was on and then we can get tracking it." Roman was sure Prey was already trying to do that, but they were focused on finding where the boat had ended up, now they needed to just find that boat.

"What's the plan when we find the boat?" Ghost asked, and Roman appreciated that the man allowed him to take the lead.

This was his mission, but one that he couldn't handle on his own. Albert Hendricks would live in a constant state of preparedness, waiting for the day when his time ran out. When you lived in the underworld you knew that sooner or later you'd wind up dead or caught. Law enforcement or a rival would eventually take you down.

"If we approach by boat he'll see us immediately," Roman said.

"So, we jump," Coach said, his eyes lighting up. The man sometimes did some skydiving training and had actually met his now wife during a lesson. During their dive, Coach had been hit in the face by a bird and knocked unconscious. Harley, who had no experience was able to get them both down to the ground safely, and the rest was history.

That was definitely up there in unusual ways to meet your future spouse as was the way he'd met Ivory.

Only he wasn't going to wind up marrying her. Was he?

Talking with Ivory had changed things. He'd known that it would when he made the decision to open up and share things with her he'd never told another living soul. His Delta team were the only people he'd ever been even marginally close to, and even then, he'd been the quiet one who kept to himself.

But Ivory with her big heart and open personality had somehow managed to hammer down his walls enough that he could peek over them now. She had been more than willing to face a man who had traumatized and almost broken her. Yet she hadn't hesitated to face her fears for him. How was he supposed to not fall for a woman like that?

"We jump," he confirmed. "Once we get a lock on the yacht, we jump far enough away he won't see the helo. Then we swim the rest of the way. Hopefully, Hendricks will never see us coming until it's too late." Roman didn't care how many men the trafficker had guarding his boat, the eight men in the room were among the best of the best, and no one had more motivation than he did to destroy Albert Hendricks.

The plan was only good if they could find the boat. If they

couldn't, then Ivory could be lost to him forever. He'd never get the chance to find out if he had the courage to fight through his issues and give her a chance. He'd never get to know if happiness was in his future.

A hand landed on his shoulder, and he looked over into Coach's hazel eyes, eyes that brimmed with understanding. "The waiting is the worst," Coach said softly, and Roman knew the man spoke from experience. After the bird in the face incident, Coach and Harley had gotten together, but then she'd gone missing, disappeared without a trace.

The only difference was that Coach had already been in love with Harley then and he and Ivory weren't in love.

While that might be true, he couldn't say he felt nothing for her because that would be a lie. He felt something for Ivory. He felt too much for Ivory. Things he wasn't comfortable with.

Since he didn't want anyone to know how affected he was by Ivory and the fact that she was missing, he merely nodded. "Yeah, waiting is the worst."

CHAPTER SEVENTEEN

December 30th
   3:42 P.M.

SHE COULDN'T STOP SHAKING.

Not good news.

Ivory knew her body was going into shock. She'd lost too much blood. Although Hendricks was careful to make sure she didn't lose too much too quickly, he was also full of two years' worth of anger he'd built up toward her because she'd almost succeeded in bringing him down. He'd been in and out of her room most of the day—at least she prayed it was only a day, it certainly felt like much longer—and when he wasn't in here having fun digging his knife into her flesh, he had one of his goons standing watch.

Seemed he actually thought she was a worthy opponent, he was afraid to leave her alone in case she did something.

He was right.

The second she was alone she was finding a way to get free.

If the blades she had stashed on her didn't work, she'd figure something else out. Bottom line was, she was getting out of here and then she was taking down Albert Hendricks.

Although she could hardly call the last few hours good, they certainly hadn't been at all pleasant, and she was now in a whole lot of pain. This had almost turned out to be a good thing. Albert Hendricks had almost broken her, thrown her into such a dark place that she hadn't thought she would be able to climb out of it. Somehow those four days being tortured and raped had broken something inside her that not even the Master had been able to touch.

Because she'd been alone.

No support system.

She was alone now, too, but somehow it was different. Ivory wasn't quite sure why. Perhaps it was because she knew that even though she'd very nearly broken last time she hadn't. She had survived. Or perhaps it was because she had something else in her life that was equally as important as Prey and her sisters.

Roman.

There was still no guarantee that he would give them a chance, but if he didn't, she wanted that to be his decision. She didn't want Hendricks to take that chance away from them.

A cell phone chimed, and her guard pulled one out of his back pocket. He spoke in a voice so soft she couldn't make out what he was saying. Not that it mattered. Her focus had to be on recouping her strength, preparing herself either for Hendricks' return or a chance at escape.

The guard muttered something in a language she didn't speak and stormed out the door.

Alone.

Finally, she was alone.

There was no time to wait. Whatever strength she'd recouped was all she had to work with, so Ivory worked to get the blade out of the bracelet on her right wrist. Even though he had cut her clothes off her, Hendricks hadn't removed her jewelry. Who knows why? It was a mistake though, and one she intended to take advantage of.

Since she was weak and her body was still trembling, it took her a little longer than it usually would have to get the blade free. This angle was awkward, usually she would be trying to free herself while having her hands bound in front of or behind her, with her arms stretched out she had nothing to use to help.

"Got it," she said triumphantly as it came free.

Next, she had to saw through the leather straps.

By the time she actually got one hand free, she was breathing heavily from exertion. This was not good. No way should it take up this much energy just to free one wrist. She still had another wrist, neck, and both ankles to go. Then she had to get out of this room. Find the jammer and switch it off. Then go after Hendricks.

Ivory was exhausted just thinking about it.

Exhausted or not, it wasn't like she had a choice. There was no point in waiting for a rescue that wasn't coming. Prey and Roman would be tracking her as best as they could, but she couldn't count on them.

She was on her own.

Reaching up, she cut the strap at her neck first, so she could at least move a little as she leaned over to free her other wrist.

As she slowly sat up, her head spun wildly and for the first time, she wondered whether she was actually up for this.

It wasn't the first time she'd had to work an op with injuries. In fact, she had already been covered in bruises from the beating by El Compradores when she and Roman headed to the resort, but this was the first time she had to wonder if she was physically strong enough to do what needed to be done.

"Not like you have a choice, Ives," she reminded herself as she breathed through the spinning and horrible nausea. Once she'd cut her ankles free, she swung her legs over the side of the table and used it to help keep her balance as she stood up.

The spinning got dramatically worse, and she moaned and pressed one hand to her eyes as her head throbbed horribly. Her other hand gripped the table, the only thing keeping her upright right now.

Time was of the essence, so she did her best to compartmentalize her pain and scanned the room. Her clothes were shredded, and there was nothing else in there, not even a blanket to wrap around herself. It wasn't that she was embarrassed about her body, she couldn't do what she did if she was, and right now it hardly looked attractive anyway, covered in fading bruises and smeared in blood from the dozens of wounds of varying sizes and depths.

More importantly, there were no weapons in there.

Looks like all she had to use were her hands.

When she got out of there, she'd have to sneak around and try to get the lay of the land. Most important was to find and disable the jammer. As much as her ego would like to think she could do this all on her own, even if she was at one hundred percent there had to be at least a dozen men guarding Hendricks.

Stopping this man was way more important than bruising her ego. This wasn't about her, this was about taking down a dangerous drug dealer and human trafficker. It was also about getting Roman the revenge he needed so he could maybe find a way to move on with his life.

If it was selfish to want him to get his revenge so maybe he could move on with her, she couldn't help that.

At the door she eased it open carefully, half expecting someone to be standing on the other side.

There wasn't. Wasn't anyone within sight.

A win for her.

Now all she had to do was search the yacht room by room until she found the jammer and got her hands on a weapon.

If only it could be that easy.

Keeping a hand on the wall as she made her way down the corridor to help keep herself upright, Ivory lost all sense of time. The yacht was huge, but it was quieter than she'd expected. Where were all of Hendricks' men?

She knew they had to be here somewhere, but she was yet to encounter a single one. That couldn't last, but she cleared room after room. It appeared she was on a lower level with all bedrooms. Most belonged to the men, they were simply decorated but quite opulent, obviously it paid to work for a man like Albert Hendricks.

When she found a staircase, she had to sink down for a moment to catch her breath. Several of her wounds were still oozing blood, at least a dozen on them would likely need stitches, and a couple might even be starting to get infected. Her head ached, her body throbbed, and she was so tired all she wanted was to curl up and go to sleep. She was going on three days now with little to no sleep unless you countered being drugged or tased.

Ivory knew she was precariously close to running out of steam.

If she did, Roman might not get his revenge, his closure.

That was enough to spur her back into action, and she

dragged herself up the stairs. At the top, directly in front of the staircase was a small room. She might have been tempted to bypass it, but the door was open, and she could see several devices on a table.

Could the jammer be in there?

Hobbling across the open space, she snuck into the room and quickly laid eyes on what was indeed the jammer. Ivory wasn't the tech person on the team, that was Lacey, but she could easily identify it and knew just how to switch it off. She didn't leave it off for long, if she did someone might notice, and Prey would only need a few seconds to get a read on her location.

Unfortunately, there were no weapons in there, and just as she limped back to the door, she heard voices heading right toward her.

There was nowhere to hide. Nowhere to go. Fighting was her only option.

At least she had the element of surprise on her side.

The first man never saw the blow coming. Ivory launched herself through the door, and delivered a swift kick to his stomach, followed by a blow to his jaw, then swept his legs out from underneath him.

His grunt of surprise quickly turned to one of pain as he lost his footing and tumbled down the stairs. He landed with a thud, his weapon a foot away from his hand.

Ivory scrambled down on her hands and knees after him and wrapped her hand around the weapon just as the other man jumped down the last few steps to land beside her.

The fact that Hendricks wanted to kill her himself was what was keeping her alive right now. He couldn't shoot her without incurring his boss' wrath, so instead, he swung a fist at her.

She might be down, but she wasn't out. Ivory swung the

weapon at him and got him right in the gut. The blow was enough to stun him, and she kicked at his kneecap, bringing him down to his knees, then delivered another kick to the side of his head.

He swayed but wasn't quite out. As easy as it would be to shoot him, she wanted to try to keep the sound to a minimum. The last thing she needed was more men joining the fight, two against one was bad enough odds right now.

So instead of shooting the man, she delivered a third kick to his stomach and followed it up with a one-two punch to his jaw, and he was down for the count.

A rush of relief washed over her. Two men down, at least another ten to go plus Hendricks, but at least she was making progress.

If she wasn't weak from exhaustion, blood loss, and pain she probably would have known the blow was coming, deflected it, but instead, it got her right in the temple and she dropped.

* * *

DECEMBER 30TH
6:53 P.M.

NEVER BEFORE HAD an hour seemed so long.

And they'd had to wait almost seven of them for this moment.

Roman wasn't sure how he'd made it through the hours without losing his mind. When Prey had called to say that they had got a very brief flash of Ivory's trackers and given them a location, he and the Delta team had worked on a plan.

Although this wasn't his first rodeo, he'd never gone on a

mission where the victim they were rescuing was a woman who was important to him. It made more of a difference than he would have thought. While the Delta team worked through everything in detail, figuring out a plan where everyone walked away alive, all he wanted to do was go running to the location where Ivory was and grab her.

Rescuing her had even caused his desire for revenge to take a back seat. If it came down to a choice between saving Ivory and killing Albert Hendricks, Roman knew he would choose Ivory.

Every single time.

A hand tapped his shoulder indicating it was his turn and he jumped.

This was far from his first time jumping from a helo into the water, he'd done plenty of jumps to land as well, and the few seconds it took till he hit the water he used to get his mind in gear. There was no time to think about what Ivory meant to him or what he was going to do about her and his feelings for her, this had to be about a rescue. He had to compartmentalize his feelings and do whatever it took to get her out alive. If he allowed emotion to play a part, mistakes could be made, and that wasn't acceptable when the stakes were this high. For now, Ivory could be nothing more than any other victim he'd rescued in the past.

Roman hit the water. His body propelled down into the inky black before he swam up to the surface. A minute later they were all ready to go. It would take them approximately thirty minutes to swim to the location where Hendricks' luxury yacht was. Once Ivory's tracker came back online Prey had been able to pinpoint the location and then send out drones to confirm whether the yacht was still there.

It was.

Which meant Ivory was still there.

Alive. At least she had been a couple of hours ago.

While he knew Ghost and his team believed it must have been a malfunction in the jammer that allowed the signal to get through for just a moment, Roman thought differently. He didn't know how he knew, but he was positive that Ivory had somehow gotten free, got her hands on the jammer, and managed to turn it off, letting them know where she was. She was smart, would know if she left it off that Hendricks would realize, so she'd given them just enough to find her.

When they reached the yacht, the first thing he noticed was the laughter.

The vessel was lit up like a Christmas tree, and even from where he was, he could see a bunch of men out on the back of the yacht where there was a pool on the top deck and then a large open space on the lower one.

Something was hanging in the midst of the group of men.

No.

Not something.

Some*one*.

"Don't."

The hand on his arm caught him by surprise. Roman hadn't realized he'd started swimming closer.

"You'll get her killed if you go running in without thinking first," Fletch continued.

"We need a distraction," Coach said.

"The rest of us will surround the yacht, board it, and draw the attention of the guards," Ghost said. "Morales and Coach, you two go in after Ivory." There was a fierceness to Ghost's voice, and Roman wondered if the man was thinking about the time he and his team had been sent in to disarm terrorists and free hostages, only to find one of the hostages was the woman he'd already fallen for, even if that hadn't been the plan when they'd met and enjoyed a night together.

Apparently, she'd been tied to a bed and been about to be raped. Roman couldn't imagine the fear and anger he would have felt walking in to find Ivory brutalized and bound.

Those couple of minutes it took for the others to get into position were the longest of his life.

Each one of them felt like an hour.

Ivory was there because the boat was lit up so brightly he could clearly see her. She was hanging upside down, blood smeared almost every inch of her creamy white skin, and the group of men was standing around laughing and throwing darts at her.

Fury boiled inside him. He wanted every single one of those men dead.

Roman would be more than happy to torture them like they were torturing Ivory. Rip their bodies to pieces with his bare hands. Hit them over and over again until he stopped feeling like his rage was going to consume him.

"We're a go," Ghost's voice said in his ear, and within a minute he saw the men on the yacht start to disperse.

They knew they were under attack, but Albert Hendricks was cocky enough to believe his men were going to be the winners. He didn't move, didn't go and hide, or make any move to get rid of Ivory so he wouldn't be found with a kidnap victim if it was law enforcement.

He and Coach swam toward the back of the boat. Coach knew he was here for backup because Hendricks was Roman's. Not only did he want the man to pay for murdering Alexa, but also for everything he'd done to Ivory.

"I'm sorry for the interruption of our fun, my dear," Albert Hendricks said as he walked over to Ivory.

While she didn't respond, Roman had to believe that she was still alive. There would be no point for the man to speak to her if he knew she was already dead. He had to take that as a win, she could heal from anything Hendricks had inflicted on her if she was alive, but dead was dead. There was no coming back from that.

Hendricks reached out and took one of Ivory's hands in his, circling his fingers around her wrist. "These hands are going to be a wonderful contribution to my collection. In fact, I think they're going to have pride of place. I'm going to cut them off and then I'm going to ride you so hard as you're bleeding out that your last thoughts are going to be of me and how much you hate me, and you'll know that you've given me exactly what I wanted."

Roman climbed out of the water, Hendricks was so busy antagonizing Ivory that he didn't even realize anyone else was there until it was too late.

He launched at the man, knocked him down, and slammed a fist into the side of Hendricks' head.

Blow after blow he rained down.

Everything else faded away.

Images from his childhood, of the times he'd tried to protect his little sister, flashed through his mind. Images of Lex high, strung out on drugs, living on the streets followed. Then Alexa as he'd seen her that last time, clean and ready to build a life for herself, the pain in her eyes as he told her he didn't believe she'd stay sober and turned his back and walked away.

Shame and guilt spurred him on.

This sickening excuse of a man wouldn't have had a chance to murder Alexa if he had believed her, offered her any help she needed, and welcomed back the sister he'd once loved instead of slamming the door in her face.

Roman had no context of time as he hit Hendricks over and over again. It wasn't until someone softly called out his name that he drew in a ragged breath and stilled.

"It's over, Roman. He's dead," Ivory whispered.

Breathing hard, his knuckles bruised and bloody, he turned around to find Coach balancing Ivory in his arms so her body was no longer hanging from her bound ankles. Her voice was weak, her eyes barely open, and her entire body covered in blood. She looked like death warmed up, and yet her concern was for him.

His heart swelled in his chest, and his anger bled away.

He'd never known what it was like to have someone care about him, put him and his needs first, and put themselves in terrible danger to help him do something important to him.

Now he did.

"Let's get you down, darlin'," he said softly as he walked over and pulled out a knife, cutting through the ropes to free her. When he held out his arms, Coach carefully placed Ivory in them, and he clutched her to his chest and dropped to his knees.

Albert Hendricks was dead, Ivory was alive, and he realized he wanted a future. A future free from darkness, drugs, and alcohol, free from addiction. What Ivory was offering was unconditional support, support that might one day grow into unconditional love. If he turned his back on this chance, he knew he would regret it for the rest of his life.

Coach was standing between him and Ivory, watching over them, a good thing because Roman suddenly felt drained.

The world spun around him.

Something was wrong.

He couldn't figure out what.

Someone said his name.

Blackness closed in around him.

CHAPTER EIGHTEEN

December 30th
7:03 P.M.

"Roman?" Ivory panicked as he suddenly slumped forward, dropping her onto the hard deck of the yacht and falling on top of her.

What was wrong with him?

She thought everything was finally over. Roman and a Delta team had shown up, Roman got his revenge and killed the man who murdered his sister, she was free. It should be over.

It was supposed to be over.

"Hold on, sweetheart," the man who had introduced himself as Coach said as he eased Roman off her and laid him down on the deck.

His black dive suit was wet, so she couldn't tell if there was any blood on him. Blood that wasn't hers anyway.

Then her eyes zeroed in on a tear in the suit.

She knew Roman hadn't been shot, but Hendricks always

had that knife on him, the one he'd spent the day using to torture her.

Stabbed.

When Roman was beating Hendricks, the man must have gotten in one stab.

Now that she realized he'd been stabbed she could see blood spilling out beneath his too-still body.

No.

This couldn't be happening.

The tears she'd held back with ease while Hendricks was having his fun with her were now flowing down her cheeks in a flood as she tried to get to her knees and get to Roman. He couldn't die on her. Not now.

"Whoa, there," Coach said, reaching out to catch her as her weak body gave out. He eased her down so she was lying close to Roman and looked down at her with grim eyes.

For her or Roman?

Right now, she wasn't sure which of them was in worse shape.

Ivory knew she wasn't doing well. She was weak, her head had that feeling that was both heavy and floaty, and she was so very cold.

She'd lost too much blood, but she was more worried about Roman.

She couldn't lose him.

They might not have known each other very long, but the time they had spent together had been intense. It was the first time she had ever opened up to a man about what she'd been through, and she knew it was the first time Roman had ever talked about his own mixed-up past.

They had shared something special, something that deserved a chance to grow. Both of them had been through so much, they deserved a happy ending.

"Here, let's get you covered up," Coach said. He was kneeling beside her, and she could hear him talking to someone else as he covered her in a blanket that did little to warm her ice-cold body.

Roman still wasn't moving, and his face was so pale it was virtually colorless.

Was he dying?

Was she?

Ivory knew she'd lost a whole lot of blood. Her body, which hadn't even recovered from the beating it had sustained a few days ago, had been abused almost beyond what it could bear. Hendricks had allowed his men to have some fun with her. They hadn't been allowed to rape her, but they had been allowed to touch her, hit her if they wanted to, and cut her like Hendricks had. The game of darts was supposed to have a winner who would get the reward of having her for the night.

"Hey, come on, kid, stay awake."

A hand slapped lightly at her face, and she blinked slowly.

She hadn't even realized her eyes had closed.

It took a moment for Coach's words to register.

When they did, her brow scrunched in a small frown.

"Not a kid," she huffed. She was often mistaken for a teen and she used that to her advantage to do her undercover work for Prey, but she was no child.

"There you go, got you back." Coach smiled down at her, but she could see the worry in his hazel eyes.

She was fading away.

Bleeding out.

Roman might have found her, but it was too little too late.

"I'm losing her," Coach yelled, and she saw more faces moving above her.

Someone dropped down beside her, but when that

someone picked up her wrist, she pushed their hands away. "Roman," she murmured. He needed help, she'd held on this long maybe she could hold out a little longer, but Roman had dropped so quickly.

"We're treating him as well," a kind voice told her, "but we're a little worried about you right now."

"Lost too much blood." Her eyes wouldn't stay open any longer, it took more energy than she had. Energy that was better spent breathing. Something that was becoming increasingly difficult.

"He certainly did a number on you," Coach said, controlled anger in his voice.

"He's evil," she said.

"Yeah, he is," Coach agreed.

Ivory felt hands roaming over her body, identifying her many bleeding wounds and bandaging them, likely with quick clot bandages which would aid her body in clotting so she stopped losing blood.

A prick inside her elbow said someone had started an IV.

"We need to do a field transfusion or she's not going to make it," Coach's worried voice said.

"We're not going to let her die," another voice said calmly.

"Roman," she murmured. She needed him to be okay. Whatever happened to her, she needed him to live, to finally find peace, to stop running from happiness.

She must have said the word so softly that no one heard her.

Something covered her face.

The soft woosh of air told her it was an oxygen mask.

Tired.

So very tired.

Everything began to fade around her.

Vaguely she heard voices yelling.

She thought she heard her name.

She'd fought as hard as she could, and now Albert Hendricks was dead.

He could never hurt anyone again.

The thought comforted her as the world suddenly seemed to grow distant.

Ivory could have sworn she was looking down on the scene beneath her.

Could see herself laid out on the deck of the luxury yacht. Could see two men bent over her. One had his hands on her chest and was pumping.

Trying to restart her heart?

Had it stopped?

The other man covered her mouth with his and breathed air into her lungs.

Dead.

She was dead.

Ivory felt like she was being pulled further away.

But then she saw Roman.

Like her, he was laid out on the deck of the yacht. Two other men were working on him but it didn't appear he was dead.

She couldn't leave him.

It would destroy him.

Somehow, she knew that with absolute certainty.

Pain suddenly knifed through her and then there was nothing but darkness.

Sometime later, she blinked open heavy eyes to find she was in a hospital bed, the room was dimly lit, and a man sat slouched in a chair beside her bed.

Not Roman though.

"Coach," she croaked.

Immediately his head snapped up, and his eyes met hers.

As soon as he saw she was awake, he smiled and moved out of the chair to stand beside her.

"Here, just take small sips," he instructed as he held a straw to her lips.

Ivory took a couple of sips, which felt like heaven sliding down her dry, sore throat. "Roman?"

There was something in Coach's gaze that she was too out of it to decipher, but he didn't look away when he answered so she knew whatever he was going to tell her was the truth. "He's fine. He lost a bit of blood but nowhere near as much as you. We brought you both to the hospital and you've been out ever since. Roman was released about an hour ago."

What?

Roman had been released but he'd just left?

No.

That couldn't be right.

He wouldn't do that.

"He's gone?" she asked, hardly able to get the words out because she couldn't believe they were possibly true. There had to be another explanation.

Had to be.

Roman wouldn't leave without at least saying goodbye.

"I'm sorry, Ivory." Coach's expression told her that he'd had a few choice words to say to Roman before he'd taken off, and while she appreciated he'd tried to stand up for her, it didn't ease the horrible ache in her chest.

How could Roman do that to her?

After everything they had shared, everything they had been through together, she hadn't thought it would end like this. She had known there was the possibility that he wouldn't give the two of them a chance, but she had thought at the very least he would say goodbye before he left.

But he hadn't. He'd just disappeared while she was still unconscious.

"Your team is on the way. I told them I'd stay with you until they got here," Coach told her.

Numb, she just nodded.

"Want to talk about it?"

Ivory shook her head. What was there to say? Roman had left. He obviously didn't care about her if he could walk away in such a cold way. What she'd interpreted as him opening up and sharing with her because he cared about her obviously wasn't so.

He didn't care. If he did, there was no way he could just leave.

Pulling the covers to her chin, she closed her eyes and let her exhausted mind tug her into oblivion where she could defer dealing with her broken heart for at least a little longer.

* * *

DECEMBER 31ST
4:16 P.M.

"THAT WAS COACH," Ghost announced.

Roman looked up from his laptop to meet the angry eyes of the Delta team leader.

No, when he looked closer, he saw that Ghost's eyes weren't angry, they were disappointed.

Which was worse.

His family had never cared enough about him to be disappointed. If anything, they'd been angry that he'd acted like he was better than them. His Delta team had seen him as the quiet guy and never expected him to talk. He'd watched their backs with a ferocity that they knew meant they were completely covered so they'd never had cause to be disappointed.

The last time someone gave him that look was Alexa when he told her he didn't believe she was capable of getting and staying clean.

Now Ghost was giving him that same look.

A look that cut right to his core because he could imagine those same disappointed eyes in ice blue from a woman who meant everything to him.

A woman he was ready to admit he couldn't walk away from.

"What did Coach say?" he asked, pleased when his voice came out calm and detached, not showing any of the pain inside him that had absolutely nothing to do with the knife wound he'd sustained.

"Her team showed up about an hour ago, she was just discharged and she's leaving for the airport to go home," Ghost replied.

Relief loosened the knot in his chest. She was okay, well enough to go home. While he was sure she should be in the hospital for at least a couple of days, she was awake, aware, and safe with her sisters. Eagle Oswald would likely have made sure there was a medic on the flight back to California so Ivory was monitored.

Following the relief came a new wave of guilt.

He should be there with her. Should have been the first thing she saw when she opened her eyes. Should be there to reassure her and help her deal with what she'd been through.

Instead, he'd just up and left, and she'd be feeling hurt and betrayed.

Roman was doing what he believed to be the right thing, but Ivory only knew that he was gone. It might have been the coward's way out, but he knew if he saw her again he wouldn't be able to leave and this was something he had to do.

"Go ahead and say whatever you want to say," he said wearily as he looked around the hotel room at each set of eyes watching him accusingly.

"Why are you here?" Hollywood asked.

"I'm not going home until this is over," he said, knowing that really wasn't what the man was asking.

"So that's it?" Beatle asked.

"You're just going to let her go?" Fish asked.

"It's more than obvious that you like her," Truck added. He knew a little about everything the man had gone through to finally get his happy ending with his now wife. They'd dealt with so much, and he was glad they'd gotten to a point where they could be together with nothing standing between them. He wanted that too. It was why he had walked away.

"Never said I didn't," he said quietly.

"And yet you're here and she's there," Fletch stated. "Why are you walking away from her?"

"I'm not." Discussing why he'd left Ivory alone in the hospital the second he'd been stitched up wasn't something he wanted to do. Not with these men who he barely knew, not with anyone. Yet it was clear they were determined to push until they got their answers.

In a way, he appreciated they were looking out for Ivory, but another part of him wanted them to just drop it.

Did it matter?

He was here, Ivory wasn't. That was the way it had to be for now.

"Looks like you just gave up on her," Ghost said, a hint of disgust in his tone. "You got what you wanted from her and now you're done? Got her help taking down the man who killed your sister, so you have no use for her now that you almost got her killed."

Roman didn't remember moving.

Next thing he knew he had the man shoved up against the wall.

He'd knocked over his chair and Ghost's in the process, and had his forearm banded across the other man's neck.

Approval sparked in Ghost's eyes, and he realized he had been played.

Ghost waved his team back when they obviously moved to haul him off their friend. "You care about her, we can all see that, so why are you hurting her?" Ghost asked, but softer this time, more gently.

He stood back, raked his hands through his hair, then paced the room once before righting his chair and dropping down into it. "I had to leave."

"Why?" Fish asked, but not unkindly.

"I messed up with my sister. Let her down. Because of that, she wound up murdered. I thought if I could avenge her death, it would ease this rock of guilt in my stomach I've been carrying around ever since."

"It wouldn't help to tell you that the only one responsible for your sister's death is the man who killed her, would it?" Beatle asked.

Roman shook his head. While he appreciated their attempts to make him feel better and even acknowledged in his head that he wasn't to blame for her death, that wouldn't take away the guilt.

"Revenge didn't help, did it?" Fletch asked.

"I was so sure it would, but that guilt is still there. I'm angry and ashamed that I treated my own sister so badly, that I didn't believe in her, cheer for her at what she'd accomplished, battling addiction is hard. Instead of that, I told her she would never amount to anything and would be back on the street within a month. The one I'm really angry at is me. Not Hendricks."

He had to pause to regain control of his emotions.

There was nothing he could do that would ever take away that regret.

Instead, he would have to find a way to live with it without letting it destroy him.

"I can't kill myself," he continued, "so I have to find a way to be a better man. The kind of man who would have rejoiced with his sister who was working so hard to overcome so much. The kind of man that Ivory deserves."

"I think she likes you just as you are," Hollywood said.

There was truth to that. Ivory would accept him as he was, but that wasn't what he wanted.

"I need to be the kind of man I can be proud of," he admitted. "I need to be the kind of man I know Ivory can be proud of. For once in my life, I need to be unselfish. I need to care about someone other than myself and what I want and need. You're right, Ivory risked her life for me. Almost died in the process. I want to find the man who kidnapped her as a baby and the little girls she was looking for. I want to bring her peace."

He needed to redeem himself, and this was the only way he could think of to do it.

If he'd stayed, Ivory would have wanted him, he would have given himself to her, but he would always see himself as the man who turned his own sister away.

His self-worth had been decimated by his family. He might not have seen himself as better than them, more as one step away from becoming them. If he couldn't learn to love and respect himself, one day he really might find himself becoming them. If he became them then he would wind up destroying Ivory.

That couldn't happen.

There was no way he could deny he was falling in love with her. Her patience, her spirit, her generosity, and her openness. What wasn't to love?

But if they were going to have anything real, he had to know that he had something to offer her besides a bitter, angry man who hadn't moved past his abusive childhood.

He wanted more for her, for them, and for the first time in his life more for himself.

"I didn't walk away today because I don't care. I walked away because I do. Because I know this is the only way for there to be something real between us, something that has a chance at lasting. I just have to pray that she understands when I go to her and explain myself."

It was a risk, but one he knew was unavoidable.

So far Ivory had been the one to fight for him and for them, now he needed to be the one to fight for her, and he would. When he got a lead on the Master and went to Ivory, he would explain himself and prove to her that he could be a man worthy of her love.

There was no way he could accept that his choices would destroy them because then there would be nothing stopping him from following in the footsteps of the rest of his family.

CHAPTER NINETEEN

December 31st
   10:44 P.M.

So that was that.

When they'd left for Mexico on this mission, Ivory would never in a million years have believed how things would turn out. She'd expected to go, hopefully, get herself kidnapped and taken to Colombia, find those missing girls, and bring down El Compradores. But seeing the Master hadn't been something she expected, and she certainly hadn't thought that she would actually lose her heart along the way.

That was exactly what had happened.

Her heart now belonged to a very sexy DEA agent who didn't want it.

She had been so sure that things would work out. When he'd opened up to her and made love to her, she'd incorrectly interpreted that as a sign that he cared.

Stupid really.

Roman had been very clear that he wasn't interested in

any relationship. Maybe he'd gotten caught up in the craziness of the week they'd spent together, or maybe he'd just wanted her to trust him since they were working together, but whatever the reason, it obviously didn't mean he cared about her.

If he did, he'd be here right now.

"We'll see you settled before we leave," Fox told her, and she turned to frown at him.

"No, you guys should go. You shouldn't even be here," she added. "It's New Year's Eve. You should be home with your families, celebrating." It had been a shock when Fox and the others were on the plane that came to pick her up in Florida and bring her home. Of course, Ivory had expected her sisters to be on the plane, that was a given, but she had expected the guys to be with their families.

Spider frowned at her. "You forget that you're family too, Ivory?"

"No, of course not, but it's hardly the same thing."

"We're a team, all of us, and we're a family, nowhere else we'd be right now, and all our wives practically pushed us out the door when they heard what happened," Chaos told her.

"I'm fine," she assured them. Not entirely true. Her whole body throbbed and ached, but the field transfusion she'd had on Albert Hendricks' yacht had saved her life, and the one in the hospital had returned a lot of her strength to her. All her wounds had been stitched and bandaged, she needed rest now, and the best place to get that was her apartment.

"Yeah," Pearl scoffed.

"The very definition of fine," Opal added with an amused smile.

"I *am* fine, and you guys *should* be with your wives." Ivory didn't want to appear ungrateful because she loved every one of these people and knew she was lucky to have them in her life, but she felt out of sorts.

"As soon as we get you settled we'll go see them, in plenty of time to kiss them as the new year starts. Does that make you feel better?" Night asked.

No.

Well, yes, she was glad they'd make it home to ring in the new year with their wives, but it also reminded her that if Roman hadn't disappeared, they could have shared a kiss and started a new year together.

"I can get myself settled," she assured them. Although the walk up to her apartment did feel a little daunting. Still, if she let them know that then her sisters would insist on staying with her, and she really needed a little time to herself right now.

"Yeah, right," King scoffed. "We'll carry you up to your apartment and make sure you're okay, then leave."

Before she could argue, everyone started sliding out of the limo until only she and Shark remained. Guess she wasn't going to convince them they didn't need to help her.

"Hey." Shark reached out and very gently took her hand when she went to move. "We're here because we care about you."

Ivory sighed. "I know. Sorry I've been ungrateful."

"You haven't. You're just dealing with an injury that no doctor can fix."

"How did you know?" She hadn't mentioned Roman to the guys, maybe her sisters had.

Shark gave her a small smile. "I know a little about messing up with the woman you love. I left Claire because I thought I was doing the right thing. When I realized I wasn't I did my best to make it up to her. Maybe your guy just needs a little time."

She really shouldn't be surprised that Shark was being so sweet and that he was so perceptive. Despite the big man's reputation for being emotionless, she knew it was a cover. While she didn't know what had happened to him, she knew he'd had a rough life, and it was his defense mechanism. She'd seen him with his wife and twin daughters, he was so soft and gentle with them. Underneath the veneer was a man with a big heart who used his silence to gather information without you even realizing it.

Just like Roman.

Suddenly teary, she squeezed his hand. "Thanks, Shark."

Obviously having said what he wanted to, he merely nodded and then reached out and picked her up, climbing out of the limo with her in his arms. Everyone followed as he carried her inside her building and over to the lift.

No one spoke on the way up to her floor, which suited her just fine. Ivory found she was precariously close to falling apart and would prefer not to have an audience for that. Family or not, she still had a little pride left and didn't intend to let her tears fall until she was safely tucked away inside her home.

Lacey unlocked the door to her apartment and switched on the lights as they all went inside.

"Couch or bed?" Shark asked.

Even though she'd spent most of the day sleeping, her body had a lot of catching up to do, not to mention she needed sleep to heal. "Bed."

Having six big, strong, tough former SEALs in her bedroom might have embarrassed her if it had been any other day. Her room was pretty and frilly, very girlie, not really the picture she presented of herself most of the time. The walls were pained a warm cream color, her curtains were cream and lacy, and an overstuffed armchair was in the corner. Her bed, nightstands, and dresser were all painted the same cream color as the walls. The quilt covering her bed was cream and lacy like the curtains, and there were half a dozen pillows in various pastel tones piled on there. The room might look bland to some, but it was her favorite color, and it made her feel safe and peaceful.

Opal pulled back the covers and Shark set her down on the mattress and tucked her in like she was a small child.

Immediately, she sank down into the softness and snuggled the blankets up to her chin. She'd been right to insist she comes back home, this was where she needed to be to rest and recover. Fox had already told her that Eagle had ordered her grounded for the next month. It would mean not being able to look for the missing girls, but she knew her body would need that long to recover.

"We'll check in on you tomorrow," Fox told her as he closed the blinds.

"Call if you need anything," Lacey added.

"And we're right down the hall," Opal said. They all rented apartments right next to one another. Opal's was to the left of hers, Lacey's to the right, and Pearl's next to Lacey's. "Unless you want us to stay?"

They'd argued about it on the plane and she thought she'd won. "I'm just going to sleep. I promise to call if I need anything."

"We'll be around in the morning to check on you," Opal said.

Pearl was the last to leave her room and paused at the door. "I was wrong you know."

"About what?" Ivory asked.

"Roman. I think he really cares about you."

"He doesn't," she said. There was no doubt in her mind that if Roman cared he'd be here right now.

"I'm not so sure about that. Sometimes you have to learn to love yourself before you can let anyone else love you."

With those cryptic words, Pearl closed the door, and Ivory eased her aching body onto her side and curled herself into a ball.

She so badly wanted to believe that Pearl was right. That Roman had another reason for staying away, but she didn't dare allow herself to hope.

Hope could be a precious gift or a way to get yourself dashed to pieces.

Unfortunately, in this instance, Ivory believed it was the latter.

* * *

JANUARY 7TH
    8:17 A.M.

FRUSTRATION WHIRLED INSIDE HIM.

He needed to find something.

For once in his life this wasn't just about him.

Yes, he wanted to find something so he could finally feel like he was something more than a self-centered jerk, but it was so much more than that. He wanted Ivory to finally have peace, to know the man who had hurt her was dead or in prison. He also wanted those little girls not to have to endure anything else and be able to be returned home to their families.

Roman had been working almost non-stop for the last week to try to find something, anything, a direction to move in. Ghost's Delta team had left in time to make it home to their families to celebrate new year's, but he was still at the hotel in Florida seven days later.

Before leaving, Ghost had suggested that he head home, take a few days to recover, then jump back into this case, but he couldn't do that.

His entire focus was on finding the man who hurt Ivory.

Sooner or later, he would have to go back. Jesse would need him to come in and give a full debrief of everything that had happened to take down Albert Hendricks. That case was over and had been the entire reason he'd accepted the job offer from the DEA. Now that it was done and he had closure on his sister's murder case, he didn't know if he even wanted to stay with the DEA. He wasn't sure what the rest of his life looked like, except that he needed to find some self-respect, become someone worthy of Ivory and then find a way to win her back.

Roman paused to rub at his tired eyes. So many hours of staring at a computer screen made them dry and gave him a headache.

Although the urge to keep working had become an obsession, he knew he needed a few minutes to reset his mind.

A shower, a little breakfast, maybe a light run, and then he'd get back to work. He was no good to Ivory if he completely wore himself down. She needed him in more ways than one, and while his body ached to be with her again, hold her in his arms, and see with his own eyes that she was okay, he still knew he was doing the right thing.

All he could do was pray she understood.

Shoving away from the desk, he grabbed a bottle of water from the mini bar and downed half of it in one go. Then he headed to the bathroom. The wound in his side was due to have the stitches removed later today. He was lucky it hadn't been worse, that the blade hadn't hit anything vital. If it had, he'd still be laid up in the hospital instead of fighting for justice for Ivory.

Taping a waterproof bandage over the white one that covered the stitches, he turned on the shower and stepped under the spray.

For several long minutes he stood there, allowing the heat and the pounding of the water to ease the aches in his body.

If only there was such an easy fix for the ache in his heart.

What would he do if Ivory didn't forgive him for leaving the way he had?

He was counting on the fact that her big heart would give him the chance to explain, and that once he did, she would understand. It felt wrong to be almost using the fact that she was sweet and caring against her, but deep down he knew this was his only shot at getting something lasting with Ivory, and once he explained he was sure she would see that too.

Didn't mean he wouldn't have some major groveling to do.

Leaving the way he had would have hurt her, and while that was the last thing he wanted to do, it didn't change things. How could he ever hope to love Ivory the way she deserved if he hated himself?

The ringing of his phone jarred him out of his thoughts, and Roman shut off the water and grabbed a towel, wrapping it around his waist as he picked up the phone from the counter and headed back into the bedroom.

His phone's screen said unknown caller, and while usually he wouldn't answer, this was the Holdon Lennox phone, and he still had a lot of feelers out trying to get information on the Master. Thankfully his cover still appeared to be intact. Word was that Albert Hendricks had put them all at risk by bringing in a spy.

While he and the Deltas had been rescuing Ivory, other

teams and agencies had been moving in to raid the resort. Almost two dozen well-known businessmen and politicians had been taken into custody. Reports that Hendricks was dead were running wild as was the rumor of a spy, but thankfully, no one had linked it to him or Ivory. She would have to lay low for a while, but in a few months, she could go back to doing what she usually did and go undercover to save girls and women from the hell she had lived through.

It was something he was going to have to get used to once they were together.

The very thought of her in danger made his blood turn to ice, but he could never ask her to be less than what she was.

Tapping accept, he lifted the phone to his ear. "Lennox."

"It's me," a voice said softly like he was afraid of being overheard.

"MacAvoy?" After their altercation at the marina, the man must not have gone right back to the resort or he would have been caught up in the raids like everyone else.

"Yes."

"Where are you?"

"I'd rather not say," MacAvoy said, clearly sounding nervous. "I assume you heard what happened?"

"The resort was raided. Guess I owe whoever stole my slave. If it hadn't been for that, I would have been there." If MacAvoy was reaching out then the Lennox cover was definitely still solid, something he could utilize to find the Master.

"Might have been Albert Hendricks who took her. Seems like he lost control. Somehow he brought in a spy who destroyed everything. Almost everything," the man said smugly.

"Yeah?"

"I don't know what's been said, who turned to get themselves a better deal, but we all have to lay low for a while. I don't know your situation, but with the raid on the resort, and one a few days before at a place in Texas, someone is out to destroy all of us. If you need a place to lay low for a while, I have one. It's a safehouse of sorts. I know a couple of guys who use it when they have merchandise they can't get rid of right away. I've reached out to all my contacts and told them about it. I don't know if anyone needs to use it, but thought it was worth mentioning."

Yeah, Roman knew exactly what MacAvoy was up to. The man didn't have the money to be top dog so he was using the next best thing. Offering favors he no doubt intended to call in at some point and building himself his own little empire.

It was almost too much to hope for but if MacAvoy knew of Douglas Chayter and the aquarium and what had happened there, and they knew the Master had sold one of the girls to Chayter, then there was a chance that the Master also knew of this safehouse.

Wasn't much, but it was better than he'd had ten minutes ago.

"Text me the address," he said.

"Will do. Stay safe," MacAvoy said before ending the call. A moment later, his phone dinged with a text.

An address. Could mean absolutely nothing or could be the key to bringing the Master down. Either way, he had to pursue it. If nothing else, maybe they could round up a few of the men who had escaped capture at the resort.

If everything went the way he hoped, it could be exactly what he'd been looking for.

It was time to go to his woman and pray that she was forgiving and understanding enough to get why he'd had to do this. Roman wanted to be a better man, leave the past where it belonged, and finally be happy.

Ivory made him happy.

Simple as that.

His hand trembled as he reached out to pick up the paper dragon. The origami gift Ivory had made for him on Christmas Day had never been out of his sight since he left her in the hospital. He'd needed the connection to it because it was all he had of Ivory right now.

Hopefully, that was about to change. It was time to make a call that would bring him back to the woman he was falling in love with. A woman who would either give him the chance at redemption and love he so badly wanted or utterly and completely destroy him.

CHAPTER TWENTY

January 7th
12:11 P.M.

S<small>ITTING</small> and staring into space wasn't the most productive way to spend her time.

It was also completely not like her.

Ivory wasn't one to mope, to wallow in self-pity, or allow her emotions to get the best of her.

But this was different.

While certainly not the worst thing she'd ever had to deal with, it was the first time she'd ever had a broken heart, and it completely sucked.

For anyone looking at her life, at everything she had been through, the way she was reacting to a simple rejection from a man seemed extreme. To them, it probably looked like she was overreacting, and she hated that she could see the truth of that.

Years of being raped and tortured by the Master had made her strong, tough, she would have thought invincible.

What Albert Hendricks had done had very nearly broken her, it had been a humbling experience, teaching her she wasn't as impenetrable as she'd thought she was. Learning she wasn't as removed from the normal human reactions to trauma had almost been a good thing.

There was nothing good about this.

Ivory knew she couldn't wallow forever, so Roman had rejected her, it wasn't the end of the world. Of course she knew that, yet part of her brain told her it was.

Falling for a guy was something she hadn't even thought she was capable of.

No one would blame her for that. Being sexually abused from the time she was ten, coupled with the violent rape at Hendricks' hand, would understandably turn her off both sexual intimacy and trusting another enough to hand over the only thing left inside her that could be broken.

Her heart.

That's what she'd given Roman, and he'd done a really good job of shattering it.

With a sigh, she shook her head as though she could dislodge the melancholy that she felt mired in.

It was like quicksand. Dragging her down until, eventually, it consumed her. Fighting against it seemed to make things worse, so for now she was going to give herself a little time to wallow before she'd ruthlessly shove aside those feelings, toughened up again, and moved on with her life.

One month.

No more than that.

When she was medically cleared and allowed to return to work, it would be time to put Roman out of her mind and heart. Maybe if she tried, she could even learn to look at the last couple of weeks of her life with fondness, see them as a blessing, and let them show her that she was capable of falling in love.

"Ives, we're coming in, and we brought lunch," Lacey announced from outside the apartment. Her sisters had keys to her place like she did to theirs, but they still tried to respect one another's privacy by announcing themselves rather than just barging on in.

Normally, she would have gotten up and opened the door for them, but her body ached too badly to bother. Unhealed bruises, almost two dozen knife wounds, she was in pain and exhausted, and walking was too painful thanks to a wound on the bottom of her foot. So she waited, and a moment later the door swung open.

"We have gooey, cheesy pizzas." Lacey grinned, holding up a stack of four pizza boxes.

"And soda," Opal added, holding up four bottles of soda.

After being restricted in their diet when they lived with the Master, when they'd finally been free they had all found they had wildly different tastes. Even now they tended to have their favorites, although most of the time they ate as healthy as possible because they needed to be in good shape for their jobs.

Although sometimes you just needed comfort food.

Now was definitely one of those times.

"Pizza and soda sound perfect," she said as Lacey set the pizzas on the coffee table.

"I'll grab plates and glasses," Opal said, disappearing into the kitchen.

"How are you feeling?" Pearl asked, setting a box of chocolates on the coffee table beside the pizza.

"Slowly getting better." Seven days wasn't enough time to recover from everything her body had gone through, but bit by bit she felt her strength returning.

"Good, I'm glad to hear it," Pearl said.

"Just wish I was back to normal."

"You'll get there. For now, you just need to keep getting plenty of rest so your body and mind can recover," Lacey said as she opened the top pizza box, pulled out a couple of slices of cheese pizza, set them on a plate, and handed it to Ivory.

"I'm sorry you guys have to take the break with me," she said, feeling bad about that. Yes, they were a team, but it still sucked that they would be out for the next month because she'd been hurt.

"We can still run training exercises," Opal reminded her as she carried in glasses of soda.

"Yeah, but what about those girls?" In the midst of the drama of seeing the Master again, meeting Roman, and bringing down Albert Hendricks and over a dozen other traffickers, it was easy to forget that she had originally been trying to find twelve kidnapped children. Six had disappeared, one was dead, and at least another five had been or were currently with the Master.

"Athena team was already looking for the other six girls after you learned they'd likely been split into two groups. And Fox gave us the okay to keep looking for the five the Master took. We can still work the case, we're just not allowed in the field again until you're medically cleared," Lacey reminded her.

"I feel like I failed them," she admitted as she nibbled on her slice of pizza, suddenly no longer hungry. She'd allowed the feelings she was developing for Roman to become a distraction and those girls might pay the price.

Maybe Roman was right.

Maybe there was no room for love in their world.

If she had gotten further involved with Roman, how

many victims would pay the price once her time and attention were split between her job and her relationship?

"Oh no, don't do that," Opal reprimanded.

"Do what?" Ivory asked.

"That." Opal waved a hand at her, indicating what was likely a look of regret on Ivory's face. "Feel guilty."

"You have nothing to feel guilty about," Lacey told her.

"But …"

"No buts," Pearl interrupted fiercely. When her sisters had first asked her if there was something between her and Roman and she had admitted there was, Opal and Lacey had both been encouraging. Pearl had been dead set against the idea. Now it seemed her sister had had a change of heart.

"You're allowed to have a life outside of Prey," Opal said gently.

"But …"

"What did I just say about buts?" Pearl teased. "I was wrong when I told you that you shouldn't do anything about Roman. I let my anger issues cloud what all three of us could clearly see was happening. That was a mistake. Some people are made to fall in love, and others aren't. You are." Her sister's clear implication was that she wasn't, and Ivory wished that Pearl could learn to let go of the anger inside her. Of all of them, Pearl was the angriest about what had happened to them and was still having the hardest time moving forward with her life.

"It doesn't matter anyway," Ivory said sadly. "Roman made his choice, and it wasn't me. I'm not angry with him for it, just disappointed. I get why he didn't want to give us a chance. It just sucks that he didn't let me have a say in the matter. He made the decision for both of us. And he didn't even say goodbye."

"His loss." Lacey reached out and squeezed her hand.

"Totally his loss," Opal agreed.

"Absolutely," Pearl added.

"You know what I really need?" Despite her earlier decision to allow herself to wallow for a while, Ivory found she couldn't do it. She was hurt, confused, and disappointed, but obsessing over that wouldn't help, and it wouldn't change anything. The best cure for a broken heart was to remind yourself of your blessings, and she had plenty to be thankful for. Starting with the fact she was still alive and surrounded by people who loved her. It would take her a long time to get over Roman, probably she never would completely, but that didn't mean she had to sit around pining for someone who didn't want her.

"What?" Lacey asked.

"To pretend we're completely normal sisters, no dark, desolate backstory, just normal women hanging out together and having fun. So, let's eat pizza and chocolate, binge-watch some cheesy comedy, laugh and talk and be happy."

Happiness.

In the end, wasn't that what everyone wanted?

To be happy?

Too bad Roman had thrown away their chance to be happy together, but she could still find a different way to be happy on her own.

* * *

January 7th

6:37 P.M.

Time to face the music.

Roman felt ridiculously nervous.

Not a feeling he was particularly used to, at least not anymore. As a child, nerves had been part of his everyday life. There had always been the worry of what kind of mood his parents would be in that day. Would they be virtually unconscious, unable to do more than lie on the couch and stare blankly into space? Or would they be vicious, looking for ways to inflict pain?

There was no way to tell until it was too late to do anything about it.

Which was exactly how he felt right now. Ivory's mood had already been decided. She felt how she felt about his choice to leave the way he had, there was no going back and undoing it. He had to take whatever she wanted to throw at him like a man. He deserved it.

As the lift opened on her floor, he strode down the corridor with a lot more confidence than he felt.

He could do this.

All he had to do was pray that she didn't cry. Ivory's tears were one thing he wasn't sure he could cope with.

At her door, he lifted his hand to knock when he heard muffled voices and laughter.

This time a different sort of pain gripped his chest. In his mind it had always been a given that leaving Ivory would hurt her. He'd just known that this was something he had to do. But what if she wasn't hurt?

What if she didn't care that he'd left?

Of course, he hadn't wanted her to sit around crying for the last week, but she was in there laughing. Was he about to make a horrible mistake?

Retreat.

That was the one thought that blared through his head. Retreat, send the information he'd found to Prey, let them handle things, then lick his wounds in private and do what he always did, pretend he didn't feel anything and move on.

Roman didn't know what choice he would have wound up making because the door to Ivory's apartment suddenly swung open. His heart stuttered in his chest at the sight of her. She was pale with dark circles under her eyes and fading bruises on the exposed skin of her face and arms. A couple of the wounds she'd sustained from Hendricks were visible on her arms and neck. Despite all of that, she was still absolutely the most beautiful thing he had ever seen in his life.

"Are you going to just stand there or were you going to knock and come in?" she asked.

Behind her, he could see her sisters sitting on the couch. Opal and Lacey looked angry, but surprisingly there was something like understanding in Pearl's eyes. It was that understanding that gave him the courage to meet Ivory's gaze squarely. "I was going to come in. I hoped we might be able to talk."

For several excruciatingly long seconds, she just stood there, and he was convinced she was about to turn him down flat and not even give him the opportunity to explain himself. He had been counting on the fact that her big heart would at least hear him out. Had he been wrong?

"All right." She stepped back to allow him to enter the apartment.

When her sisters didn't move, he asked, "Alone?"

Before anyone could protest Ivory nodded. "It will be fine."

Even though they clearly didn't like it, Opal, Lacey, and Pearl all stood and gathered their cell phones and keys, heading out the door and closing it behind them. Finally, he was alone with Ivory. All he wanted to do was grab her and hold her like he'd ached to do for seven very long days, but he knew he owed her an explanation first.

Better to just get the words out, like ripping off a Band-Aid. Roman paused only to take Ivory's elbow and guide her to the sofa. She looked so weak like a gentle breeze could knock her over. Once she was seated, he began. "I'm sorry for the way I left things. You'll never know how hard it was to walk away from the hospital without you."

"Then why did you do it?" Ivory asked, a rare hint of vulnerability in her blue eyes.

"Because I needed to be the man you deserved," he answered honestly. No more secrets, no holding back, Ivory had given him all of herself and she deserved the same in return.

"I liked and understood the man you were."

He gave her a sad smile. "I know, sweetheart, and that's why I had to leave the way I did. If I had told you this before you would have insisted that you already liked me, that you already respected me, that you didn't deserve any more than what I already was, and I would have let you convince me that was true. I would have been weak and stayed, but it wouldn't have been true. I've been selfish for most of my life. It was the only way I knew how to survive. You deserve better than that. I knew I was falling in love with you, but unless I could learn how to respect and love myself, sooner or later I'd wind up hurting you. That wasn't acceptable. For once in my life, I had to put someone else first. Can you understand that?"

Tears shimmered in her eyes, and he had no idea if that was a good thing or a bad thing.

Roman had been under no illusions. While he was counting on her sweet heart and forgiving nature, he had known there was a chance she would turn him down flat. It had been a risk he had been willing to take, but losing her would slice through him in a way nothing else ever had, damaging a part of him his family couldn't touch. His heart. He hadn't loved them, even as a small child, and while they'd destroyed his soul, they hadn't touched his heart.

A heart that now belonged to the woman staring at him with an expression he couldn't decipher. She was the only one who could destroy it because she was the only one he'd ever given it to.

Slowly, she reached out and placed her hand over his.

Willing to take whatever she was offering, he immediately turned his hand over so hers was cradled in it and laced their fingers together.

"You risked everything for me," he continued, "almost died in the process, so I would have justice for Alexa. I thought killing Albert Hendricks would ease the guilt inside me over how I treated my sister, but it didn't. Revenge was for me. For my sister I needed to do more. I needed to put someone else first for once. You. I needed to start working on myself so I could be there for you. For the last week I've worked non-stop to try to find the Master, and I think I might have found a lead."

He'd expected her eyes to light up at the news, but instead, her gaze was tender. "For the record, even though it hurt because you didn't explain yourself, you made the right choice. My love can't save you, only you can save yourself. You took the first step toward doing that. You realized you're worthy of love and affection and determined to start by learning to love yourself."

Relief crashed down upon him. He'd needed to hear those words so badly. "You're not mad?"

Ivory grinned. "Oh, I'm mad. Hurt too. But I understand. Besides, we have the rest of our lives for you to make it up to me, and I think you made a good start by finding information that might help us find the Master."

Grabbing her, he lifted her and pulled her onto his lap, wrapping his arms around her and holding her tight. "Baby, I swear, I'll make it up to you."

"I don't doubt it." Her smile was sweet, her understanding a precious gift, her love a shining beacon that had saved him whether she knew it or not.

Roman touched a light kiss to her lips, then framed her face with his hands. "You are the most beautiful gift I've ever been given."

There was a hint of self-consciousness in this gorgeous woman he hadn't seen before. "I'm all gross. With all the stitches, I haven't been able to take a proper shower, and I'm dying to wash my hair. I haven't been able to do it because my arms are too sore, and I'm too weak, plus the whole can't get all the stitches wet thing."

When they'd been very small before Alexa had given in to drugs, he used to take care of her, including washing her hair. Swinging Ivory into his arms he stood. "I'll wash your hair for you."

"You will?" From the look on her face, he could tell she was trying to hide a smile.

"I used to wash Lex's hair sometimes when we were little, and I'd make up stories to keep her still. Our shower rarely worked so I used to do it in the bathroom sink." Assuming her bedroom would have its own bathroom, he located the master and set her down on the counter. Then he went to the kitchen, grabbed a chair, and returned to the bathroom, where Ivory had set her shampoo and conditioner on the counter.

Sitting her down, he wrapped a towel around her shoulders and then turned on the faucets. When the water was warm but not too hot, he tilted her head back and ran the water over her hair.

"I think you're forgetting something," Ivory said as he poured a little shampoo onto his palm.

"Oh, yeah, what's that?"

"My story."

Roman laughed. A genuine sound that surprised even him. Laughter had never been part of his life, but Ivory was opening up whole new worlds to him.

Massaging the shampoo into her hair, he started their very own fairytale. "Once upon a time, there was a very angry prince. He was angry at the world, hated himself, and thought he would never get a glimpse of the sun that lit up other people's worlds. Then he met a princess. A princess unlike any other. She was tough, strong, caring, compassionate, and the most beautiful woman to have ever existed. Only in this story, the prince doesn't save the princess. The princess saves the prince."

CHAPTER TWENTY-ONE

January 8th
    10:02 A.M.

HAND IN HAND, they walked up the steps and onto the plane.

Ivory was grateful that Roman hadn't tried to talk her out of being part of this. Even though she was far from healed, and was supposed to be grounded from participating in missions, he knew how important this was to her.

After he'd washed her hair—which was quite possibly the sweetest thing anyone had ever done for her—they'd talked some more before she'd asked what he found. While catching the Master was important to her, it wasn't more important than reconnecting with Roman. What she'd told him was true, she was hurt and perhaps just a little angry, but she also understood. He had done what he felt was the best thing for them in the long term, and since she wanted him to find peace and happiness, and agreed that it started with him learning to love himself, she had no choice but to forgive him.

Especially since she knew he'd been right when he'd said she would have taken him any way she could have gotten him. And while she would have, Roman had wanted to give her only the very best version of himself that he could be. That knowledge made the seven long, lonely days without him worth the wait.

Holding grudges usually ended up hurting you as much as the person you couldn't forgive. What was the point of that? She wanted what normal people had, what the Oswald siblings and their partners had, and what the team of former SEALs who managed her team had with their partners. She wanted someone to share her life with, a home, maybe kids. She wanted to be more than just someone who rescued the innocent. That would always be an important part of her life, but those days without Roman had shown her that she wanted—perhaps even needed—to be more.

If this was all she ever had in her life, then it felt like the Master won. While she might be using the skills he had taught her to bring down evil rather than to work as his own personal assassin, she was still doing what he intended.

Fighting.

She wanted to be more.

Rescuing innocents would always be a huge part of her life, but she wanted Roman to be just as big a part.

"Coach." She grinned as she stepped inside the jet and saw the man who had played a big part in saving her life. She didn't hesitate to walk over and throw her arms around the big man, hugging him tightly. Ivory would always be grateful that he had sat by her side so she wouldn't be alone in the hospital, it was a sweet move, but she already knew tough guys like the Delta operative had sweet sides they didn't like anyone to see.

"You're looking better than the last time I saw you," Coach said, returning her grin and hug.

"Barely," she said as she straightened and ran a hand over a lingering bruise on her cheek. Still dealing with daily pain, unable to walk without a limp, and yet to have her stitches removed, Ivory knew she was lucky to be allowed to be part of this mission and was grateful to Eagle for okaying it and Fox for fighting for her.

"You look gorgeous." Roman kissed her cheek and guided her into an empty chair.

"I see you two kissed and made up," said a tall man with a scar on his face who looked like he might have broken his nose a few times. He looked vaguely familiar, so she assumed she'd seen him on Hendricks' yacht, although most of her memories of her rescue were hazy at best and non-existent at worst.

"Since you didn't get to meet everyone, that's Ghost, Fletch, Hollywood, Fish, Beatle, Blade, and Truck," Coach said, pointing to each man as he said their names.

Most of them didn't look familiar, but she'd passed out fairly early on, and Coach had been the only one she'd seen in the hospital. "You saved my life," she said to Truck, the man with the scar. "Thank you." Going to him, she hugged him hard.

"Didn't think you'd remember that," Truck said, returning her hug.

"My memories are fuzzy, but I do recall your and Coach's faces hovering above me. Coach told me you guys did an emergency field transfusion which saved my life. I'm guessing it was you two who did that." Ivory knew she was lucky to be alive, and when she caught sight of the stricken look on Roman's face, she knew he was thinking the same thing.

Returning to her seat, she took Roman's hand and squeezed. Both of them had dangerous jobs and they would have to get used to that idea. Other than her sisters, there had never been anyone to worry that she wouldn't make it home from a mission. Of course, her sisters would be devastated to lose her, but it wasn't the same thing as having a man who loved her, who might one day ask her to marry him and have babies with him.

"I didn't know you guys would be joining us," she said as the jet began to move down the runway. "I thought it was just going to be me, Roman, and my team."

"Roman asked if we could help," Ghost explained.

"I appreciate it. All of us want the Master pretty badly," she said, indicating herself and her sisters.

"We'll get him," Roman assured her. "If not today then one day. He won't go unpunished."

"Want to fill us in on what you got from your contact?" Fletch asked.

"You all already know about my Holdon Lennox cover. One of the contacts I cultivated was Zeke MacAvoy," Roman explained.

"MacAvoy wasn't caught with the rest of the men at the resort," Opal said.

"He was likely still on his way back from coming out to pick us up," Ivory explained. "He called Roman and said he was coming to get us because Roman was in, but Hendricks got to us first. As far as Hendricks believed, Roman had no idea who I was, he thought I was playing Roman the same way I had played him in the past." That was the only thing that had saved Roman's life, and she was eternally grateful that Hendricks had been too focused on her to even consider an alternative.

"Yesterday I got a call from MacAvoy. I had no idea if my

cover had been blown, but thankfully, MacAvoy believes that Ivory—although he didn't know her name—was the one who brought the cops. He told me that a lot of the men who weren't there at the time of the raid were looking to go to ground and he offered me use of a safehouse," Roman told them.

"Safehouse is in New Mexico. We have no idea if anyone will be there, or how many, or even if the Master has ever set foot in it, but we're hopeful," Ivory said.

"Given we know the Master was recently in Texas, we're hoping that this is where he might have gone after he got word that Douglas Chayter was taken into custody," Roman said. "Maybe it's stretching things a little, but it's all I could come up with, and ..."

"And this is important to all of you," Blade said, his eyes full of understanding.

"Yeah, it is," Roman said, his hand tightening around hers. "I didn't tell MacAvoy that I would use the safehouse. I don't want him figuring out I'm not who I say I am. I probably won't use the Holdon Lennox cover again, but I'd prefer to keep it intact if possible, just in case. If raiding this house can help us get a lead on the Master, we have to check it out. At the very least we might be able to take down a couple more human traffickers."

"Once Roman gave us the address, we did a little recon," Lacey explained to the Delta team. "Property is owned by a shell corporation. We haven't been able to figure out who the actual owner is yet. It's remote, not a lot of cover. It's out in the desert, approaching quietly isn't going to be easy. Darkness is about the only friend we'll have."

"There are at least five buildings on the property," Opal added. "So we're going to have to split up."

"We'll need to hit them all at once," Ghost agreed.

"Could be booby traps," Hollywood said thoughtfully.

"And if they're smart there will be a good security system," Fish added.

"Best we can hope for is that they'll be arrogant enough to believe no one will ever realize who the property belongs to," Beatle said.

"Arrogance has taken down more than one criminal," Roman said.

And Ivory prayed that it would bring down the Master. While she knew she could move on with her life, be happy with Roman, and build a future with him, even knowing the Master was still out there, it would be wonderful to start her new life with a clean slate.

* * *

JANUARY 8TH

10:59 P.M.

AS BADLY AS Roman wanted to wrap Ivory up in cotton wool and tuck her away somewhere she would be safe, he knew that was unfair of him. This was who Ivory was. She saved people, she took down evil men and women, she was well trained, smart, and while she certainly took risks with her own safety, he trusted that she wouldn't take any unnecessary risks.

They were just at the beginning of their relationship, and he was determined to prove to her that she had made the right choice in forgiving him, and that he was serious about putting her and her needs first. She needed this. Needed to be part of taking down the man who had hurt her so very badly.

All he had to do was keep reminding himself of how she'd brought him to his knees that very first day they'd met. Yeah, he'd been unprepared thinking she was a kidnap victim, but she had still legitimately managed to take him down, which considering her size was no small feat.

"I can do this, even injured," Ivory whispered beside him.

Leaning over, he touched a kiss to her cheek. "Never doubted that for a moment, darlin'."

The smile she shot him did that thing to his heart he was beginning to associate with what love felt like. A strange feeling for someone who had never been loved.

If the Master wasn't here, he would make it his life's mission to find the man. There was no way he should be allowed to continue to walk free. He needed to pay for every horrific thing he'd done to Ivory. That she had managed to come out of it a strong, confident, and loving human being was a testament to the woman she was.

A woman he was pretty sure could do absolutely anything.

Finding a heart in his cold, empty chest proved it.

"Everyone ready?" he asked into the comms unit. Since there were at least five buildings and the drones they'd used earlier showed more than a dozen heat signatures, they had divided up into five teams. He and Ivory, her sisters, and the eight Deltas had split into two groups of three and a pair. Ivory's sisters were tackling the main house, the two groups of three Deltas were taking the other larger buildings, and the two pairs would take the smaller ones.

Although he was sure she'd noticed, Ivory hadn't said anything about him assigning them the smallest and most out-of-the-way building. Since she wasn't one hundred percent, he wanted to give her the easiest assignment with the least potential for danger.

"Ready," Ghost said.

"Good to go," Coach said.

"Yep," Truck replied.

"More than ready, been waiting a lifetime to do this," Pearl muttered, making him smile and hope that the Master was here. Ivory and her sisters deserved to be able to live without knowing he was out there somewhere hurting more girls. Girls who might not be as lucky as they had been.

"Let's do this," he said.

With their night vision goggles on, they could all move easily through the dark. The lack of cover wasn't ideal, but it was what it was. They just had to make the best of it. They had decided they would hit the compound late evening rather than in the early hours of the morning when whoever was inside would be more likely to expect an attack.

The property was a little over two acres. With the five buildings spread out, he had to wonder if that was to give whoever was staying here the privacy to do whatever they wanted with any victims they might have brought with them.

A few trees were around, and they were just passing one when he heard Ivory gasp.

Swinging around, he aimed his weapon, ready to take out whatever threat had dared to put his woman in harm's way only to find no one there.

Instead, Ivory was hanging upside down four feet off the ground.

"That's the second time in a week that I've been hung upside down," Ivory muttered.

Roman couldn't help his lips quirking up into a small smile. "No worries, honey, I'll get you down. Put your hands on my shoulders," he ordered as he stepped closer and pulled out a knife. "Can you still shoot?"

"Really? You have to ask?" He could hear the humor in her

voice. "I can shoot upside down, right way up, sideways, and spinning in circles."

"Spinning in circles, huh?"

"One of the Master's games. He had this old merry-go-round thing. It was metal and rusty, and he used to love to put us on it, spin us around, and make us aim at our targets."

"You can hit a target spinning in circles?" He sawed through the rope, impressed that Ivory could do that. Not many people would be able to, including highly trained operatives.

"Not at first. Had good motivation to learn though."

"He punished you if you missed?" Roman asked even though he knew the answer.

"Yeah. Pearl used to get dizzy really easily, she couldn't do it. He'd get so angry at her, one time he beat her so badly we were sure we were going to lose her."

"We'll get him, Ivory. I promise you that. Neither of us will stop until he pays for what he did." It wasn't a vow he had made lightly, and he meant it. If not today, one day they would get the man.

"And make it so he can't ever hurt another innocent girl."

It shouldn't—and didn't—surprise him that she cared more about keeping other girls from going through what she did than getting revenge on the man for what he did to her. "You ready to get down from there?"

"Totally."

Carefully cutting through the last of the rope, Ivory's hands on his shoulders kept her from falling. Roman wrapped an arm around her waist as he slowly lowered her down. Before he set her on her feet, he crushed his mouth to hers. "You're amazing, you know that?"

"I think you're pretty amazing too," she said, kissing him again.

Roman knew he had done nothing to deserve this woman. She was so far out of his league they were in different universes, but he would always be grateful that she had chosen him and he would become a man she could be proud of.

With her feet back on the ground they both started moving again. The building they were heading toward appeared before them, and they both paused to scan the perimeter.

"I don't see anyone," Ivory said softly.

"No lights on inside either."

"You think it's empty?"

"Only one way to find out."

They both started moving again but hadn't gone more than a few steps before a pained scream came through the comms.

"Pearl?" Ivory asked. Despite the black paint on her face and the NVGs, he could see the terror on her face.

"What happened?" he demanded, feeding off Ivory's fear.

"Pearl is down," Opal said. It was clear from her voice that it wasn't good.

"How bad?" Ivory asked.

"They had traps set, an arrow hit her in the chest," Opal explained.

"Truck?" he asked the medic.

"I'm on my way," Truck replied.

"Everyone be careful. Ivory got caught in a trap as well," he said.

"Ives?" Lacey asked.

"I'm fine," she assured her sister.

"Truck, get to Pearl, get her out, the rest of us proceed." Even if the Master wasn't here, other men needed to be stopped. They couldn't leave until they'd taken them into custody and freed any victims being held here.

"You hold on, Pearl," Ivory said fiercely.

"Are you going to be good to do this?" he asked her. As much as they needed to check out the building, if Ivory was going to be distracted worrying about her sister, then it was better if she waited outside. He wasn't questioning her skills, but she was already hurt, not fully recovered from her injuries. He wouldn't blame her for not being able to compartmentalize, he just wasn't willing to risk her life.

"Absolutely," she said fiercely. He could tell that her sister being injured had only made her more determined. Although he wouldn't have thought it possible, his admiration for her grew. It wasn't easy to shove aside worry for someone you loved to focus on the job at hand.

"Then let's go do this."

Watching each other's backs, they approached the house just as someone started shooting at them.

CHAPTER TWENTY-TWO

January 8th
   11:21 P.M.

"THERE'S a basement door over there, you keep his attention, and I'll go in and get him from behind," Ivory said as she fired back at whoever was shooting at them.

"We stick together," Roman said firmly.

"That's what he'll expect." It was a better plan, she knew that, but she also knew that Roman was protective of her. The idea of her being in danger made him want to go all alpha male on her, and while she understood why, she was just as trained as he was to do this.

"Fine," he said tightly. "I'll keep laying down cover fire, you get to the door."

Feeling the same protectiveness toward Roman that he felt toward her made it hard to walk away from him. Together they were stronger than they'd be alone, but sometimes they had to fight apart. This was one of those times.

Her plan was solid. If Roman stayed out here firing at

whoever was shooting at them, she could slip inside, go up into the house, and take the guy down from behind. If she was lucky it was the Master, nothing would be sweeter than being the one to destroy him, but whoever this man was he deserved a lifetime in prison.

Actually, he deserved a whole lot worse, but she couldn't condone cold-blooded murder.

Still, if it came down to it and he gave her no other choice, she would kill the Master and wouldn't lose a second of sleep over it.

"If you get yourself shot, I'm going to be pretty mad, darlin'," Roman said as she yanked open the door.

"Back at ya, handsome," she said with a grin as she walked down the steps and closed the door behind her.

The quiet suddenly seemed too quiet.

She could still hear the gunfire, but it was dull now like she had stepped into an alternate reality, connected to hers but once removed.

Ivory continued down the steps and soon found herself in a large open basement. The room looked like something out of a horror movie. There were cages over to one corner and chains hanging from the ceiling, embedded in the floor, and in the walls. On another wall were several whips, paddles, and dozens of other torture devices hanging on hooks.

Even if she hadn't lived the kind of childhood she had, and even if she didn't have the job that she did, it wasn't hard to figure out what went down in this basement. Even when hiding out in a safehouse, these men couldn't keep control of their evil and sadistic vices.

Across the other side of the large space was another set of stairs. This one led up into the house, probably into a kitchen. Although the house was small, she was sure she'd be able to get up there without whoever was in the house shooting at Roman knowing she was even there.

It wasn't until she was halfway to the other staircase that she saw them.

Five little girls.

The same little girls who had been with her in El Compradores' house the day she'd met Roman. They were the little girls she'd been originally searching for. Half of them anyway, so far there were no clues as to where the other six girls had been taken. But minus the one who had been dead in the aquarium at Douglas Chayter's place, these were the rest of the girls.

Did that mean the Master was here too?

"Everything is going to be okay now," she soothed as she headed for the cage where the five little girls were huddled together.

None of them spoke, just clung to one another and watched her with wary eyes.

While it made sense they no longer trusted anyone, it hurt to see their sweet little faces so afraid and the darkness in their eyes. She knew they would be forever changed and haunted by what had happened to them.

There was nothing she could do to undo it, but she could at the very least make sure they were returned home to their families.

"I'm going to get you out of there, all right? Is anyone hurt?" she asked as she scanned the room looking for the keys to the padlock that kept them locked inside the cage.

Reinforcing her belief that the smallest of the girls was the toughest, the little one finally stepped forward, leaving the safety of the huddle. "He hurt Anna," the child said. Despite the fear in her eyes, a burning anger also told Ivory that the girl had what it took to bounce back from this. Who knows, maybe she was even looking at a future Prey operative.

"What did he do to her, sweetie?" She couldn't find the keys, but there was an ax amongst the tools on the wall. She could use that to break the padlock.

"He did ..." There was confusion in the little girl's eyes. "He took her clothes off and put his peepee inside her." The innocence of the child's words broke her heart. While the little girl knew it was a bad thing that had happened, she was too young to even know what sex was.

"Okay, baby," she soothed as she grabbed the ax. "Did he hurt the rest of you?"

"No, just Anna."

"What's your name, sweetie?"

"Maria."

"Okay, Maria, you are being so brave, I'm really proud of you, but I need you to keep being brave. Can you do that?"

The little girl nodded.

"I want you to go over with the others while I break the padlock. Then I'm going to get you out of here."

"Are we going to see our mommies and daddies?" another little girl asked.

"You sure are, baby."

"My mommy is going to be angry," Maria said, somewhat sadly.

"No, baby, she won't," Ivory assured the child.

"I didn't listen. I'm not supposed to talk to strangers, but he had a puppy," Maria said.

"Trust me, sweetie, your mommy is not going to be angry." With the five girls huddled together again, she swung the ax at the padlock.

It took her a few tries, but finally the lock broke and

dropped to the concrete floor. As soon as it did, she wrenched open the door.

"Okay, girls, I need you to come here. Can you all walk? Anna?"

"I can walk," said a little girl with messy red braids who she assumed was Anna.

"You are the bravest little girls, but I'm going to need you to be brave a little longer, okay? Do you know who the man is who took you?"

"He said we had to call him the Master," Maria told her.

Perfect.

They'd been right. It had been a huge gamble coming here, but it looked like it was their lucky day. The Master was here in the house and wasn't walking out of it alive.

"He won't hurt you again," she promised. "I need you to hide for me, okay."

"Where are you going?" asked a little girl with dark hair that fell down her back all the way to her backside.

"I need to go upstairs and find the Master." She scanned the room looking for a place to stash the children.

Her gaze landed on a small window.

An adult probably couldn't fit through it, but the children likely would.

"Girls, I want you to break that window, climb out, and hide right beside the house. Don't go running off okay, no matter what." The last thing she needed was for one of the kids to get hit by a stray bullet. "Can you all do that?"

Five serious little heads nodded.

Handing the ax to the girl who looked the oldest, the one with the long dark hair, she ushered the girls over to the window.

"All right, sweetie, I'm going to lift you up. I want you to swing this at the window and break the glass," she instructed.

The child nodded so she hefted the girl into her arms, and a moment later glass was raining down around them.

"You need to be really careful of the glass, okay," she said as she lifted the girl higher so she could climb out the window. The window was too high for her to reach properly on her own so she could clear away any shards left behind, and she had nothing to cover them with. There was also an urgency that said she needed to get the children out of the way as quickly as possible.

She had the oldest girl out, then Anna went next, then a quiet, little blonde, and a very pretty brunette, but when she went to reach for Maria her heart dropped.

The child had a gun pressed to her temple.

The man of her nightmares stood behind the little girl, that evil half-smile she remembered from her childhood on his face. It had been five years, but he hadn't changed much. His smooth bald head reflected the light, and his small, beady, dark blue eyes stared down at her with the same superiority she'd always hated.

He really was an ugly man. Inside and out.

"Hello, Ivory. It has been many years," the Master said in his softly spoken manner.

Her weapon didn't waver as she pulled it from her waistband and pointed it at him. "It's over."

"Tut, tut, tut," he said, holding the child higher so the little girl's body blocked most of his.

The child was small, only five or six, but she was big enough to cover the man's head and torso so Ivory couldn't get off a good shot. She would risk going for his leg, but she was concerned that if he even thought she was going to shoot he'd make sure the little girl was the one who took the bullet.

"I am disappointed in you, Ivory. You should know that

nothing is ever as simple as it seems. Have you forgotten all of our lessons so quickly?"

He had an escape route planned.

That was the only thing that made sense. He was too calm to feel like he was trapped. Maybe he'd heard the glass breaking, or maybe he'd decided Roman wasn't going to stop shooting at him. Whatever it was, he'd come down here for a reason.

All she had to do was keep him occupied just for a minute or two. When no more shots were fired, Roman would enter the house, clear it, then come down here looking for her.

"I won't let you go," she warned.

"You would really kill your own father?" he asked, tone mocking.

"You aren't my father, thank goodness. None of your evil blood runs through my veins."

"All blood is evil. That was one thing you never understood."

"No. Most people are good. No matter how hard you tried you couldn't corrupt my soul. Couldn't corrupt Pearl, Lacey, or Opal either. Is that why you've been laying low for five years? You're too scared to try again?" This time she was the one who mocked.

"You'll always be mine, Ivory," he sneered.

In rapid succession, he fired at her, the bullet hitting her square in the chest.

Then he produced a knife and slit Maria's throat.

Darting backward, he pressed on part of the wall which opened to reveal a hidden passage.

Even as she was falling backward from the bullet's force, she fired her own weapon at the man disappearing into the tunnel.

"Ivory!" Roman screamed her name. A second later he dropped to his knees at her side. "Are you hit?"

"Vest," she muttered. The bullet had been stopped by the Kevlar vest she was wearing, it had knocked the air from her lungs, had probably cracked a couple of ribs, but it hadn't pierced her heart ending her life. "Maria."

Struggling onto her knees, she shoved away Roman's hands and crawled to the little girl, pressing her hands to the child's neck where blood was flowing far too fast.

The Master had gotten away, Maria might die, and she saw blood on Roman's arm.

This hadn't been a successful mission.

* * *

January 9th
9:49 A.M.

"COME ON, BABY, YOU NEED REST," Roman said as he grasped Ivory's shoulders and tried to guide her out of her chair.

For the last eight hours, she'd alternated between sitting at her sister Pearl's bedside in ICU and beside six-year-old Maria Sanchez's bedside. Somehow the child had survived the gash to her neck. Just. It had taken fourteen stitches across her small neck to close the gash that should have ended her life.

The girl's family had been notified that she had been found—as had the families of the other children—and were on their way to New Mexico, but Ivory didn't want the little girl to be alone so she was sitting with her. When Ivory went to check on Pearl, she begged him with huge, scared eyes to stay with the child.

It didn't matter to her that the doctors had said the girl would sleep for a few more hours, she was paranoid the child would wake up alone and afraid. Although letting Ivory out of his sight was the last thing he wanted to do, he stayed with Maria to ease Ivory's mind. Anything to get that terror out of her eyes.

She saw herself in the little girl, he knew that and didn't like the idea of the child being alone after everything she'd been through either, but Ivory looked dead on her feet. She was still recovering from what Richard Bouquet and Albert Hendricks had put her through, and the Master had shot her tonight. If she hadn't been wearing the bulletproof vest, she'd be dead right now.

What she needed was uninterrupted rest.

"I can't leave," Ivory said in a soft voice. It was part sadness, part frustration, and part pain. The bullet had cracked two ribs, and even though they'd found the five girls, and all of them had survived their ordeal, it wasn't without casualties. Maria had almost died, and Anna had been raped. One of the girls had died in Douglas Chayter's aquarium, and six of the girls were still missing. This mission had been both successful and not, and he knew she was struggling to deal with that.

Plus, she had winged the Master when she shot at him which meant they now had his blood, his DNA. It would be run through every database that existed and hopefully they'd get a hit.

"You have to, you need rest."

"But ..."

Turning her chair around, he touched a finger to her lips. "No, darlin', no buts. Pearl has Lacey and Opal there with her. Maria's parents are due to show up any moment now. It's time for me to take care of you."

"I'm fine."

Roman shook his head. "No, sweetheart, you're far from fine."

Her eyes narrowed, and he was sure she was about to give him a whole retort on how she believed she was fine. He almost welcomed it, anything to get the desolation out of her eyes. But then he saw the fight drain out of her, and she just looked exhausted.

"I'll go when her parents get here."

"Nice try, but this isn't a compromise situation. Opal is going to come and sit with Maria, Lacey will stay with Pearl, and I'm taking you to a hotel so you can shower and rest." When she'd been checked out in the ER, she'd had her stitches removed so now she could take the shower she'd been longing for.

"She almost died because of me," Ivory said, pain lacing every word.

"No. You saved her life."

"I was so busy trying to get the girls out, I didn't hear the Master coming down the stairs. I should have tried to shoot him in the leg, but I was worried if he thought I was going to shoot he'd hurt her. Turns out I didn't need to worry, he hurt her anyway."

He would do anything, give anything, to take away her pain, but he couldn't, all he could do was be here for her. Take care of her, be there for her when she was ready to let go, break down, and talk it out.

"We'll get him, and he'll pay for hurting Maria," he assured her.

The look in her eyes told him she didn't believe him, but he knew without a shadow of a doubt that one day the Master would be taken down.

"Come here, baby." Gently he gathered her into his arms

and carried her out the door. Opal was waiting for him. She gave a soft smile at her little sister and smoothed a hand down Ivory's hair before disappearing into Maria's room.

Roman carried Ivory through the hospital halls, pleased that she had curled into him, her hands fisted in his sweater, her face pressed against his neck. Coach was waiting for them in their rental. After taking him and Ivory to the hotel he and the rest of his team would leave. The rest of them would likely remain in New Mexico until Pearl was strong enough to travel back home.

None of them spoke on the drive to the hotel. Roman sat in the backseat with Ivory on his lap. Her eyes were closed, but he could tell she wasn't asleep, feeling the tension still buzzing inside her.

"Thanks," he said to Coach when they pulled up outside the hotel.

"Take care of her."

"I will."

They already had a room booked, and Coach had given him the key card, so he headed straight to the elevators. Prey had rented them a nice suite and by the time he reached it, opened the door, and locked it behind him he felt drained. Tonight hadn't gone the way he'd hoped. He had hoped by the time they got to the hotel the Master would be in custody, the girls ready to return to their families, and everything would be over. Still, they were all alive, and that was what mattered most.

Carrying Ivory straight to the bathroom, he set her on her feet, opened the shower's glass door, and turned the water on.

Ivory stood where he'd put her looking small and lost. Fragile. But his girl was the opposite of fragile, and he knew after a shower, some sleep, and something to eat she would bounce back.

With gentle but efficient movements he stripped off her clothes. They'd changed into jeans and sweaters at the hospital and washed the paint from their faces. A bullet had winged his arm. The wound hadn't even needed stitches, but the sight of the dark black bruise on Ivory's chest, right above her heart, made his own heart stutter in his chest.

So close.

So very close to losing her.

Steam filled the room, and he nudged her toward the shower. "There you go, honey. Take your time, relax, and enjoy."

He turned to give her privacy, but her hand darted out and grabbed his. "Stay."

The one word was all he needed, and he quickly stripped out of his clothes and then guided her into the shower. They just stood there for a moment, letting the water pound down around them, slowly easing the tension inside both of them.

Their toiletries weren't unpacked so he grabbed the hotel shampoo, turned Ivory around, poured some into his palm, and began to massage it into her scalp.

A small moan fell from her lips, and he felt his body respond.

It wasn't the right time, this was about taking care of Ivory while she was vulnerable not sex, and he didn't intend to do anything about it, but he couldn't not react to this gorgeous woman. If Ivory noticed his hard length prodding her back, she didn't mention it.

"Here we go, baby," he said, moving her into the spray and rinsing the soapy suds from her hair. "Conditioner next."

Before he could pick up the bottle, she turned and

reached for him, closing her fingers around his throbbing length.

"Stop, sweetheart," he said, covering her hand with his own. He didn't want her to feel pressured just because his body had responded to her.

"I want to."

"You're vulnerable right now, I don't want to take advantage."

The smile she gave him showed some of the spunk he was used to seeing on her face. "It's not taking advantage if I want this too."

With a groan, he shifted them so he was leaning against the warm tiles, and turned Ivory so her back was flush against his chest. Then he let his hand dip between her legs. Circling the pad of his finger over her little bud a couple of times, he slid that finger inside her, stroking deep.

Ivory moaned and arched back against him. Roman groaned as the movement ground against his pulsing length. It was aching to be buried inside her but not until she came first.

Adding another finger, he thrust in and out while his thumb went to work on her little bundle of nerves, working it harder and faster as her body undulated against him, taking him deeper with each thrust.

"Roman, I need ... more," she murmured.

Curling his fingers around, he stroked that spot inside her that would make her fly apart, pressed hard on her bud, and touched a line of kisses along her neck.

With a cry she came, his name falling from her lips.

While her pleasure was still rippling through her, he lifted her, turned her to face him, and slid himself inside her tight, wet heat.

Her internal muscles were still quivering, and when she

crushed her mouth to his he found his control snapped, and his release hit him hard and fast.

By the time it had faded, Ivory was watching him with a sleepy smile. They'd both pretty much hit a brick wall.

Setting Ivory back on her feet, he shut off the water then they both stepped out of the shower. Grabbing one of the fluffy white towels, he dried Ivory off, then himself before gathering her up into his arms again.

Bed. That was what they both needed right now. Not putting her down, he pulled back the covers, lay down, and held her close.

Touching his lips to her forehead, he held them there for a long moment. "I love you, sweetheart. Thank you for fighting for me. Nobody had ever done that for me."

Ivory touched her lips to his. "I will always fight for you, Roman. Always."

CHAPTER TWENTY-THREE

January 9ᵗʰ
    6:14 P.M.

"Mmm," Ivory blinked and stretched. Her chest still ached, but she felt much better now that she'd gotten some sleep. "Hey," she said when she lifted her head to see Roman watching her. His expression was tender, and it went straight to her heart. This was the guy she had known he was hiding beneath his cold, hard exterior.

"Morning. Well, evening really since it's after six." One of his large hands palmed her cheek, and he tilted her face up so he could kiss her.

"I could get used to starting my days like this," she said when she could finally tear her lips away from his. Almost as soon as the words were out of her mouth, she regretted them. The last thing she wanted to do was pressure Roman. This was new to him. He had never had anyone love him before, it was a little much to expect him to want to jump right into something serious. He loved her, but that didn't mean he was ready to move in with her or marry her, or anything else.

His reply surprised her. "I could too. I love watching you sleep."

"You were watching me sleep? For how long?"

"Just a couple of hours."

"A couple of hours? You're really turning into Mr. Romantic, aren't you?" she teased. This was what she had to do. Keep things light, teasing, and fun. When Roman was ready to make things more serious, he could let her know. For now, she was more than content to know that he loved her and wanted to be with her.

"Only with you, baby." His words practically turned her into a puddle of goo. Earlier today he'd been so sweet with her, from worrying about her at the hospital, taking care of her and bringing her back here, then helping her relax and making sure she got sleep.

"I like that. I like knowing you're tough and protective, but also that you're sweet and softer when it's just us. I don't need anyone to protect me, but I like knowing that you can, you make me feel safe in a way I've never experienced before," she admitted. So much for her keeping things light plan. Nervously, she chanced a glance at him, but he still had the tender expression on his face.

"I like the same thing about you. I never thought I wanted a woman in my life, not permanently anyway. But you're everything I need, everything I didn't even know I wanted. I love your big heart, compassion, and your ability to see the light in a dark world, and I love that you can take care of yourself. I love you, Ivory."

"I love you, too. Always. So, you want to order room service before we go back to the hospital to check on Pearl and Maria?"

When she went to climb out of bed, Roman grabbed her and pulled her sideways so she was lying draped on top of him. "I'm not ready to let you go yet."

Snuggling closer, she touched a kiss to the side of his neck. "You don't have to, you know. You don't have to let me go. Not at all. Not ever." Even though she didn't want to pressure him, she also wanted him to know that she didn't care about timelines or speed. Didn't care that their relationship had developed so fast. All she cared about was loving this amazing, complex man.

"I don't want to let you go, Ivory. Not ever. I know it's soon, but I was thinking of moving to California, maybe getting an apartment in your building."

"Really?"

"Really."

Ivory drew in a breath. If Roman was already willing to pack up his life and move to San Diego just because she lived there, then surely he wouldn't think it was pressuring him to ask. "You know, if you want, you don't have to look for a new apartment."

A frown furrowed his brow. "You don't want me to move to California?"

There was so much anxiety and doubt in his dark eyes that she couldn't help but smile. "No, silly, I was trying to ask you to move in with me. I just don't want to pressure you in case it's too much too soon."

The smile that transformed his face stole her breath. He was stunning, when he smiled like that and let go, he was completely and utterly the most gorgeous thing she had ever seen. "You want me to move in with you?"

"Yep. I like seeing your grumpy face first thing in the morning and then last thing before I go to sleep at night."

"Then I think we're going to have problems, darlin'."

Since his voice was still tender, the smile still on his lips, and his fingers were trailing up and down her spine, making her bare skin tingle, she didn't worry he was going to say anything she wouldn't like. "Oh, yeah? What's the problem?"

"I don't think I'm going to be using my grumpy face so much anymore."

"Oh? And why is that?" she teased as she propped her chin on one fist while she slipped her other hand between their bodies to stroke his morning hard-on.

"Because of you." His lips touched her forehead in a gentle kiss, then he captured her lips in a kiss that quickly turned fiery. "Definitely could get used to this every morning." His hands curled around her hips, and he moved her so she was on her knees right above him.

"Definitely," she agreed as she guided him to her entrance. "We didn't use a condom last night." She'd been so out of it at first, and then so filled with a need to have him inside her she hadn't even thought about it. "I'm on birth control and clean."

"I'm clean too, been almost two years since I was last with a woman."

"Then I guess we don't need to worry about condoms again," she said as she took the first inch of him inside her. "I like there being nothing between us."

"There is nothing between us, sweetheart," he said as he reached out and palmed one of her breasts, kneading and then taking the sensitive little bud between his thumb and forefinger, tweaking it.

"Nothing," she agreed, thrusting her chest forward, seeking more as she slowly sank down, taking him inch by inch inside her.

"Touch yourself, baby. Let me watch you."

The heat in his eyes sent a flush of heat right through her

body, zinging from her breasts to right between her legs where she could feel him throbbing inside her.

Touching herself where their bodies joined, she worked her bundle of nerves with her fingers as she lifted her hips until just his tip was still inside her before sinking down again to take him deep.

She felt pleasure building. With each lift of her hips, each swirl of her fingers, it built until it reached a crescendo sending pleasure coursing through her. Her head fell back, her fingers worked faster, Roman's hands gripped her hips, and he began to thrust inside her hard and fast, making the pleasure go on and on until it felt like it consumed every part of her body, heart, and soul.

When at least it started to ebb, she sank down against Roman's hard chest. "I love you so much," she whispered, tears of joy in her eyes.

"I didn't even believe I was capable of the love I feel for you," he said softly.

"You're capable of so much more than you think you are. You're a wonderful man, Roman. A man who had horrible things happen to him, who thought that shutting down was the only way to survive, but you have a big heart, and you can love just as large as anyone else."

"Not larger than you, baby. You have the kind of love that heals, that brings out the best in others. The things you've overcome make you nothing short of miraculous. My miracle. My beautiful, sweet, brave, wonderful miracle."

"You gave me the last piece of myself back to me," she told him, lifting her head so she could look at him. "I knew I could love, I knew I could survive, I knew I could fight to find happiness no matter what, but I didn't know I could love a man. I thought the Master might have broken that part of me."

"He didn't break you, not any part of you, sweetheart."

"And your family didn't break you," she reminded him. "We might have had to fight through things most people couldn't even imagine to get here, but we are here. Together. And we have the entire rest of our lives to be happy together."

"Together. For a guy who never had anybody you don't know how good that word sounds."

"Well, get used to it because you're stuck with me."

"I want to be stuck with you."

Ivory laughed as she felt him starting to grow hard inside her again. Never could she have envisioned that her life could turn out to be this perfect.

The fight it had taken to survive, to get here, had been more than worth it.

Pearl Smith will do anything for a chance at rescuing six little girls and having another shot at getting The Master including working with a man she can't stand in the second book in the action packed and emotionally charged Prey Security: Artemis Team series!
Pearl's Fight (Prey Security: Artemis Team #2)

ALSO BY JANE BLYTHE

Candella Sisters' Heroes Series

LITTLE DOLLS

LITTLE HEARTS

LITTLE BALLERINA

Broken Gems Series

CRACKED SAPPHIRE

CRUSHED RUBY

FRACTURED DIAMOND

SHATTERED AMETHYST

SPLINTERED EMERALD

SALVAGING MARIGOLD

River's End Rescues Series

COCKY SAVIOR

SOME REGRETS ARE FOREVER

PROTECT

SOME LIES WILL HAUNT YOU

SOME QUESTIONS HAVE NO ANSWERS

SOME TRUTH CAN BE DISTORTED

SOME TRUST CAN BE REBUILT

SOME MISTAKES ARE UNFORGIVABLE

Detective Parker Bell Series

A SECRET TO THE GRAVE

WINTER WONDERLAND

DEAD OR ALIVE

LITTLE GIRL LOST

FORGOTTEN

<u>Count to Ten Series</u>

ONE

TWO

THREE

FOUR

FIVE

SIX

BURNING SECRETS

SEVEN

EIGHT

NINE

TEN

<u>Christmas Romantic Suspense Series</u>

CHRISTMAS HOSTAGE

CHRISTMAS CAPTIVE

CHRISTMAS VICTIM

YULETIDE PROTECTOR

<u>Conquering Fear Series</u>

(Co-written with Amanda Siegrist)

DROWNING IN YOU

OUT OF THE DARKNESS

ABOUT THE AUTHOR

USA Today bestselling author Jane Blythe writes action-packed romantic suspense and military romance featuring protective heroes and heroines who are survivors. One of Jane's most popular series includes Saving SEALs, part of Susan Stoker's OPERATION ALPHA world! Writing in that world alongside authors such as Janie Crouch and Riley Edwards has been a blast, and she looks forward to bringing more books to this genre, both within and outside of Stoker's world. When Jane isn't binge-reading she's counting down to Christmas and adding to her 200+ teddy bear collection!

To connect and keep up to date please visit any of the following

Email – mailto:janeblytheauthor@gmail.com
Facebook – http://www.facebook.com/janeblytheauthor
Instagram – http://www.instagram.com/jane_blythe_author
Reader Group – http://www.facebook.com/groups/
janeskillersweethearts
Twitter – http://www.twitter.com/jblytheauthor
Website – http://www.janeblythe.com.au

There are many more books in this fan fiction world than listed here, for an up-to-date list go to www.AcesPress.com

You can also visit our Amazon page at:
http://www.amazon.com/author/operationalpha

Becca Jameson: Destiny's Delta
Lynne St James, Gwen's Delta
Elle James: Ivy's Delta
Riley Edwards: Hope's Delta

Police and Fire: Operation Alpha World

Freya Barker: Burning for Autumn
B.P. Beth: Scott
Jane Blythe: Salvaging Marigold
Julia Bright, Justice for Amber
Hadley Finn: Exton
Emily Gray: Shelter for Allegra
Danielle M. Haas: Crossroads of Betrayal
Deanndra Hall: Shelter for Sharla
Jenna Harte: Dead But Not Forgotten
Amber Kuhlman: Protecting Paisley
Reina Torres: Justice for Sloane
Aubree Valentine, Justice for Danielle
Maddie Wade: Finding English

Tarpley VFD Series

Silver James, Fighting for Elena
Deanndra Hall, Fighting for Carly
Haven Rose, Fighting for Calliope
MJ Nightingale, Fighting for Jemma
TL Reeve, Fighting for Brittney
Nicole Flockton, Fighting for Nadia

As you know, this book included at least one character from Susan Stoker's books. To check out more, see below.

SEAL Team Hawaii Series

Finding Elodie
Finding Lexie
Finding Kenna
Finding Monica
Finding Carly
Finding Ashlyn
Finding Jodelle (July 2023)

Eagle Point Search & Rescue

Searching for Lilly
Searching for Elsie
Searching for Bristol
Searching for Caryn
Searching for Finley (Sept 2023)
Searching for Heather (Jan 2024)
Searching for Khloe (TBA)

The Refuge Series

Deserving Alaska
Deserving Henley
Deserving Reese
Deserving Cora (Nov 2023)
Deserving Lara (Feb 2024)
Deserving Maisy (TBA)
Deserving Ryleigh (TBA)

Delta Team Two Series

Shielding Gillian

Shielding Kinley
Shielding Aspen
Shielding Jayme (novella)
Shielding Riley
Shielding Devyn
Shielding Ember
Shielding Sierra

SEAL of Protection: Legacy Series

Securing Caite (FREE!)
Securing Brenae (novella)
Securing Sidney
Securing Piper
Securing Zoey
Securing Avery
Securing Kalee
Securing Jane

Delta Force Heroes Series

Rescuing Rayne (FREE!)
Rescuing Aimee (novella)
Rescuing Emily
Rescuing Harley
Marrying Emily (novella)
Rescuing Kassie
Rescuing Bryn
Rescuing Casey
Rescuing Sadie (novella)
Rescuing Wendy
Rescuing Mary
Rescuing Macie (novella)
Rescuing Annie

Badge of Honor: Texas Heroes Series

Justice for Mackenzie (FREE!)

Justice for Mickie

Justice for Corrie

Justice for Laine (novella)

Shelter for Elizabeth

Justice for Boone

Shelter for Adeline

Shelter for Sophie

Justice for Erin

Justice for Milena

Shelter for Blythe

Justice for Hope

Shelter for Quinn

Shelter for Koren

Shelter for Penelope

SEAL of Protection Series

Protecting Caroline (FREE!)

Protecting Alabama

Protecting Fiona

Marrying Caroline (novella)

Protecting Summer

Protecting Cheyenne

Protecting Jessyka

Protecting Julie (novella)

Protecting Melody

Protecting the Future

Protecting Kiera (novella)

Protecting Alabama's Kids (novella)

Protecting Dakota

New York Times, USA Today and *Wall Street Journal* Bestselling

Author Susan Stoker has a heart as big as the state of Tennessee where she lives, but this all American girl has also spent the last fourteen years living in Missouri, California, Colorado, Indiana, and Texas. She's married to a retired Army man who now gets to follow *her* around the country.

www.stokeraces.com
www.AcesPress.com
susan@stokeraces.com

39222365R00163